D1206756

DIANE CAPRI

JACK FROST

ISBN: 978-1-942633-48-8 (ebook)
ISBN: 978-1-942633-49-5 (paperback)
ISBN: 978-1-942633-50-1 (hardcover)

Additional format available:
ISBN: 978-1-942633-51-8 (large print edition)

Original cover design by: Cory Clubb

DEDICATION

Perpetually, for Lee Child, with unrelenting gratitude.

JACK
FROST

CAST OF PRIMARY CHARACTERS

Kim Otto
William Burke
Reggie Smithers
Charles Cooper
Carlos Gaspar
Lamont Finlay
Fern Olson
Duff Keegan
Liam Walsh
Petey Burns

and
Jack Reacher

61 HOURS
Lee Child

Reacher didn't answer. He was adrift. The world had flipped underneath him. All his life, to be taller had to be better. More dominant, more powerful, more noticed, more advantaged. You got credibility, you got treated with respect, you got promoted faster, you earned more, you got elected to things. Statistics bore it out.

You won fights, you got less hassle, you ruled the yard.

To be born tall was to win life's lottery.

Born small, two strikes against.

But not down there.

Down there to be tall was a losing ticket.

Down there was a world where the small guy could win.

CHAPTER 1

Friday, May 13
Carter's Crossing, Mississippi
5:00 a.m. Central Daylight Time

Her phone pinged, awakening her from a sound sleep fueled by exhaustion. FBI Special Agent Kim Otto rolled over to read the text from her boss.

The first thing she noticed was the delayed transmission. Cyberspace didn't work nearly as well as people assumed.

The text had been sent at 3:55 a.m. Eastern Daylight Time, but she'd received it two hours and five minutes later.

The Boss had booked her on a flight out of Memphis, departing shortly after one o'clock, Central Daylight Time, to Rapid City, South Dakota. From there, she'd travel to Bolton. A place she'd never heard of before.

No objections entertained.

She'd rolled over for a few more hours of shuteye before she'd packed up, said goodbye, and left Carter's Crossing for the drive to Memphis.

Nine hours after the Boss had sent the text. Seven hours and five minutes after she'd received it, Kim sidestepped the mass of passengers waiting for screening and approached the TSA checkpoint at Memphis International Airport.

The Boss had notified TSA's Officer Garrett, who was expecting her. Garret would ask to see her badge, and he'd simply pass her through. Without examining her bags or confiscating her service weapon. Which was absolutely against the rules.

Ideally, none of the other passengers would notice that she'd skipped the screening devices and systems required for everyone else. The last thing she needed to deal with was an angry mob.

Years after 9/11, a surprisingly large number of casual flyers remained edgy about the security measures applied at all U.S. airports. Anything a passenger proposed to carry past the security checkpoint was subject to inspection. Even though there had not been another U.S. jetliner hijacked in years.

Everything is screened. Whether passengers liked it or not.

No exceptions.

Mrs. Otto's daughter, Kim, a petite Asian-looking woman dressed in a black suit, with a travel bag, a laptop case, and a suspicious bulge caused by a holster resting under her arm, should have been subject to the same security measures as everyone else.

The list of contraband not allowed beyond the TSA checkpoint was long and, sometimes, overreaching. At least in the eyes of the public.

Tensions could run especially high among civilians asked to stand inside a scanner and raise their arms to be checked for explosives residue. Especially if other passengers weren't required to submit to the indignity of it all.

Some passengers were nervous flyers. Others were belligerent citizens. Still others were mentally or physically impaired. All of them went through screening, regardless of individual concerns.

TSA officers never came to work expecting the day's routine activities to flow smoothly. Agent Garrett was likely as skeptical as the rest of his fellows. Kim didn't plan to give him any reason to apply that skepticism to her.

She scanned the area until she located Garrett at his duty station. He was a gray-haired guy carrying about twenty extra pounds around his waist. She'd have placed him at about fifty if forced to guess.

He was working the center checkpoint line, standing with his hands on his duty belt, ten feet beyond the conveyor that trundled carry-on items through the X-ray system.

The female agent operating the screening device noticed something that had been placed on the belt by a flamboyantly dressed man near the head of the line. Kim hadn't seen the item, which was enclosed by the X-ray machine.

The agent stopped the conveyor belt that had been running through the scanner and called Garrett over for a second opinion. They whispered, the woman pointing to the screen and glancing at Garrett for confirmation.

While she waited, Kim's phone buzzed with a new text. Instead of connecting as planned in Rapid City, he'd been rerouted to meet her here in Memphis.

She looked around for her new partner, William Burke. She'd never met the guy. But she'd pulled up his photo on her phone before she came into the terminal. She'd recognize him instantly in any crowd.

Not that he was especially memorable.

Burke wouldn't stand out in any particular way. He was six feet tall, fit, dark hair, dark eyes, boring haircut. In short, everything a solid FBI agent should look like if he wanted to blend into a group of regular Americans.

Kim was the lead agent on the Reacher assignment, and Burke was her new number two. She was younger than Burke by a couple of years, but she had more time in the field and a lot more experience on the Reacher case.

She didn't see him standing around in the security screening area. Maybe he was already at the gate.

Kim rubbed her neck and rolled her shoulders. The drive from Carter's Crossing had been uneventful. But she was tired. She'd been running on her standard triple As for way too long. Adrenaline, ambition, and anxiety could only carry her so far. Eventually, she also needed sleep and a good meal.

A strong whiff of freshly brewed java reached her nose. As soon as she was done here, she'd make a beeline for it. Maybe they'd have a sandwich or a bagel or something, too. Her stomach had been growling for an hour. Food and coffee would help.

"What the hell are you doing?" The flamboyant passenger who owned whatever was holding up the line at the screening machine had run out of patience.

Kim looked ahead. People in line behind the guy were restive, too. They wanted to move through security and get on to the next phase of what had become the nightmare of air travel.

Add in a couple of crying babies, and cranky toddlers, and things were about to get ugly. Kim could feel the vibe.

She moved closer, hoping to catch Agent Garrett's eye, but he was focused on the unruly passenger now.

"Sir, please step aside. We'll need to ask you a few questions," he said, indicating a chair on the other side of the trace portal machine. He stretched his palm forward to indicate the entrance. "Walk through the puffer first, please."

"Absolutely not," the man said, much louder than necessary. "I want my bag. Give it back to me right this minute."

Agent Garrett was an old hand at his job. He wasn't about to let things get out of control. He gestured to a third agent standing on the other side of the checkpoint. She walked his way, as the passenger's belligerence increased exponentially instead of throttling down.

"I said, give me my bag!" he shouted. He moved closer to the X-ray machine and lifted his arm, trying to reach inside. But his arms were too short to clear the Plexiglas shields mounted on either side.

Agent Garrett grabbed the man's bicep firmly. "Sir, I need you to step over here, please. You're holding up the line."

The second agent was almost there. Whatever had seemed so essential in the passenger's bag just a moment before was quickly abandoned. He jerked his arm up and away from the X-ray scanner and turned to run toward the exit.

He elbowed aside two women in line behind him. One of the women had a toddler belted into a stroller, which she held onto. Both the mom and the stroller fell over, and the toddler began to scream.

The second woman, perhaps the grandmother, shouted in outrage. "What the hell is wrong with you?"

The man kept going, picking up speed as he pushed passengers aside with both arms like a fullback on the field, rushing toward the game-winning touchdown.

He was approaching Kim's position. Plowing through, head down, clearing his path as he moved.

Agent Garrett lumbered along behind him in hot pursuit. "Stop! Hey!"

When the passenger reached a point just a few feet in front of Kim, before he had a chance to correct his trajectory, she shoved her bags into the runner's path.

He swung one arm in a wide roundhouse to knock her aside.

She stepped out of the sweep's arc.

He whiffed.

The momentum of his swing kept him going.

His arm continued to travel around his body, twisting his legs while his feet were still planted on the carpet.

He lost his footing and stumbled while attempting to keep his balance.

When he staggered and fell forward, Kim stepped to one side, shoved her right leg out, and tripped him. Momentum and gravity did the rest.

He flailed both arms and stepped around his own feet in an attempt to stay upright. But he failed at that, too.

Kim moved out of his way. The last thing she wanted was to end up on the floor with the guy. As it was, she'd have a bruise on her leg where he'd come into contact with her.

As he went down, arms flailing, the sharp edge of his pinky ring scraped Kim's neck, deep enough to draw blood.

Half a second later, he'd fallen hard in a crumpled heap of howling outrage, cussing and screaming the whole time.

A man walked up and put a booted foot on the passenger's chest. He applied just enough pressure to keep him on the ground.

"You're bleeding, Agent Otto," he said with a grin. Which was when she looked at his face for the first time. William Burke. No doubt about it.

Kim reached into her pocket for a tissue and applied pressure to the stinging scrape on her neck.

A second later, the two TSA agents finally broke through the crowd. Kim confirmed Garrett's name on the brass plate above his breast pocket.

"Thanks, Agent Garrett." She showed her badge and nodded at Burke to do the same.

Garrett glanced briefly at both badges.

"Nice work, Burke," Garrett said, bending down to cuff the passenger, who was still spewing curses.

"You were right on him. But glad to help," Burke replied with a grin. He moved his booted foot off the passenger and set it firmly on the floor again.

Kim resisted the urge to glare at Burke's smirking face. Hogging credit for her takedown? Conduct unbecoming.

It was a small thing. But small things showed the measure of a man. Details revealed character. This was not a good opening gambit from her new partner. Gaspar would never have done it, for damned sure.

CHAPTER 2

Friday, May 13
Memphis, Tennessee
12:30 p.m. Central Daylight Time

A crowd had gathered, watching the show. A few passengers had pulled their cell phones out and recorded the whole sequence. The video would be posted online within the next ten minutes. The world would know who took the guy down. No need for her to make an issue of it now.

"We need to get going," Kim said.

"Yeah," Garrett nodded toward a gated area while still attempting to subdue the belligerent passenger. "Go through the swinging door there. We'll take care of this guy."

Burke grinned again. "Just curious. What's his problem, anyway?"

Garrett shook his head. "Guess he thinks a concealed carry permit lets him take a loaded Glock on a plane. Dumbass."

"It's my gun. I can take it anywhere I damned well please." The passenger was still on the floor, squirming in his effort to stand while wearing handcuffs. "I'll have your badge for this. Then who's the dumbass? Do you know who I am? Do you?"

"These folks in the crowd here seem to know." Garrett shook his head. He pulled the guy up off the floor. "Come on, Mr. Celebrity. You can tell me all about it back in the office."

When he walked the guy away, the remaining passengers in the security line applauded.

Kim collected her bag and pulled it toward the door. Burke followed her.

"Who was that guy?" Burke asked.

"No clue," Kim replied. She went through the security door and followed her nose straight toward the coffee. She had fifteen minutes to make her flight.

Burke sauntered easily along behind her.

At the java stand, she grabbed a muffin and paid for two coffees. "We'd better hustle. They're closing the door."

"I'm on it." Burke grabbed his cup and strode off, faster than Kim's legs could carry her without running. Which she flatly refused to do.

Burke made it to the gate with two minutes to spare. He spent them chatting up the pretty gate agent while Kim approached.

"She's with me," Burke said. The gate agent nodded, and they rushed into the jetway half a moment before she closed the door behind them.

She'd known the guy fifteen minutes, and he'd already rescued her twice. Which was annoying. Just what had the Boss told him about her and the assignment, anyway?

A short line of passengers was waiting to board inside the jetway.

The flight attendant standing just inside the bulkhead doorway said, "We have a full flight today, folks. We need you to take your seats and stow your belongings as quickly as possible."

Burke flashed her a megawatter smile before he turned to Kim and said, "My seat is 1A. Where are you?"

"3B. Have you reviewed the files?" She shuffled ahead, the line of passengers moving in fits and starts and making little progress.

"Yeah. We're headed to Bolton Correctional Facility. A prison two hours' drive east and north of Rapid City," Burke replied. "Before we get there, we're to interview a local jailhouse lawyer named Fern Olson."

His accent was slightly southern U.S., Kim thought. But she'd just spent a few days in Mississippi, so maybe she was hearing things.

"Why are we going out there?" she asked.

This was the first time the Boss had sent her to a prison. It was a strange task. Reacher rarely let criminals live long enough to be tried and convicted.

"Interview one of the inmates. Guy worked as an informant for the Bolton PD seven years ago when Reacher came through, I guess." Burke shrugged. "The file's a little vague on what the guy is supposed to know or why it matters. Care to fill me in?"

The line had finally begun to move and Kim walked onto the plane. When she reached Burke's seat, she said, "Let me get settled and read the files. Then we'll talk. We've got five hours to get up to speed."

"Sounds like a plan," he replied as he hefted his bag into the overhead bin and slid into his seat.

Kim walked back two rows and slid into the aisle seat in row three. She stowed her bags, snugged her seatbelt tight, and waited for the plane to defy gravity.

Once the plane had reached cruising altitude at thirty thousand feet, the flight attendant brought coffee, and Kim opened her laptop to work.

She'd downloaded the encrypted files from her secure server from the Boss earlier and set them aside. She'd also downloaded encrypted files from Gaspar. She'd asked him to research her new partner. Now that she'd met Burke, she opened Gaspar's file first.

Her initial impression from Burke's behavior back at the airport confirmed he was no Gaspar. That impression was firmly cemented as she read through the file.

She covered the basics quickly.

William David Burke. Age thirty-six. Two years older than Kim. Birthday April 10. Aries the Ram. No surprise there. He'd already shown a few of the classic Aries personality signs when he jumped right into the situation she already had under control back at TSA.

Aries was a fire sign. He was likely to have an abundance of ambition, which was okay. She was ambitious herself.

A flash-fire temperament was not okay. He'd need to keep his anger on a leash. She wondered if he could actually do that. *Time will tell.*

No siblings. Parents deceased. Divorced. No kids.

Employment history was somewhat common for certain kinds of agents. After college, he'd joined the Navy SEALs and stayed for ten years before moving to the FBI. He'd been employed at FBI for four years. After the required two years as a field agent, he qualified for the Hostage Rescue Team.

The interesting part of his resume was the most recent entry.

The details were classified, so Gaspar's hurriedly gathered report was sketchy. He was still digging for more details. What he knew so far was that Burke got mixed up in some sort of situation. Whatever it was, Burke ended up sideways and could have been fired.

But the Boss, for reasons of his own, didn't want to let Burke go. So he parked Burke with Otto, out on the fringes of the FBI, where no one could see or complain about his behavior. Which was okay. Kim had been in this no-man's land for a while now and she could use a guy with Burke's skill set.

The whole Reacher assignment was temporary anyway. If Kim didn't finish it soon enough, Burke would stay until things cooled off inside the HRT for him. Then he could go back to hostage rescue and other feats of daring-do, she supposed. That sort of stuff was a young man's game, but Burke wasn't too old for it. Yet.

She closed the file and the laptop to think about what she'd learned.

Reading between the lines, she suspected that the Boss had sent Burke in to do what Kim had failed to accomplish so far: Find Reacher. Which pissed her off royally.

Not that she could do anything about it. The Boss made all the decisions. He held all the cards.

The question was whether or not she could trust Burke. With his background, he should be more than capable. The hunt for Reacher was dangerous business. Burke's skill set would be helpful and maybe even crucial.

Maybe, like Gaspar, Burke could be relied upon to think like Reacher. Kim had understood from the first minute of this assignment that if she was to succeed, brains, not brawn, was her best weapon. To deploy it, she had to understand Reacher's moves before he made them.

Gaspar had been helpful with that issue. Maybe Burke would be, too.

But unlike Gaspar, Burke was Cooper's boy. No doubt about that at all.

So the real question was: why was he here?

The answer was not contained in these files.

She closed the file and stashed it. Time to get up to speed on her assignment in Bolton, South Dakota. She ordered fresh coffee, opened the files from the Boss, and went to work.

CHAPTER 3

Friday, May 13
Bolton Correctional Facility
4:55 p.m. Mountain Daylight Time

"Sorry, but no. And I gotta go. I'm here, and I'm running late. I'll call you when I'm done," Fern Olson said into the blue tooth speaker as she pulled her red BMW into the mostly empty visitors' lot and parked in the area reserved for lawyers.

The vibe was different, somehow. She'd felt it for the past week, right after she'd delivered the messages from last Friday's regular visit to Bolton Prison. Something was off. She didn't know what. Regardless, she didn't want her son wandering the streets today, even in the small town, five miles south.

Her regular client conferences at the prison were a chore. Necessary, yes. Lucrative, sure. But like many things any lawyer does every day, most prisoner conferences were pure drudgery. Usually.

"How long are you gonna be?" the kid whined. Like every teenager on the planet, he wanted his mother's world to revolve around him.

"My goal is always to get in, get it done, and get out," she replied, glancing around the compound. Everything looked the same as always. Solid. Impenetrable. Secure. "I'll call you when I'm on my way home."

The day was sunny and clear, but colder than she liked. Spring had blown into Bolton a few weeks ago, stayed for about forty-eight hours, and fled south again. The change of seasons was, as always, unpredictable.

No one living in Bolton expected different, except her son. He wanted to go swimming in the lake with his friends.

"But, Mommmm," Noah whined, drawing out the single syllable until it seemed to last forever. "All the guys are going. It's not too cold. People swim in the Arctic Ocean, for cripe sake."

"Heaven help me," Olson muttered under her breath, shaking her head. "We'll talk about this when I'm done here. I've gotta go. Love you."

He hung up.

"Was I ever that obnoxious?" she said looking up to the roof of her car.

She grinned and spoke to one of the women she'd admired most as a child. Long gone, now, Janet Salter had been an inspiring role model to young girls growing up in Bolton.

She said, "I'm so sorry, Mrs. Salter. I'm not half the woman you were. I've done the best I could with him."

For a brief moment, she considered changing her mind about the swimming.

Elevation in Rapid City was three thousand feet and in Sioux Falls, it was fourteen hundred feet. Bolton lay between them and farther north. The land was flat here. All the interesting elevations were closer to Mount Rushmore. Weather fronts came and went. Mostly warmer in summer and colder in winter.

But sometimes Mother Nature could act more than a bit drunk. Like this year.

Now it was mid-May and the trees were still bare, but daffodils and tulips had pushed up through the thawed ground. Roads were clear, and the last of the snow piles had finally melted. Flurries last night had left a light dusting of new snow in the grassy areas, but it had melted before noon.

Still, it was way too cold to go swimming.

Any halfway intelligent fifteen-year-old should know that, shouldn't he?

She shook her head, still mumbling to herself. "The weather will get better, Fern. Mid-July, he'll be complaining about the heat."

Olson had worn jeans and boots to work because she visited the prison every Friday afternoon. She'd gathered her hair into a bun at the base of her neck to tame the long, unruly curls she preferred to leave free.

The chill in the air had prompted her to don a brown leather blazer over her crisp white shirt. She tossed her sunglasses onto the passenger seat, slid her phone inside the console and locked it, and grabbed her briefcase.

Cell phones were on the long list of prohibited items, including things like cigarettes, drugs, and weapons, not allowed inside the federal prison.

If she had the phone on her, she'd be required to leave it in a locker. Her entire world was stored on that phone. No way would she leave it where one of those idiots could grab it.

The prison guards insisted that they wouldn't open lockers or try to breach the security on phones.

"And if you believe that, you're not a jailhouse lawyer, for damned sure," she muttered to herself.

Unlike everyone else in Bolton, Olson locked her car and dropped the key fob into her pocket. The BMW was new. She didn't want some kid taking it for a joy ride.

She trudged across the parking lot, avoiding the puddles as she made her way toward the visitor's entrance. It was late. She'd already had a long day. She didn't plan to waste any time she had left before the prison locked down for the night. The last thing she wanted to do was be forced to come back tomorrow.

She could find her way with her eyes closed. She'd made the same trek every Friday for a long time, regardless of the weather. Just like her predecessor.

Olson had been a junior partner when she got this gig. The senior partner who'd handled the legal needs of prisoners before her had been murdered seven years ago.

In all law firms, shit work flows downhill. Which was how she got the prison detail. She shrugged. When her kid went off to college, maybe she'd make a change. Until then, there was nothing she could do but suck it up and do the job.

She reached the building, pulled the heavy entrance door open, and walked through. A slight citrus scent disinfected the air.

There was no line inside. Friday wasn't a regular visitor's day. But the interior was no less depressing. Linoleum on the floor and green paint on the walls and fluorescent bulbs in the ceiling cast a greenish tint everywhere.

The prison was thirteen years old and built to last a hundred. But the money was spent on design elements that had more to do with basic human needs, security, and function than a homey appeal.

When the heavy door snugged solidly closed behind her, it seemed to suck the life out of the room right along with the possibility of breathing free air.

Ahead of her was the big lobby, an empty X-ray belt, a walk-through metal detector, and three prison guards standing around doing nothing, discussing the weather and the baseball season.

She nodded and they nodded back. She wasn't friends with them. Didn't even know who they were. Personnel seemed to rotate through the visitor's entry duty on a randomized schedule she hadn't bothered to figure out.

But they were all on the same side, really. Prison was a binary world. Either you were locked up, or you weren't. She wasn't. They weren't.

Olson removed her visitor badge from her jacket pocket and placed her folded jacket into a plastic bin. She clipped the badge onto her shirt. Then she pulled down another bin and placed her briefcase in it. She opened the briefcase, stashed her car key fob inside, and closed it again.

She stacked the two bins together and carried them across the room to a window. A uniformed woman took the bins from her and gave her a claim ticket to collect them after they'd been hand-inspected.

"Running late today." the officer said. "How long are you planning to be?"

"Couple of hours, probably," Olson replied.

The officer nodded. "Warden has extended hours in the exercise yard since daylight saving time kicked in. Gives the inmates more fresh air. We won't be locking down until eight o'clock tonight. All interviews end by seven-thirty."

"Okay," Olson replied. "I've got three clients scheduled. One hour each. I'll do my best to hurry them up."

"Unless you'd like to stay overnight, we'll be escorting you from the building before seven-thirty." The woman frowned. "Whether you're done or not."

"Understood."

This was a federal government facility. She had no idea how many employees were on the site at any given time. The staff was mostly veterans from all branches of the military. Regardless of their backgrounds, they were all trained in law enforcement.

Bottom line was that Bolton personnel operated pursuant to thick stacks of rules and regulations and manuals and plans and backups and contingency plans, too. They'd no doubt trained to deploy such practices in a regimented way, precisely as and when needed.

Olson returned to the metal detector and stood waiting for the go light overhead. One of the guards pushed a button and the light turned green. She walked through slowly. She'd learned long ago to leave her jewelry and her underwire bra and anything else metallic at home.

Nothing beeped.

On the other side, one guards watched and another wanded her. The third, a female officer, patted her down.

Olson showed her photo ID and another card identifying her as a member of the South Dakota Bar Association. After she'd passed all of the screening tests, she exchanged her claim check for the return of her briefcase and her jacket. Then she collected her briefcase and jacket and followed the guard who escorted her to the meeting rooms.

Olson didn't need the escort. She could have found her way in the dark. The building was clean and tidy but depressing just the same.

All prisons ran on protocol and this one had as many rules as any other.

No unescorted visitors. Period.

Which was a precaution against something. Olson wasn't sure exactly what the warden was worried about. She had never heard of mobs trying to get inside the place. As far as she knew, they'd never had a single inmate escape, either.

Olson's escort walked her deeper into the complex. Through heavy doors, around tight corners, and past thick green glass windows with watchful faces behind, until they reached her destination.

Four interview rooms, each divided exactly in half by a wall-to-wall counter with impenetrable safety glass above it, like a bank teller's cage in an old movie. Each side of the room had a separate entrance door. The prisoners entered from the other side.

Olson had never been on that side of the wall. She had no firsthand experience over there. Nor did she want any.

Her escort opened her door and then locked her inside and took a few steps away to offer the appearance of privacy.

In theory, lawyers and clients were allowed confidential communications inside these rooms. Savvy lawyers like Olson never relied on those promises.

Smarter to assume nothing was private inside any prison. Every inch of the place, even the parking lots, was under constant surveillance. Maybe the cameras should be off at certain times. But mistakes were made. Olson had read about them in the law books.

She glanced at the clock. She had plenty of time before lockdown. Three clients. The first and last were okay, but the second guy was flat out terrifying.

Olson put her briefcase on the desk, pulled out a yellow legal pad and a cheap plastic pen, which was all for show.

The first and last clients never told her anything important enough to write down.

The second client carried a list of demands in his head. Not for himself. For other inmates.

He passed the demands to her.

Like her predecessor, she memorized the list and passed it along to someone else.

They were both being used.

He knew it.

She knew it.

Neither one cared.

Ryan Denny's skin was pale and translucent white. He was bulked up and overweight and shackled at the wrists and ankles. He would never leave Bolton Prison alive. His eyes were dull, but he must have been some kind of savant. He memorized orders from other inmates and passed them along to her.

Olson shook her head. Denny was too frightening to focus on. He'd long ago invaded her sleep, causing nightmares after every visit. She forced his image from her mind and glanced at the clock again.

Her first client was eight minutes late, which was unusual. Not that she cared. She'd allotted him exactly forty-five minutes. No more, no less. And she was billing every second, whether Liam Walsh showed up or not.

CHAPTER 4

Friday, May 13
Rapid City, South Dakota
5:35 p.m.

Captain Wayne Romone sat alone in the big old bird. Nervous about the operation and satisfied that he'd made it this far, all at the same time.

When he got the word from air traffic control, he pushed the throttle on the A320 to the max. With fifty tons of metal on board and a full load of fuel, every ounce of thrust he could get from the plane counted.

Once airborne, he kept the wings level for a couple of minutes, building airspeed before banking to the east.

The flight plan said Rapid City, South Dakota, to Minneapolis, Minnesota. Ninety-eight minutes in the air, nonstop. Piece of cake.

Except he wasn't flying nonstop today.

Romone wasn't worried. He'd had a good run. The love of his life had married him a couple of decades ago and they'd built a strong family. Four kids. Good kids. Three boys already at college and his daughter was going off in the fall.

He was proud of them all. His wife, especially. Her work as a teacher had given her many happy years.

When he'd daydreamed about his future, he'd planned savings for the kids' college, and to care for elderly parents, and funding pensions.

But he'd never seriously considered how his own death might happen.

If he'd thought about the matter at all, he'd simply have assumed death would come to him in its own way and its own time and nothing he might want would trump the Grand Plan on that score.

Romone simply lived his life as if every day might be his last. In his line of work, it was a better strategy than most.

Romone had started his career with ten years in the military, flying transports into hot spots the world over. When the defense spending cuts came, he'd transitioned into the civilian world as a pilot for a big airline.

He'd flown lots of international trips. Lots of jet lag. Lots of days away from home.

When his fourth child had arrived, he'd transitioned to a smaller airline, flying domestic freight. What the job lacked in salary, it made up for in other ways. Most days he could sleep in his own bed and be a part of his family's lives.

Which made everything he'd sacrificed to make it happen more than worth it. No regrets. Even as his world began to change.

Over time, the big air freight operators had gobbled up more and more of the market. There were still opportunities for small businesses like his, but the competition was fierce, and the money wasn't there.

He'd accepted pay cuts to stay employed.

Which was okay.

His life was better spent with his family than chasing more money, anyway.

He'd have a lifetime to accumulate wealth. His kids were young only once. So he hadn't questioned his career choices. No reason to.

Until that day at the doctor's office when his whole world changed. Terminal cancer. "No way out," the doc said. But Romone couldn't wrap his head around it. It was damned unfair.

He'd always exercised and ate more salads than steaks. His mind was a sharp as ever. Passed his annual physicals with flying colors. Hell, he didn't even need reading glasses. He was a good pilot, too. Knew all the routes, the approaches, even the air traffic controllers by name.

Sure, he'd been tired sometimes, but he was getting older, after all. He liked to fly later in the day. Less air traffic to worry about. Most of the time he flew on autopilot anyway, so it didn't matter if he took a nap now and then.

He had a good copilot. Reliable. Younger. Easy going. Only too happy to babysit the electronics that were getting them from here to there and back again.

Which explained why Romone had to push hard to convince the young dude to call in sick this afternoon. But he couldn't take any chances with the copilot's career.

In a small outfit like theirs, everyone was essential and had to pull his own weight. Persuading the younger man to take the day off hadn't been easy, but Romone had finally managed.

With no first officer available, Romone should have been grounded. His A320 was converted for freight haulage, which fell under the same rules as a commercial aircraft full of passengers.

But hauling freight isn't a forgiving business. Given a chance, bigger operators would steal the clients in a hot New York second. Missing a big delivery like the one Romone was scheduled to fly next would give the competition the break they'd been salivating for.

So after his copilot called in sick, Romone convinced his boss that he could fly solo, just this once. The boss knew the score. He knew the flight would be a challenge. But the freight had to go, and the boss had no one else to fly the A320 today.

The boss argued with Romone, but in the end, agreed, as Romone had known he would.

A few false notations in the logbook and he was good to go.

Both Romone and his boss knew the messed up notes would be construed as minor mistakes. Mere oversights. At most, he'd get a slap on the wrist and be told not to do it again.

If the authorities found out.

Which they wouldn't.

Nothing out of the ordinary about the cargo. Specialized engines for heavy earthmovers. It was the sort of freight that usually went by rail. But the manufacturer had a rush order and using air transport would get it there sooner.

If today's flight went well, there were more contracts promised for the future.

Which was all well and good.

But the only thing Romone really cared about was that the cargo didn't require a supervisor onboard. When the big aircraft started rolling, he'd be the only one on the plane.

Risking his own life for a big payoff to his family was one thing. Risking the lives of others was not at all okay.

Several times during the planning stages, he'd thought the operation might go off the rails. But it hadn't. He'd managed to push through all the problems until, finally, he sat patiently waiting his turn for takeoff on runway one.

Daylight saving time had kicked in a few weeks ago. But he'd still be flying in daylight for the first leg. Sunset was three hours away. A nighttime return flight from Minneapolis would be fine, too. Easier than flying into the setting sun. Visibility clear all the way.

Twenty minutes into the flight, he pulled a sheet of paper from his pocket and read through it again. It was an informal checklist he'd created after significant research containing the steps and procedures he'd need to hide the planned detour of seventy tons of plane and cargo.

"Talk about flying a herd of elephants," he muttered under his breath without cracking so much as a grin at the ridiculously apt mental image.

Romone had wrestled the situation around in his head for hours at night while the family was asleep, making his checklist. Transporting a herd of elephants was difficult under any circumstances. Maneuvering the A320 in total secrecy was damned impossible.

Finally, he'd accepted that he couldn't hide his actions entirely. There were simply too many rules and regulations and eyes watching all the time.

At the moment, he felt more like an elephant wedged in a shoebox. No wiggle room at all.

He'd get as close to perfect as possible. He'd handle the inquisition afterward. That was the best he could do.

The payoff would be worth it. His family would be set for life. He'd never need to worry about them again. He could rest in peace when the time came, knowing he'd done the right thing.

CHAPTER 5

Duff Keegan's outdoor exercise period was the last on the schedule today. With late spring's warmer and longer days, the inmates were allowed more time outside, which was perfect. Sunset was later. Nights were shorter. Which wasn't perfect, but he could work with those challenges. He'd handled much bigger issues already.

He'd showered and shaved and dressed in a clean white T-shirt and jeans before he donned a larger than normal orange jumpsuit over his street clothes. He sat on the edge of his cot to tie the new and aptly named running shoes. He smiled before he stood and stretched a bit, lifting on the balls of his feet, trying them out.

He looked around the cell for the last time.

A few books rested on a small shelf near his bed. His cellmate had gone outside already, too excited to stay cooped up, he'd said. Denny wasn't much of a reader. He liked to memorize things and recite them back in perfect order, like replaying a recording.

Keegan wasn't sure the scary-looking idiot could read at all. But he'd been useful with the lawyer, and maybe he'd develop the reading habit over the next thirty years. He'd have plenty of time.

Nothing else noteworthy caught Keegan's eye. He'd accumulated little since they'd sent him to serve his time at Bolton Correctional and he cared nothing for sentiment anyway. He'd have everything he could possibly want when he reached his destination on Monday.

When the automatic door lock opened, he rested his hands in his empty pockets and walked straight out of his cell and into the corridor, without a backward glance or an ounce of remorse.

His mind was on the future.

There was nothing worth caring about here.

Two cells down the row, Liam Walsh stood waiting. Keegan nodded, and Walsh joined him. They walked casually side by side toward the yard, as they'd walked everywhere, every day since Keegan was first locked up at Bolton.

Any crime boss always had a protective presence around him. Keegan's reputation as the most vicious gangster in Boston was usually protection enough, inside or outside any prison.

The few times Keegan's cloak of extreme menace wasn't enough, Walsh handled things in a more violent way. That's what protective muscle was for.

Keegan didn't keep Walsh around because of his brains and good looks. It was brawn Keegan paid handsomely for, and Walsh had never failed to deliver. Nor would he.

Not more than once, anyway.

Keegan had been squirreled away in this stinkin' place because the feds were stupid. No other way to look at it.

The feds thought he'd be out of his element here. He was a big man in Boston. He was nobody in Nowheresville, South

Dakota. That's how the feds had figured it. That Keegan would be controllable, away from his organization.

Keegan shook his head. How stupid could they be?

Just before his armed escort had uncuffed him during his check-in at the warden's office, the scrawny bespectacled FBI agent had said maybe, after a couple of winters in South Dakota, Keegan would take the witness protection offer they'd dangled.

He shook his head again. For smart guys, these feds weren't at all wise in the ways of Keegan's world. Not even a little bit.

"You see your lawyer today?" Keegan asked. The lawyer was part of the plan. She just didn't know it. Which was as it should be.

Walsh nodded. "She was late. I was later. She had Denny and Burns after me. She's still here."

Both men grinned and kept walking.

Up ahead of him in the corridor, the line of men wearing orange jumpsuits waited to exit the cell block to the exercise yard. Keegan applied patience in these sorts of things. His turn would come. He had plenty of time.

All prisons had rules, and at Bolton, forty-six men at once were allowed in each exercise yard for a one-hour period. The groups of forty rotated through the one-hour schedule like civilian teams renting a sports facility on the outside. The cell blocks rotated the schedule.

On Fridays, Keegan's cell block took the last hour of the day. Since daylight saving time had kicked in, the last hour of the day had moved to after dinner instead of before. Which worked better for him. Keegan had terrible indigestion if he went to bed right after dinner.

No prisoners were allowed out in the yard the other three days of the week. That was when visitors were on the premises.

Seven days a week, week in and week out. This had been his life. Which was about to change.

The forty-six men in orange jumpsuits shuffled along until they reached the door and then walked through the exit, one at a time.

Keenan and Walsh were in the middle of the group, protected from the front and the flank. Just in case.

Ahead, Keenan saw daylight before he reached the exit. The weather was sunny and clear and not a cloud in the sky, just as the weatherman had predicted. The temperature was still a bit cool, which was perfect for running.

He pushed himself up on his toes to stretch his calves as he shuffled toward the front of the line. At the exit, he walked deliberately across the threshold, for the last time, savoring the moment.

As he did, he vowed to himself that he would never take another breath inside Bolton or any other prison. Never.

It was a promise he meant to keep.

Keegan walked toward the picnic table in the far corner of the fenced yard. Walsh walked alongside him. They sat on the table, feet planted on the benches, facing west.

He'd quit smoking back in Boston after he was sentenced. Cigarettes were an addiction no inmate should entertain. Otherwise, he'd find himself at the mercy of dealers inside. Keegan had more self-control.

He reached into his pocket for a stick of chewing gum, unwrapped it, and folded it into his mouth.

He looked into the empty sky, toward Rapid City.

"What do you see up there, Walsh?" he asked.

"Nothin', Boss," Walsh replied.

"That's right. Nothing but cloudless blue space," Keegan said, flexing his feet in the running shoes.

He wasn't worried. His ride would be here soon.

CHAPTER 6

Friday, May 13
South Dakota
6:30 p.m.

Captain Romone was getting close. He ran through everything one more time.

The A320 aircraft carried a slew of instruments that were monitoring and recording every flight parameter on a constant basis. His employer was required to review the parameters and file reports of any and all deviations.

FAA regulations governed aircraft movements and tracked position and speed through data broadcast from the aircraft as it traveled, too.

Hiding his actions would be neither easy nor foolproof. He couldn't do an actual practice run. He had one chance to make this work.

Which was why Romone had prepared his list late at night using a flight simulator.

Before anything else, he had to buy a little time. The flight schedule was way too tight.

Under normal conditions, descending from cruising altitude, landing, and climbing back up would take twenty minutes. But every moment of his flight time was scheduled and monitored at all times.

Which meant he needed to find a way to create twenty extra minutes of maneuvering room.

First, Romone keyed the microphone to call the company dispatcher to report nonexistent headwinds.

Headwinds made a difference. Flying into a hundred-knot breeze took a hundred knots from his speed across the ground. Ninety-eight minutes of flight time would be stretched to 110.

If such headwinds existed.

Which they didn't.

The dispatcher noted the pilot's reported headwinds and Romone ended the transmission without further discussion.

He'd bought himself twelve minutes with the false report.

Twelve minutes.

He needed twenty.

There was no way to get permission for the next step. Neither his dispatcher nor FAA controllers would allow it. Too dangerous, they would have said.

If he'd asked.

Which he didn't.

Romone wasn't concerned. He could do this. He'd flown in every condition imaginable. Today's flight conditions were as close to perfect as Mother Nature could produce.

Regulators, on the other hand, were another thing entirely. Over the years, he'd learned it was easier to get forgiveness than permission from the regulators. He'd worry about them when, and if, they investigated the flight later. Chances are, if he pulled this off, they wouldn't have any reason to investigate at all.

No one would ever know. He'd take the secret to his grave.

Romone took a deep breath and dialed the autopilot height down from FL300 to FL200, which reduced the cruising altitude from thirty- to twenty-thousand feet.

Landing from the lower altitude was not in the flight plan, but it would trim the remaining minutes he needed.

The aircraft systems reduced the engine power and went into a gentle dive.

The descent still took too long. Eight full minutes.

Because the aircraft's flight control system prioritized passenger comfort over a more rapid descent.

Which was stupid. The old bird hadn't carried a passenger in twenty years.

Romone's next steps would be where his personal risk really kicked in. His internal controls snapped to full attention.

Aircraft are designed to handle failures. Which meant, given the chance, the systems would thwart Romone's unauthorized activities.

The flight control system had multiple physically separate computers calculating how the aircraft should respond to the pilot's joystick and throttle changes. Romone knew that any onboard computers that generated such risky moves would be rejected by the safety systems, so he turned them off.

The system was designed to prevent an errant computer from crashing the aircraft.

But it also limited the plane's performance, minimizing fuel consumption and maximizing the life of the plane's components.

Romone couldn't allow the safety systems to get in the way. His mission needed to succeed on his own terms.

"I'm in control here, baby. You computers can take a little nap," Romone said aloud, partly to reinforce his own choices.

He taped his phone to his leg and started a timer to display big digits he could see at a glance counting down on the screen.

Romone reviewed his private checklist and traced his fingers over the switches he would activate and buttons he would press, further committing the whole process to memory.

The faster he worked, the more plausible his cover story would be later when he claimed the A320 had experienced a power failure. Intermittent electrical problems were a fact of life on complex aircraft, and he'd use that reality to cover his ass.

He'd flown over Bolton prison twice a week as it was being built a few years ago. He knew precisely where the compound was located. Smack dab in the middle of nowhere USA. Surrounded by open land. The closest town was Bolton, five miles south, and it was a tiny burg, itself.

He peered into the distance, looking for the prison.

At the limits of his vision, a smudge on an empty landscape marked his target. The smudge resolved into a long black line of runway beside a series of mottled earthy colors.

He'd studied the layout carefully during his satellite research and while creating his checklist.

Large open concrete areas with smaller buildings dotted the perimeter around the prison. Guard towers.

The runway and three much larger buildings were coming into view.

The buildings were separated by strong steel fences topped with serious amounts of razor wire because Bolton was a maximum security facility.

The runway was likewise fenced off. Physically, of course. And also by government regulation. A permanent FAA NOTAM, a notice to airmen, restricted the prison runway to emergencies and authorized flights only.

Such access was rarely requested and even more rarely granted.

The feds, the state, and the county were not kidding about keeping the extremely dangerous prisoners inside their respective compounds at Bolton Correctional and keeping the rest of the world out.

The runway itself was a good size for smaller birds, but for Romone's fully loaded A320, it would be tight.

He'd completed similar jaunts in the military and knew the drill.

Slow in.

Touchdown at the very start of the runway, and straight onto full reverse thrust to slow the big bird down.

He'd use any remaining speed at the end of the runway to turn on the tiny parking apron.

The timer on his phone reached zero, alerting him with a loud buzz. He inhaled deeply and began to work his checklist, mumbling as he covered each point.

Romone's fingers darted over the controls above his head like a concert pianist moving surely over the keys, in precisely the correct order, with exactly the right touch, following years of practice.

Powering down computers and responders. Disabling the radio and flight recorder. And finally, shutting down all but one of the flight control computers.

CHAPTER 7

Numbers and displays in front of Romone blinked off until only the standby instrument was illuminated.

He'd transformed the old bird in an instant, from one of the most sophisticated commercial aircraft in the world, to a basic cockpit any World War Two pilot would have recognized.

The aircraft shuddered.

One computer controlled the aircraft, and Romone controlled that computer.

"Just you and me, now, baby," he murmured as he touched the joystick.

The aircraft responded immediately. The safety nets were gone.

He had become the pilot in command.

It was a simultaneously exhilarating and nerve-wracking feeling of power that he hadn't experienced in years.

Romone savored the feeling only for a brief moment. He had no time to waste.

He pushed the joystick forward, nosing the aircraft down, while also pulling back on the throttle.

As if she lived to serve his every command, the big old bird started down fast.

Normal descent rates for the A320 were in the region of 3,000 feet per minute. But Romone had neither time to waste nor passengers to worry about.

He kept pushing and the plane descended more than 4,000 feet per minute.

He felt his stomach drop through the floor.

To the aircraft's designers, the sharp dive traded potential energy for kinetic energy. To Romone, the maneuver meant gaining airspeed, just like rolling down a hill faster and faster.

If he didn't bleed off the excess speed before touchdown he could cook the brakes, or worse, blow out a tire.

Cooking the brakes might be okay. He could deal with that.

But blowing a tire was not okay. It presented a major risk for takeoff on the way back up. Romone and his new passenger would be lucky to survive.

He was a good pilot, but not a miracle worker.

"Come on, baby. Slow it down," he said softly, like a lover.

The runway was neatly aligned along his flight path. The skies around him were clear. He'd been paid to land, collect a passenger and leave, and that was what he intended to do.

It was a matter of pride now. The money was simply proof that he'd done what couldn't be done. He was old and sick, but he was still a damned fine pilot.

He was told not to radio for permission to land. So he didn't.

"Just don't shoot me," Romone said under his breath to the prison guards who couldn't hear him anyway.

At 15,000 feet, he pushed the lever for speed brakes to twenty-five percent.

But the A320 didn't slow down.

Even in big planes, pilots get used to the bumps and vibrations caused by actuating mechanical components on the way down, but there was none of the expected noise and vibration now.

Romone cycled the lever to zero and back to twenty-five percent.

Still no response. The big bird didn't slow. Instead, his airspeed was increasing.

At 10,000 feet, he pushed the speed brakes to one hundred percent and idled the engines.

The brakes didn't slow the plane, either.

He was coming in far too hot to land.

Which left him with two choices.

Circle and get his airspeed under control and try again.

Or maneuver hard and hope to bleed speed somehow before the A320 crashed and burned on the runway.

He ran through possible options, but he knew he only had one choice.

Circling the airport would alert too many people. It would take time he didn't have. The mission would definitely fail. He wouldn't land or collect his passenger.

He wouldn't get paid.

His family wouldn't collect the money he'd risked so much to earn.

"Unacceptable, dammit!" he said.

After everything he'd been through to get here, he wouldn't give up now. He had to slow the big bird down and land.

Right now.

He banked right.

Fifty degrees of roll and pulling two Gs as they said in all the good movies. The prison disappeared from view as the plane's nose veered away.

He felt the force of gravity pushing him into his seat.

His airspeed began a steady decline caused by the aerodynamic drag.

He counted to fifteen before banking left. Another fifty degrees. Another two Gs. Another fifteen count.

The prison came back into view.

After a third roll, he was breathing hard but back in line with the runway.

With the engines idling, the maneuver had put him closer to landing speed, but he wasn't there yet. He was still about five miles out from the prison runway.

"Let's do one more. Just to be safe," he muttered.

Romone pulled the joystick over to roll the big aircraft again. He needed to slow down.

Nothing happened.

The horizon stayed level. The runway remained straight ahead.

"What the hell?"

He stared at the joystick. It was exactly where it should be.

"Tipped over in roll and pulled back in pitch," he reminded himself, unnecessarily, like a plumber's "righty tighty, lefty loosey." He knew the stick was in the correct position for a coordinated banked turn. *Knew it.*

He shoved the stick to center and pulled it over again.

Still, nothing happened.

The sweat on his forehead ran down into his eyes and he blinked furiously to get rid of the stinging salt.

His gaze ran over the switches above his head. Had he powered down a vital system? Severed a crucial link? Fat-fingered the wrong switch?

Nothing looked out of place except the too-rapidly growing view of the prison.

Romone yanked back on the joystick as hard as he dared. Still no response from the plane.

His heart raced, even as he made every effort to control his panic.

He couldn't keep going. He needed to stay airborne to solve the problem.

Now he needed airspeed.

He shoved the throttles to max.

Again, the A320 did not respond.

He felt no vibration. No tremble. No thousands of pounds of thrust pushing him back into the sky.

"Come on, you big bitch! Move!"

He rammed the throttles back and forth as his left hand stabbed at the power switches to bring the big aircraft's computers back to life.

But the lights behind each switch remained dark.

"Two miles out," he said incredulously. He truly could not believe what was happening.

The prison's tiny windows were clearly visible. He could see movement in the guard towers. There were prisoners outside in the large exercise yards.

He was still losing altitude, but at 300 knots he had no hope of landing.

The undercarriage doors would be torn off. The tires would burst on contact. The undercarriage itself could collapse.

He literally could not make it happen.

But he was still lined up on the runway.

Romone took a deep breath and accepted what his experience was telling him in no uncertain terms.

The A320 was about to crash. No way to avoid the truth.

His best hope was a glancing blow in a crash landing.

He whipped his head around.

The first officer's seat was empty, but his joystick functioned independently of the pilot's. Whatever failure had happened might have left the copilot's controls operational.

Romone hammered on the seat belt release and fought to escape his four-point harness.

The prison and runway loomed larger. He was almost there.

And he had no control over the hurtling A320.

No control at all.

He struggled to get his legs out of the harness, stretching over the center console.

The throttle levers stabbed into his back, but he didn't care what switches he hit.

When half his body reached into the copilot's seat, he grabbed the joystick and yanked it back.

Nothing happened.

He grunted as he rammed the stick back and forth with strength borne of desperation.

The aircraft began to roll. He couldn't believe it. He grinned and snorted a quick burst of laughter.

Today wasn't the day he'd been fated to die after all.

Only thirty seconds from the runway, the nose of the A320 began to edge away. The roll continued. He felt Gs. Same as he'd felt maneuvering at higher altitude.

It was working. The damned bird was rolling. He felt hot tears in his eyes, blurring his vision. He blinked furiously to clear them.

"Thank you, God," he said, feeling relief all the way down to his toes.

He wasn't saved yet.

Romone fought his way to the copilot seat and pulled the joystick left, towards the runway, and back, to gain altitude.

But it didn't work.

The Gs remained strong.

The bank angle didn't correct.

The side of one of the big buildings crept into the aircraft's curving flight path.

The aircraft rolled out, righting itself, as if it was controlled by invisible hands. Wings level. A straight path.

The A320 was headed straight ahead at a shallow angle. In seconds, it would collide directly into the side of one of the large prison buildings.

Romone inhaled sharply as the ground came up fast.

Pilots call it ground rush. At 300 knots, it was amazingly fast.

He leaned over as far as he could reach. He had the joystick pulled back hard.

From his position, he glimpsed grass and concrete.

Small windows with bars.

In the distance, a stripe of black. The runway.

Everything was close. Too close.

He didn't think about death at that moment.

No, Wayne Romone was massively annoyed.

Aircraft didn't just fly itself.

And no possible systems failure could disable both the pilot's and copilot's controls.

It simply wasn't possible.

His anger grew hotter. Only one thing was possible.

He'd been set up. Used as a pawn in a deadly game.

Someone had taken over the controls of the A320.

The hacker had steered the jet directly into the prison at the precise point when Romone could no longer save the plane.

Or his life.

The last thing he felt was monstrous outrage.

After a cascade of mechanical problems, the pilot was no longer controlling the plane. He was just along for the ride.

There was nothing Romone could do to avoid disaster.

Nothing at all.

CHAPTER 8

Friday, May 13
Bolton Correctional Facility
7:05 p.m.

Fern Olson glanced nervously toward the clock above her client's head on the other side of the partition. The guard had knocked on the glass and pointed.

"Last call, Ms. Olson," he said as if she were sitting in a bar waiting to be served her last drink of the night.

Olson gave him a wave to acknowledge the warning. She'd never spent a night in any kind of jail, and she didn't plan to start now. She was almost done anyway. She still had twenty-five minutes to finish up and get out before lockdown.

Petey Burns, the scruffy, rakishly young hottie seated on the other side of the glass, seemed even more hyped up today than usual. He'd become a guest of the feds before the age of thirty after he'd been convicted of grand theft auto for the last time. His specialty was high-end luxury vehicles, and his skills were much in demand, he'd told her. His criminal history reports supported the boast.

"I mean, a guy's gotta eat, Ms. Olson, right? Customer comes calling with cold, hard cash? What's a guy to do?" Petey said when they were discussing his latest appeal.

He had a lilting Southern accent acquired in south Alabama, he'd told her, where he'd worked at the Mercedes plant. Which is how he'd developed his particular craft.

Petey saw himself as a sophisticated thief with a smile on his face and filled with good cheer. "Stealing German vee-hicles ain't no job for amateurs, you know? Takes skill and cunning, right? I'm an artiste, not a car thief? Car makers oughta hire me to keep 'em out of trouble, don't cha know?"

Olson was skeptical about Petey's artistic talents, but she had to admire his guts. He rarely stayed out of trouble for more than a few months. He'd run out of money and get right back into the game.

She smiled at him, wondering why he was so antsy today. Petey was pleasant enough every time she'd met with him. It was hard not to like the guy.

He'd described his process earlier in their relationship. Mostly, he knew how and where to acquire gadgets that he could use to "rejigger" the security systems on the vehicles. Then he'd use the altered equipment to steal the signal for a keyless entry system and start the vehicle and drive it away.

He'd bragged that the security systems were upgraded all the time by the manufacturers. But as soon as new security systems were developed, hackers figured out how to bypass them. Petey knew a few sophisticated hackers.

"The biggest weakness in the systems is the car owners, right? They're not careful with their keys? And they don't buy a new car every day? So a guy wants last year's model?" Petey slapped his palms in a glancing blow and cackled with glee. "I'm outta there! Piece 'a cake!"

As good as Petey was at stealing cars, he wasn't equally good at running from the law. Obviously. Which was how he'd acquired such a long record at his relatively young age.

When the guard had signaled the last call, Petey craned his neck around and looked at the clock. He signaled to the guard on his side and stood. "Sorry we gotta cut this short today, but I gotta run, Ms. Olson."

"Okay. Your appeal's another month away. We can talk more next time," she said as she tossed her legal pad and pencil into her briefcase and snapped it closed. When she looked up, Petey was already hustling through the door on the other side, hands in the pockets of his orange jumpsuit.

Olson shook her head. After all these years, she'd seen just about every kind of inmate there was. Petey was a lot less threatening than most. She approached the door and realized the guard had stepped away. She sat down again to wait, watching the clock tick closer to lockdown.

When he returned, he noticed she was alone in the interview room and opened the door with his key. "Sorry, Ms. Olson. Nature calls, you gotta go, you know?"

"No problem." She stepped through into the hallway, and they retraced the route toward the lobby that they'd taken earlier.

Just as they walked through the last locked door, the entire world became chaos. Everything seemed to happen at once.

Olson heard something like a thunderous sonic boom that seemed to come from the other side of the prison building.

She felt the very earth move beneath her feet.

She lost her balance and landed on her stomach on the floor.

Ear-splitting noises she couldn't process or describe filled the lobby, feeling as if they were crushing her from all sides. Both hands flew up to cover her ears.

Emergency sirens and alarms began shrieking and blaring from every direction.

She twisted her head to look frantically, everywhere at once.

The guards who had been standing in the lobby rushed through the doors, deeper into the prison.

All of a sudden, Olson was alone in the room.

She scrambled along the floor toward the exit.

She crouched and then lunged to her feet and pushed hard on the heavy steel with her full weight. The door didn't budge.

There were no windows. She couldn't see outside.

"Now what?" she said.

She smelled disaster next.

The ventilation system began to circulate heavy smoke, possibly generated by a big fire somewhere within the building.

She glanced at the clock on the wall. It wasn't 7:30 yet.

Even so, the entire prison had been locked down.

Whatever disaster had occurred, Olson couldn't fathom.

But she knew for sure she had no way out.

"I hope to hell a tactical team is on the way," she said, wishing she'd made the time to study the prison's vulnerability analysis.

Detailed knowledge of the prison's risks and readiness might have been helpful. Except for the emergency lighting, she was alone in the dark.

CHAPTER 9

Friday, May 13
Near Bolton Correctional Facility
7:15 p.m.

Two miles from Bolton prison, the hacker sat on a lawn chair on top of a Suburban. The SUV was parked on a hillock. A pair of binoculars stood on a tripod in front of him. His gloved fingers stabbed at the keys on a laptop connected to a large mobile phone antenna.

Even in the unseasonable South Dakota cold, he sweated. Nerves.

He'd watched a hundred Hollywood movies that showed aircraft controls hacked and the plane flown by a computer from a remote location. Unlike a lot of things they put in movies, this particular stunt was actually true.

But it wasn't like playing a video game.

Controlling an A320 so stealthily that no one knew it, including the pilot? Well, that required another level of skill entirely.

First there was the preparation of the aircraft.

Wiring had to be changed. Control signals had to be routed through new boxes.

Those boxes had to mimic the aircraft's original commands well enough to fool the aircraft computers into accepting that the pilot was doing the flying. And then those boxes had to be expertly controlled from a remote location.

While hacking into the A320's systems through a radio link was technically feasible, cellphones offered a much simpler solution.

But cellphones came with a huge drawback, which was one of the reasons the hacker was sweating.

Without good cell coverage, connecting with the plane's signals was a hit or miss affair.

And finding good cell coverage with strong signals that didn't blink, out in the middle of nowhere like this, was about as likely as, well, he couldn't think of anything less likely at the moment.

As the A320 had descended, he'd held his breath, struggling to make that connection.

Ninety seconds before impact, he finally established a solid signal strong enough to take control from the pilot.

He'd had only the briefest of time to change the plane's flightpath.

The hacker got lucky.

The pilot screwed up. He had brought the aircraft in way too hot to land.

Which made the big plane more maneuverable using the hacker's equipment.

He breathed a relieved sigh when his last-minute changes immediately took effect.

The hacker watched through the binoculars as the Airbus hurtled toward the prison and slammed into it.

"Yes!" he said, fist-pumping the air.

A satisfyingly hard hit. Not the angle he'd hoped for, but a significant glancing blow.

More than good enough. Maybe good enough to get a performance bonus, even.

He glimpsed chunks of white flying through the air as the A320 broke up. The wings and tail, probably. Ripped off by the prison wall before the long, hollow body slammed into the concrete.

The prison wall buckled, peeling outward as the aircraft tore along the side. A giant plume of dust welled up, only to be engulfed by roiling flames.

The A320 was traveling at 300 knots at the time of impact, generating enough heat to ignite the fuel.

The fuselage continued its carnage. Ripping through the prison wall like a hot knife through butter.

He nodded with satisfaction as he watched the results of his work unfold. His client would have to be totally thrilled with this. The results were awesome! Well beyond his expectations.

The big fuselage traveled past the edge of the building.

It was on the ground now.

Sliding across the concrete exercise yard, cutting through the razor wire fence, and churning its way across the grass. It left a trail of flame rising from a point under the jet's belly and mushrooming out in yellow and black.

The plane covered the earth along a straight line. Its path entirely predictable.

The hacker moved his binoculars to see along the plane's destructive trail. One of the perimeter guard towers came into view. He could see activity behind the glass.

The guard inside saw what was coming. His face contorted in horror.

The plane smashed through the lower half of the tower, toppling it in painfully slow motion. The manned room at the top pirouetted over the fuselage before it became engulfed in the overwhelming flames.

Two hundred feet beyond the prison perimeter, the aircraft eventually came to a stop. A trail of fire led all the way from its initial impact point to its resting place.

The building had been peeled open. The interior floors and wall were laid bare. Survivors were scrambling to get away from the edge as debris rained down and flames billowed up.

The hacker wanted to stay and watch the destruction unfold. Instead, he reluctantly turned his attention to the exercise yard.

Initially, the inmates had run toward safety and from the chaos caused by the crash. But in mere moments, they realized the escape opportunity that had inexplicably presented itself.

The guards soon realized it, too.

All hell broke loose.

He unplugged his laptop, slid off the roof of the SUV, and dived into the driver's seat. The engine was already running and he'd pointed the vehicle down the road.

He rammed the accelerator to the floor, and the Suburban took off. Tires squealed. The lawn chair and equipment he had used to hack into and control the aircraft tumbled from the roof and scattered across the ground.

The hacker didn't care. No one would ever find the debris. And even if they did, nothing would tie it back to him.

He had no time to spare.

The road ahead was straight. The speedometer needle climbed past a hundred. The SUV weaved as a crosswind hit.

His stomach churned, and he gripped the wheel harder, but he kept his foot planted.

When the big prison had been built, the feds had made an arrangement with the local police for additional support in the event of an emergency.

This was the mother of all emergencies, and they were at least ten minutes away. He had to get in and get his passengers out before reinforcements arrived.

The hacker accelerated into a sharp bend using the full width of the road. Sweeping out to the curb, kissing the apex, and kicking up clouds of dust on the far side.

The prison was to his right, black smoke billowing high into the sky as the fuel continued to burn. Lights flashed ahead, and sirens wailed.

His stomach flipped a couple of times and he clamped his mouth shut to hold back the vomit.

He liked creating disaster. But he was terrified of running toward it.

He took a concrete road to the right, smashing through a barrier marked with lawyer's gobbledygook to cover the government's ass if trespassers got shot.

He put his hand on the side of his seat and wrapped his fingers around the Glock. He'd come prepared to cover his own ass with bullets, not words.

Ahead, the remains of the old Airbus were still spouting flames. Fire and black smoke poured out of the windows and a hundred open holes in the fuselage.

The line of fire the A320 had laid down had taken hold on the grass to the north of the buildings.

The plane had uprooted the razor wire fences as if they were a child's toy. The fence posts hung at lazy angles, still swaying with the weight of wire.

The hacker aimed for the largest gap in the fence and slowed.

The inmates in the exercise yard had been quick to act. Some were running and some were staring, probably trying to decide if they'd make it or get sent back to do even more time.

He shivered when he noticed a huge white guy dangling what had once been the connections between shackles from his wrists and ankles. His eyes were dull, but he moved like a man escaping from hell.

At least two dozen inmates were running like rabbits. Maybe more.

The hacker locked the SUV's doors and kept going toward the exercise yard. He'd been paid to collect three inmates. Only three.

He steered along the left side of the approaching crowd rushing in the opposite direction. Unsure whether the Suburban carried friend or enemy, they gave him a wide berth.

Fifty yards away, two inmates had shed their orange jumpsuits. One man ripped off his T-shirt and waved it around his head.

Something no one would think to do. A bizarre action amid the chaos. A signal.

He slowed and angled the SUV toward them. As the SUV came closer, the hacker recognized his targets from the photographs.

The hacker pressed the door locks to open the doors.

Keegan jumped into the passenger seat. Walsh, holding his left bicep with his right hand to staunch the blood that seeped through his shirt, struggled into the back seat.

The third passenger, the big white guy with the shackles, was slow, but he was close and still coming. He expected to join them in the Suburban.

"Let's go," Keegan commanded.

"Aren't we taking him along?" the hacker asked, pointing.

Keegan glanced out the window and shook his head.

"Are you sure? He's on my list. He's expecting to come with us," the hacker said, alarmed. Not only because of the money he'd been paid and already spent. Failure wasn't an option. That had been made crystal clear to him from the outset. His life was on the line.

Walsh cast a worried glance toward Keegan, who shook his head sharply.

"Get going," Walsh ordered.

The hacker's eyes widened and his nostrils flared. His breath came in short spurts. He glanced into the rearview mirror.

Walsh glared toward him. "Are you deaf? Get us the hell out of here. Now!"

The hacker stabbed the lock button again before the other inmates tried to breach the SUV.

Walsh was the bagman. Keegan was calling the shots. If Keegan said to leave the big guy behind, no argument was allowed.

Keegan was even more ruthless than the hacker had been told. Which raised his blood pressure considerably.

The hacker stomped on the accelerator and swung the wheel hard. The Suburban kicked up dust and stones as it spun around. He glanced into the rearview mirror and saw the big man's face settle into a deeply angry scowl.

The escaping inmates had reached the perimeter fence, crowding the way ahead. He opened the window on his side and fired a burst of gunshots over their heads. The inmates scrabbled back, and the Suburban tore through the gap.

At the end of the drive, he turned onto the concrete road and accelerated the heavy SUV up to speed. He'd need as much distance between him and the prison as he could manage. Two miles away, when they were out of surveillance range, they'd transfer to another vehicle.

The hacker had researched the three men before he'd accepted the contract. Money's great but knowing who he'd be dealing with kept him alive. Having seen Keegan's cold-blooded disregard for Denny's life, he struggled to control his nerves. He really wanted to stay alive.

Keegan shrugged his shirt back on, turned up the temperature, and looked out the window.

His passengers didn't speak. He didn't expect them to. Men like Keegan and Walsh didn't make small talk.

He'd have appreciated a "nice job" at least. He'd pulled off a feat not many hackers out there could possibly match.

Oh, well. He shrugged. It was what it was.

CHAPTER 10

Friday, May 13
Bolton, South Dakota
7:20 p.m.

Almost three hours ago, after landing in Rapid City, Kim and Burke had deplaned and located the full-sized navy blue Lincoln Navigator waiting in the parking lot, exactly where the Boss had said they'd find it.

"Black SUVs practically scream 'federal agent' these days," Burke had explained after they'd stowed the bags in the back and climbed into the front seats. "Navy blue is a solid compromise when we're working undercover."

Burke had settled behind the steering wheel, adjusted the mirrors and the seat to his satisfaction. He'd entered the address of their hotel into the GPS.

"You know we're not officially undercover, right? This operation is strictly off the books. Which means we haven't been approved by anyone except the Boss," Kim said, as she settled into the passenger seat.

He should know the parameters of their assignment already, but she wanted him to be clear on the protocols. Meaning, there were none.

Burke shrugged. "Yeah, I know. Our orders are to do the job on our own. We have zero support through the usual channels. We can reveal our official mission, but that's all."

Kim nodded. "So, we just tell people that we are assigned to the Special Personnel Task Force, and we're conducting a thorough background check on Reacher. He's being considered for a special classified assignment. We don't know what that is because it's above our clearance levels."

He cocked his head and slipped his sunglasses on as they exited the parking garage. "And people buy that?"

"It's up to us to sell it. So be convincing."

Kim was the lead agent on the case, and Burke was number two. Number two drives, Gaspar had always insisted. Truth was Kim preferred the passenger seat anyway. More operational flexibility.

Not that she intended to let him know it. He seemed to need the feeling of control. Or maybe he had something to prove to her.

He was new on the job. He deserved time to tackle the learning curve. As long as he didn't put lives at risk, she'd let his pompous attitude go. For now.

"Speaking of the job at hand," Burke said once they reached the highway that would take them to Bolton. "I read your reports. So I'm up to speed on the official details."

Kim nodded.

"I'd like to know what you left out, though." He turned his head to glance in her direction. She couldn't see his eyes behind the sunglasses. He couldn't see hers for the same reason.

"What makes you think I left anything out?"

"Good agents always have a cover-your-ass file. You're telling me you don't?"

"You think I need one?"

Burke had returned his attention to the traffic. But his tone clearly conveyed his opinion. "I think this Jack Reacher guy is someone I'd have been proud to serve with, back in my SEAL days. But I doubt he's fit for civilian life. Most guys I've met, with service records like his, are too rough around the edges, you know?"

Kim nodded and said nothing. But she wondered if Burke was describing himself. Was he too prone to solve problems with combat solutions? Was that what had happened on his last Hostage Rescue Team operation? And was that why she was saddled with him now?

When she didn't respond, Burke turned on the satellite radio to a classic rock music station and they passed the miles accompanied by the best years of rock. At least, that's what Kim's dad had called it when she was growing up.

The soundtrack of her childhood was mostly the Rolling Stones and Bob Seeger and the Eagles, with a little bit of Beatles thrown in, even though they were on their way down when she was still a kid. Classic rock reminded her of home.

They'd been on the road for almost two hours when Burke glanced at the GPS. "We're about twenty miles out. There's a truck stop coming up on the right. How about we stop for coffee?"

"I never say no to coffee," Kim replied from behind her sunglasses. Sunset was almost another hour away and the sky was still bright enough to force a squint.

"I'll make a note of that," Burke grinned as he slowed the big beast down for the turn and dialed down the music. "From the files I got, looks like Bolton, South Dakota, owes its prosperity to government spending."

"Nothing special about that. Thousands of small towns across America are in the same situation."

But Bolton's revenue came from a slightly less common expenditure. The relatively new maximum-security federal prison brought development money, jobs, visitors, and notoriety to Bolton in a way nothing else would have. The state and the county piled on by adding their own prisons and jails to the compound. The final result was that the prison compound became a walled city in itself.

"You ever been to a prison town?" Burke asked when he steered the SUV away from the fuel pumps toward the store and parked. He stretched his arms over his shoulders.

"Probably. Why?" Kim unlatched her seatbelt and removed the alligator clamp she'd placed at the retractor to keep the stiff webbing from slicing off her head.

"Prison towns are a different world. Totally artificial in some ways," Burke said. He opened the big Navigator's door and stepped outside.

Kim did the same from her side and stretched the kinks out of her back. She'd been sitting a long time today. Maybe the hotel would have a treadmill where she could run a bit before bed.

She walked toward the store and Burke walked alongside her, shortening his steps to match hers.

"I lived in a prison town for a few years," he said. "Every week supplies roll into the prison, and waste management contractors haul away the trash. Visitors arrive at the prison by bus from the town, where cheap motels and fast-food restaurants of every kind pop up to serve them."

She pulled the door open and walked inside.

Burke followed, still talking. "Employment will be of the minimum wage variety, mostly."

"A new hospital was built on the outskirts of Bolton, though. A medical complex grew up around it, too. Those will be better jobs," Kim replied, searching for the coffee counter inside the store. She followed her nose to find the setup in the back.

Burke shook his head. "Turns out visitors, workers, inmates, and prison employees all need medical care. Most of that is government funded, too. Schools, services. All government."

"What's your point?"

"Bolton is a company town. And the company is the government. And, if you were a philosophical sort, you might say the government was the people," Burke finished, finally.

It was about the tenth long-winded philosophical lecture upon which he'd pontificated since they'd left Rapid City.

Which was more than enough.

"Or you might say that people need work to put food on the table, and a job's a job." Kim poured black coffee.

That was one of the best things about truck stops. They always had good fresh coffee. She found the lid and pressed it onto the large Styrofoam cup.

"They need a job after whatever half-baked crime their dumb loved ones tried didn't pan out, you mean?" Burke said with a snarky edge.

Kim frowned.

Burke said, "We don't catch the smart ones, you know."

"No?" She grinned and gave him a cheeky, "Speak for yourself."

For half a moment, he seemed speechless. But that didn't last.

His eyes crinkled, and he laughed out loud, and she liked him a lot better, instantly.

It was the first time he'd exhibited any ability to take a joke, which was one of the things she missed since Gaspar retired. Jousting with wit and humor against a worthy competitor was fun.

Would Burke be so worthy? Not yet. But it was early days for their partnership. She could hope.

After a quick bathroom break, they returned to the SUV, and Burke pulled onto the road.

They'd driven five miles farther east when Kim peered ahead, squinting as she pointed off to the north. "Do you see that?"

Burke lowered his sunglasses and stared into the distance. "Looks like a big fire. All I can see for sure is a lot of black smoke."

"Yeah. And from here, it looks like the fire might be close to Bolton prison. Check the radio. See if you can find breaking news," she said as she fished her cell phone out of her pocket and speed-dialed Gaspar.

CHAPTER 11

Friday, May 13
North of Bolton Prison
7:35 p.m.

The hacker had his foot hard on the accelerator. His hands gripped the steering wheel, which was the only thing controlling his shaking. The kid was a fool. He should have known Keegan couldn't be trusted. He should have understood that from the start.

Keegan checked his watch. They'd been traveling a full five minutes already. The prison siren must have been damaged in the crash and the fire that followed. Or maybe the cacophony was so loud that the siren was overcome.

Either way, the prison guards would be calling reinforcements. No point in escaping from prison just to be recaptured on the road. They had to get out of the area and do it fast.

Bolton PD would be sending all personnel to their prearranged checkpoints. Keegan had seen the map. The checkpoints were along a one-mile radius from the prison.

Which meant he needed to get beyond the one-mile limit before Bolton PD arrived and set up the blocks. No doubt, their orders would be shoot to kill.

Five minutes was too long.

Over the years, Keegan had honed his ability to appear calm in every situation. He'd also learned to control his quick-flash temper embedded in his Irish DNA.

A casual observer wouldn't know that from the moment he'd seen the A320 hurtling from the sky toward the prison, his heart rate had pounded hard. Even the top of his head seemed electrically charged. His breathing had quickened and his entire body alerted, poised for escape.

The plan had been meticulously sequenced by his most trusted guys. He'd rehearsed the steps in his head over and over for weeks, looking for the slightest mistake. He'd found a few, told Walsh, who had passed them along through Denny to the lawyer, and they were resolved long before the jetliner set him free.

Keegan had trusted no one but Walsh, and only with the most necessary details of the escape plan. Until and unless he proved otherwise, which Keegan didn't expect to happen, Walsh could be counted on to do his job. He'd be handsomely rewarded when they reached Canada, but that's not why Walsh was so reliable.

It was old-fashioned loyalty to Keegan that kept Walsh alive. Keegan trusted Walsh and no one else.

Keegan was getting antsy. Walsh must have felt the vibe.

"Where's the Ford?" Walsh demanded from the backseat.

The young hacker glanced into the rearview mirror nervously. He tried to speak, but no sound passed his vocal cords. He cleared his throat and tried again. "Two miles down the side road up ahead. Four miles north of the prison. Just like you said. We're almost there."

"How long?" Walsh said.

The hacker choked on his own saliva before he coughed out, "Five more minutes, tops."

"Get there in three," Walsh insisted.

The kid didn't object. He pressed the accelerator and the Suburban lunged ahead.

Keegan kept his senses alert for the sound of approaching helicopters and sirens from law enforcement and first responder vehicles likely to be speeding toward the prison. He didn't expect to hear any. There were no real towns north of the prison for at least a hundred miles.

The point of the jetliner crash was to do maximum damage to the prison building and its surroundings.

Keep them all busy, giving Keegan time to get away.

Everything had worked exactly as planned.

So far.

He wasn't in Canada yet.

But he would be.

The kid kept his speed for another couple of minutes before he began to slow, peering out the side window.

"What are you looking for?" Walsh asked.

"A big rock," the kid squeaked.

"There's rocks all over the place," Walsh said, annoyed.

"Yeah. This is a pink rock. I put a mark on it. And I checked the mileage. We're almost there," he slowed, lowered the window, and stuck his head out like a dog, looking at the ground as the SUV moved past.

Keegan's patience was at the breaking point, but he held his temper.

Walsh would deal with the hacker soon enough.

A few more minutes and the kid spotted his rock. He slowed the SUV and turned left onto hard ground, moving through the underbrush toward a stand of trees.

He pointed, "I parked it back there."

Walsh grunted as the Suburban bounced along the dirt path. Keegan had said nothing, but he'd noticed when Walsh's left arm had been sliced by flying debris back at the exercise yard. Walsh had sucked it up and kept moving.

But the wound must have been worse than Walsh let on. Fresh blood had soaked through his street clothes underneath the sleeve in his orange jumpsuit.

Keegan was starting to worry that Walsh wouldn't be able to complete the job. Maybe they should have let Denny come along after all. Too late to do anything about that now.

The kid drove around the stand of trees and pulled up next to another SUV. Keegan's stomach tensed when he saw it.

The kid had been instructed to get a second vehicle, but the directions should have been more specific.

This SUV was silver instead of black. It was a Ford instead of a Chevy. They were too similar for Keegan's comfort level.

He shook his head. The hacker had been hired to crash the plane and hustle them away from the prison during the inevitable chaos that followed.

He'd done all of that.

He'd earned his money.

But like a lot of geeks, his intelligence didn't run to the practical aspects of criminal life.

After the kid stopped the vehicle, Keegan opened the door and stepped onto the first free ground he'd experienced in months.

He took deep breaths, imagining the free air smelled better here than the exercise yard at Bolton. Which was nonsense, of course. Air was air. And they were not even five miles away from the prison.

"Where's the stuff we told you to bring?" Walsh asked.

"In the back of the Explorer," the kid replied.

Keegan walked over to the Ford, opened the driver's door, and saw the key fob on the seat. Keegan walked around to the back of the SUV. He saw the guns and supplies and gave Walsh a thumbs-up signal.

"Come on. We need to wipe down this cabin with the bleach you brought," Walsh said to the kid. "It's in the back, right?"

"Yeah."

Walsh used his right arm more than his left, but he didn't complain about the damage to his bicep. Keegan hoped that was a sign that the pain wouldn't overwhelm him. They had a long way to go before they'd be safe from recapture. Canada wouldn't extradite him because of the death penalty. But they had to get across the border first. Seven hundred miles north.

The kid was nervous, but he climbed out of the Suburban and trudged around to the cargo hold. He opened the back hatch, reached in, and collected the spray bleach and a roll of paper towels.

"Hurry up. We've got to get this done and get the hell out of here," Walsh said. The kid went right to work. "I'll be right back. I gotta take a leak."

Walsh walked around to the other side of the tree and into the bushes. Keegan lost sight of him. A couple of minutes later, Walsh howled and cursed loudly. Two more sharp howls followed.

"What the hell?" Keegan said as he hurried toward the tree, gun in hand. When he came around the big tree trunk, he saw Walsh stomping the ground with three large rattlesnakes clamped onto his calf.

All three of the snakes were at least five feet long. They thrashed and squirmed, bodies writhing, tails rattling. Each triangular head was affixed to Walsh's leg like a vise.

"Get them the hell off me!" Walsh yelled. "They came at me out of nowhere. Stabbed me with their fangs. No time to move."

Keegan looked into the brush. A nest of pit vipers writhed like worms in a pile near Walsh's left foot.

"Move this way, Walsh!" Keegan said. He didn't want to shoot at the nest of snakes. The risk that someone might hear the gunshots this close to the prison was too great.

The kid came running with a shovel in his hand. "Stand still! Stand still!"

Walsh did the best he could to comply. The kid raised the shovel and stabbed the blade down hard onto the biggest of the three snakes. He raised the shovel and stabbed again.

On the third strike, he severed the snake's body into two pieces. But still it didn't let go of Walsh's leg.

Walsh struggled to drag the weight of the snakes and moved farther away from the nest.

The kid began stabbing the shovel at the second snake. He managed to sever the second one with the first blow. Two more blows to the third viper and Walsh was free of the long bodies.

Keegan scanned the ground until he found a fallen tree branch about four inches in diameter. He picked it up and walked over to Walsh. He bent and shoved the stick under the rattler's head, pushing upward, until it released Walsh's flesh and the head fell to the ground.

He did the same thing twice more until Walsh was free. Then the three men moved farther away from the nest.

Keegan turned to the hacker. "Finish up with the bleach. You got a first aid kit?"

The kid nodded. "In the back of the Suburban."

The kid went to work, vigorously spraying bleach over every surface inside the passenger areas of the vehicle. He swiped it around and then sprayed it all again.

Keegan nodded approval. Soon, all evidence that Keegan and Walsh had ever been inside the Suburban would be destroyed or degraded beyond any hope of analysis.

Walsh found the first aid kit. He stripped off his clothes and stood in the cool air in his underwear. The kit contained a small bottle of alcohol, which Walsh opened and poured over the six puncture wounds in his left calf.

He winced as the alcohol hit the wounds. "These bites hurt like a son of a bitch."

Keegan didn't see much blood. Six streams ran down Walsh's calves, but that was all. The only thing he knew about rattlesnake venom was what he'd learned from old western movies, which was probably exaggerated anyway.

"You think that alcohol will fix those bites?" Keegan asked.

Walsh shrugged. "Hell, I don't know. I've got no idea what to do for rattlesnake bites."

"Any swelling?"

"Maybe a little. Hard to say."

"How are you feeling? Any sort of reaction to the venom?"

Walsh shrugged again. "I could use a bottle of water."

Keegan nodded and collected a bottle from the back of the Suburban for him. They'd lived in Boston all their lives. The only snakes they'd had to contend with were the two-legged variety.

While Walsh and the kid handled their tasks, Keegan changed into different street clothes and stuffed his old ones, along with the orange jumpsuit, into a garbage bag.

When he'd finished dressing, he caught Walsh's gaze and gave him a solid nod. He glanced at the digital clock on the dashboard and noted the time.

Walsh quickly overpowered the kid. Knocked him to the ground and, even with his own injuries slowing him down, managed to choke the kid to death.

At first, the kid kicked and bucked and tried to pry Walsh's strong right forearm from his neck. None of his efforts made any difference. Walsh kept the pressure hard and strong.

The kid stopped struggling after twenty seconds. He lost consciousness sixty seconds later.

Walsh kept his weight against the kid's neck, never letting up until the deed was definitely done.

Keegan glanced at the clock again. The whole thing, start to finish, lasted eleven minutes.

He'd watched closely while Walsh worked. He was sloppy. Not as fast or solid as he normally was. Again, Keegan wished he'd let Denny into the Suburban back there in the yard.

When he'd finished the kid off, Walsh rolled off his chest and stood up, a little breathless. "Take the body with us? Dump it with the Ford when we drop it off?"

"No." Keegan shook his head. "Spray him down good with the bleach. Then roll the body under the SUV. With luck, those snakes and a few other predators will get him before he's found in a few days."

"I can set this Suburban on fire. Burn the evidence," Walsh suggested, still breathing harder than he should have been.

"No. The fire would draw attention that we don't want. We'll be long gone before they find him," Keegan said, moving toward the Ford. "Come on. Get changed. We need to get on the road."

Keegan donned a pair of latex gloves, sprayed the kid's body with the bleach, paying extra attention to potential evidence transfer spots. He rolled the kid under the Suburban with his running shoes.

Then he rummaged through the contents of the Suburban. He found the kid's wallet, cell phone, and another laptop.

Walsh pulled everything out of the wallet and tossed the contents into the weeds. Then he smashed the cellphone and removed the SIM card and battery. He threw most of the pieces as far as possible and flung the rest into the water-filled ditch near the rattlers' nest.

He destroyed the laptop and tossed the pieces as far as he could fling them, saving a few of the more fragile looking electronics for the ditch.

Nothing he did would thwart the discovery of the hacker or his role in the prison break. But it might slow the feds down enough. All he wanted was a bit more breathing room.

When he'd finished, Walsh found his fresh street clothes in the Explorer. He pulled off the white T-shirt and tore it into a wide strip. He tied the strip around his bicep, hoping to staunch the bleeding that had started again when he strangled the kid.

Then he changed quickly, shoved his bloody prison wear into another bag, and moved in behind the wheel of the Explorer.

Keegan got into the passenger seat. Walsh slipped one of the pistols into his pocket, started the SUV, and drove slowly to the roadway, his left elbow on the armrest with his forearm raised.

Walsh rolled onto the northbound county road. He looked into the rearview mirror. Keegan turned his head and glanced south toward the prison. Flames and black smoke rose high in the sky.

"We lost a little time, but we can make it up on the road," Walsh said. "It'll be nothing but chaos back there at the prison for a while."

Keegan replied. "Yeah. The building was severely damaged. Dead inmates and guards. At least a dozen escapees, and probably more."

"All the cop shops will be scrambling. Can't see helicopters yet." Walsh peered upward through the windshield.

"They'll be on the way if they're not out there already," Keegan said.

"What do you guess is going on at the prison?"

"Right now, they're overwhelmed, I'd imagine," Keegan said. "Trying to get an accurate headcount, rounding up the escapees, getting the injured to medical care, locking down the destroyed prison for the night."

Walsh chuckled. "All of that should keep them occupied for a while."

With any luck, they wouldn't even know Keegan and Walsh were gone. At least, not right away.

The more distance they could put between them and the prison, the better.

CHAPTER 12

Friday, May 13
Bolton, South Dakota
7:45 p.m.

Fern Olson looked at the big clock high on the wall. Forty minutes had passed since she'd left the client meeting room. No one had come through the heavy doors to check on her. Perhaps they didn't realize she was there.

Something had happened, but she didn't know what it was. Thinking it through, she'd narrowed down the options.

She'd ruled out tornadoes and derechos because the weather forecast had been clear. No storms anywhere in the area.

Fires and explosions were possibilities. Terrorism was too, she supposed, although terrorism was a rare thing in South Dakota.

Prisoner escapes were even rarer. If Bolton Prison had ever experienced an escape attempt, she hadn't heard about it. And she would have heard, she thought.

Most likely, the cause of the disturbance was a prison riot. They'd had a couple of those out here in the past. They'd had a couple of false alarms, too.

One of the firm's clients had been charged in a riot years ago. As she thought about it, she recalled that was when her friend Janet Salter had died.

Olson was a junior lawyer and she'd been forced to learn the case so she could write the briefs. With her forefingers, she kneaded the headache that began behind her temples as she thought about her friend and the rest of the facts, as well as she could recall them.

The prison had a crisis plan back then. If a riot started, Bolton PD would serve as the backup for the prison guards. Secondary backup was the Highway Patrol.

Riots could start without warning, and that's what had happened. Maybe the riot was to cover up an escape, too. She couldn't recall exactly.

Anyway, when the siren went off, all of the Bolton PD rushed out to the prison, and while they were gone, someone killed Janet Salter.

Olson remembered more of the facts as she thought it through. It turned out to be a false alarm, hadn't it? "There had been no escape. No riot, either. Janet died for nothing."

Olson looked around. The emergency lighting cast a red pallor over the empty waiting room. The smell of burning petroleum had wafted through the ventilation system but had not filled the room with characteristic heavy black smoke.

Maybe this was a false alarm, too. Just like all those years ago, maybe there was nothing terrible occurring now, either.

"A training exercise? Maybe that's all it is."

Even as she spoke the hope quietly, she knew this was no false alarm. Whatever was actually happening, this was not a drill.

She heard sirens continue to blare around the prison. Occasionally, she heard footsteps and clanging and heavy boots pounding on the floor and shouting between men.

She'd heard no shots fired and she imagined that was a good sign. Or it could be that the solid walls surrounding her were muting the noises outside.

Olson shivered slightly and pulled her jacket closer around her body. It was a visceral reaction. The room itself was climate-controlled. It wasn't too hot or too cold. At least, not yet.

She wished she had her phone. Or any phone. But she didn't.

How long would she be required to sit here? Her son would be wondering why she'd never made it home. Maybe he'd call her office. Maybe someone would call the police.

"Or not," she said. "Someone will find me eventually. Could be a long night's wait."

She stood up and walked around the room, just to work the kinks out of her muscles. On the third lap, she thought she heard sirens coming up the driveway and stopping in the parking lot out front.

"Hallelujah," she said, feeling a smile spreading along her face when a gloved fist pounded on the heavy exit door.

"Open up! Bolton PD!" the guy yelled.

Olson hurried over to the door and pounded and yelled back. "It's Fern Olson. I'm locked in. Let me out."

"Ms. Olson, it's Captain Irwin Mitchell. Bolton PD. Hang tight. We've got to find someone to open the door," he shouted through the reinforced steel.

She put her back to the door and waited. Her legs were rubbery. She needed the support of the heavy door. Tears of relief sprang to her eyes and she wiped them away and sucked in a deep breath before the tears became a flood.

She'd be out of here, get debriefed, and on her way home in no time. She whispered as if her son could hear her. "I'm coming, Noah. I'll be there soon."

Another ten minutes passed before Mitchell returned with a key to unlock the door. Olson had regained her composure and began to notice the outrage deep in her gut.

When Mitchell opened up, Olson grabbed her briefcase and stepped outside into the fading sunlight. She took a deep breath of outside air and coughed when the pollution hit her throat. The smoke was stronger out here where it hadn't been filtered through the ventilation system.

A group of four Bolton PD officers, suited up in anti-riot gear, dashed past her into the lobby.

The parking lot swarmed with official vehicles, lights flashing, personnel weighed down by various gear, scurrying to and fro like moths circling bright light.

"You okay?" Mitchell asked, concerned about her coughing probably. "You need a medic or anything?"

She shook her head. Her limbs had begun to quiver again. Shock, probably. "No. I'm good. I just want to get in my car and go home."

"Tell me what happened in there," Mitchell said, feet apart, hands on his duty belt.

"I don't really know. I was here for client meetings. I'd finished up and left the room with an escort. We made it to the lobby. Next thing I know, everything's locked down, and I'm alone, literally in the dark." She heard the catch in her voice and cleared her throat again. The irritating smoke had settled quickly into every crevice.

Mitchell nodded. "Okay. We'll need a detailed statement from you. But right now, I don't have anyone who can do it. We'll contact you as soon as we can."

He turned to walk away and she grabbed his arm. "Wait. Tell me what happened here. I deserve to know, don't you think?"

Mitchell ran a palm over his weary face and gave her the bare facts. "We're still gathering intel. But it looks like a cargo plane crashed into the exercise yard out back. It hit the prison wall, too. Did some damage. We don't know how much. Might have a few prisoners on the loose. We're not sure."

She stared at him as if he was speaking an alien language.

"Can you drive yourself home?" Mitchell asked, turning to wave to one of his officers who was calling to him from inside.

"Yeah, I've got a car. Over there," she turned to point into the parking lot where she'd left her red BMW a few hours ago. She gasped. "It's gone!"

Mitchell turned toward the empty parking space. "Okay. I'll get you a ride. We'll talk about the car later."

A female officer came over when Mitchell waved. "This is Officer Flax. She'll drive you home. Give her the details on your car. I gotta go."

He turned and walked into the building while Olson stared after him, mouth agape.

Officer Flax said, "Come on. I'll take the stolen vehicle report and get that going. So you won't have to wait so long. How's that?"

They walked side-by-side to the Bolton PD vehicle and climbed in. Flax started the engine and drove toward the exit.

"How many prisoners escaped?" Olson asked.

"We don't know. We're trying to get a headcount. The ones in the exercise yard just scrambled. And it looks like the area of the building that was damaged might have opened up an escape route for a few more."

"Give me a ballpark number," Olson said, fastening her seatbelt and cinching it tight.

"Forty. Fifty, maybe." Flax shrugged, watching the road, dodging oncoming traffic. "We'll find most of them in short order. We've got plenty of personnel out there. A couple of helos and a lot of cars, and these guys are on foot. Highway Patrol is on the way. The fugitives will be getting tired and cold and hungry, too."

"Where are you planning to take them?"

"We'll house as many as we can. Otherwise, there's an evacuation plan in place. It's just a matter of transport. It'll take us a few days, but we'll get it all sorted out. Don't worry," Flax said, like a mom talking to a five-year-old. "Now, tell me about your car. I'll put out a BOLO. They'll run out of gas and they don't have any money to refill. So it'll turn up. We'll find it. Don't worry."

"One of the inmates probably stole it, I guess," Olson said with a sigh. "And I think I know who it was."

CHAPTER 13

Friday, May 13
Bolton, South Dakota
7:55 p.m.

Burke had increased the Navigator's speed well over the legal limit and they'd covered significant ground. As they approached Bolton, the fire north of town became more visible, even as it seemed to weaken in strength.

Black smoke billowed skyward in the distance. Burke kept one hand on the steering wheel and his eyes on the road while he turned the radio dial attempting to find local breaking news.

Kim removed her sunglasses and peered into the distance. She listened to the radio with one ear while she waited for Gaspar to pick up her call. Her former partner was always available to her. The fact that he didn't answer seemed ominous somehow.

She stopped counting the rings after six and waited for his voicemail to kick in. When it did, she left a message and disconnected.

Only one choice now.

She located the Boss's cell phone and hit the speed dial button.

When the Boss didn't pick up her call, Kim didn't leave him a message. She was the only person who had access to this phone and the burner he'd connected to it on his end. He knew she was calling. He was deliberately ignoring her. He'd return her call when and if he felt like it.

She frowned. Situation normal.

The Boss was way less reliable than Gaspar in every way that mattered.

"I'm not finding anything on the airwaves," Burke said as they sped eastward along the highway.

Big ditches had been dug on each side of the road to carry running water. Maybe it was snowmelt. Maybe spring rains. Either way, it looked deep and fast from her vantage point.

Kim replied, "Might be too soon. If it just happened, the locals are scrambling to get whatever it is under control."

"We didn't hear an explosion."

"If it's the prison, we're too far away. Sound travels slower than light, and we saw the aftermath, not the event itself."

"That's a lot of black smoke. And what looks like a huge fire to go along with it," Burke said, still messing around with the radio. "Some kind of petroleum fire, probably."

Kim nodded. The familiar thrashing in the pit of her stomach worsened. She reached into her pocket for an antacid and popped it into her mouth.

Not many things were capable of producing a big petroleum fire like that. She mentioned the least likely option first. "Are they drilling oil out there?"

"No idea." Burke shrugged. "South Dakota is an oil-producing state. Most of the drilling is done down by Sioux Falls, as far as I know. But I didn't see anything about oil drilling near the prison or the town. Not in the reports Cooper gave us."

He glanced across the cabin and seemed to notice the pained expression on her face for the first time. "You're not going to vomit, are you?"

The back of her reptilian brain kicked into high gear. Every nerve ending in her body began to vibrate. She struggled to control the quivering in her voice.

"Where were you on nine-eleven?" she said quietly.

He frowned. "What? SEAL training. Why?"

"I was living in Washington, DC. Still in law school. Ten minutes after nine-thirty-seven in the morning, I saw smoke in the sky exactly like that. When Flight 77 crashed into the Pentagon."

"Are you kidding me?" He'd seen a lot of things in his life, but he hadn't been close to those attacks.

She paused, inhaled a deep breath, and held it for a count of four before she said, "From the looks of that smoke and the flames, if there's no oil rig out there, then I'm guessing we've got a downed jetliner."

"That's a pretty big leap, isn't it?" Burke's eyes widened, and his nostrils flared as he considered the idea. "Let's think this through. There're no railroads nearby. Might have been a big rig. A tanker. Those trucks can carry ten thousand gallons."

"Sure. But there're no roads for that kind of tanker anywhere near Bolton Prison. What would a big rig hauling that much petroleum be doing out there in the middle of nowhere?" Kim said just before her phone rang.

Gaspar.

She picked up the call. "Thanks for calling me back."

"Tell me you're not anywhere near Bolton Prison, Suzie Wong." His words were light, but his tone was deadly serious.

"Can't do that, Chico. Much as I'd like to," she replied. He was tracking her phone. He knew precisely where she was. The teasing was his way of telling her that he didn't like it. She didn't like it, either. "I'm going to put you on speaker."

She nodded toward the phone as she made the introductions. "Burke, this is Gaspar, my former partner. Gaspar, this is Burke. Just assigned to replace you. What's going on?"

"We don't know much yet." Gaspar paused a moment. "Looks like a cargo plane crashed into the side of the federal prison building. Only the pilot on board."

"So they are defending in place," she acknowledged the only reasonable alternative at the moment.

"They might be forced to evacuate. Too early to say," Gaspar replied. "Details are coming in piecemeal. You know how these things go. So far, reports we're getting say no damage to the state penitentiary or the county lockup, which are on the same site. And most of the federal facility is intact."

Burke glanced her way and gave her a solid nod to acknowledge she'd been right before he cleared his throat. "The plane exploded on impact or shortly after?"

Even before nine-eleven, Kim had hated to fly. Planes were reliable and crashes were rare. But mechanical things and human error being what they were, the chance that someone would screw up something was always a risk she preferred not to take.

Events like this crash cemented her opinion. People laughed at her, but she was right. Flying was dangerous. Every time.

She popped another antacid in her mouth, but her stomach felt like a creature clawing its way out.

Gaspar said, "An A320, based on what we can see from the satellites. Took out one side of the biggest prison building and destroyed one of the exercise yards. Locals are scrambling to get a handle on it and help is on the way."

"How many dead?" Kim asked.

"Don't know for sure. All we can say right now is that the damage appears to be contained to the north side of the building," Gaspar replied.

"How many prisoners escaped?" Kim asked, looking toward the sky. Helicopters would be swarming like mosquitos at a campfire, even if she couldn't see them from this distance.

"Don't know that, either. Maybe forty, give or take."

"What *do* you know?" Burke demanded sharply, like the superior officer he'd once been barking orders to the young seaman Gaspar never was.

A long pause hummed along the empty air.

Gaspar owed Burke nothing. In a bar, after a few drinks, late at night, maybe this was the point where the big dogs stopped sniffing each other and settled things with their fists.

Kim waited out the silence for several seconds before she turned off the speaker and raised the phone to her ear again. "Thanks, Chico. Any chance you've got video or still shots or anything at all to help us out here?"

A few more seconds of silence followed. It wasn't like Gaspar to pout. So he must have been seriously annoyed.

"We'll talk about Burke later. There're a lot of things about the guy that you don't know, and I don't like," Gaspar finally said, not in the least amused. "Meanwhile, keep your puppy on his leash."

"More like a Rottweiler. When we've got more time, maybe you can tell me exactly how I'm supposed to do that." Kim kneaded the headache that was just beginning between her eyebrows.

Gaspar's reservations about Burke raised her internal threat level meter into the red zone and held it there, needle pressing hard against the extreme position.

She took another breath and tried again. "So, FAA?"

Gaspar relented. For now. "Classified. Not for sharing."

"Okay," she said.

Although he knew she would tell Burke the facts. No way around it at this point.

Gaspar meant she wasn't to mention where he'd obtained the intel. Not to Burke or anyone else.

Gaspar's new job at Scarlett Investigations gave him access to all sorts of data the Boss and the law wouldn't allow her to reach. But that didn't mean Gaspar was authorized to access it or to share what he found.

"FAA says the plane was most likely an A320 cargo hauler out of Rapid City headed for Minneapolis. Fully loaded. They'd lost contact with the pilot," Gaspar said, wearily, as if the news was too exhausting to repeat. His tone became more somber. "So far, it looks like he flew straight into the building."

"Intentionally?" Kim widened her eyes and felt her heart thumping in her ears. Terrorists didn't usually hijack planes solo. The intel made very little sense. "Like a kamikaze or something?"

Burke flashed an angry stare her way. He didn't like being out of the loop, even temporarily.

Kim turned her gaze skyward. The intense flame and black smoke seemed to be growing as they came closer to the town.

Gaspar said, "Sounds crazy, I agree. I haven't seen the video. Just got a report, so far. Based on eyes and ears on the ground out there. I'm working on acquiring the rest. I'll send it to you as soon as I have it."

"Copy that," she said, mimicking his style of old. He chuckled before he hung up, and she was glad his good humor had partially returned. At least where she was concerned. Burke might be another matter entirely.

Man, she missed working closely with Gaspar.

"One more thing," he said before he hung up. "Smithers is on his way. He was in the area, and when the locals requested FBI assistance, he volunteered. He'll probably arrive before you do. I told him you were en route. He's expecting you."

She slipped the phone into her pocket. The news settled Kim's nerves a bit. Smithers was a solid agent. She'd worked with him in extremely tense situations twice before. Unlike Burke, she had no reservations about Smithers.

Peering into the distance, she saw a helicopter heading west, flying above the road. It was moving away from the fire, not toward it.

She lowered the window. The scent of burning in the distance filled her with dread.

The helo was still too far away to see clearly through the smoky haze.

"Burke," she said pointing skyward. "Eleven o'clock. Headed this way."

Burke glanced up to look. "What the hell?"

He reduced the pressure of his foot on the accelerator.

CHAPTER 14

Friday, May 13
Near Bolton, South Dakota
8:05 p.m.

Moments later, Kim could make out a car headed westward coming out of the smoke at a high rate of speed. The helo might have been chasing the car. Or might have been observing it. Either way, the pilot would be calling for officers on the ground to assist.

Burke said, "This would be a good time to have a radio car connected to local law enforcement. Without it, we have no idea what's going on."

She pointed the vehicle out to Burke. "There. Do you see it? A red car. Maybe a mile away?"

Burke leaned toward the windshield, peering ahead. "The helo is what? Chasing him?"

"Looks like it to me, but I'm really reading tea leaves here. Could be a guy involved in whatever's going on at the prison."

"Yeah. Or he could be rushing his wife to the hospital or something. Regardless, he's in one helluva hurry," Burke said.

"If he's running from the helo, they'll be calling ahead for backup. Let's get behind him and follow along until we get more intel."

Burke slowed the SUV, waiting for the red sedan to speed past. When it did, Kim saw a white male wearing an orange jumpsuit at the wheel.

She snapped a quick photo as he sped past. The photo was mostly useless, but maybe it would be better than nothing.

Burke turned the Navigator and followed the speeding sedan.

Kim snapped a photo of the car's license plate. The rental SUV had a dash cam in it, and Gaspar had eyes on her from the sky. She hoped they'd get solid intel pieced together shortly.

"Call 9-1-1. Get the word out to highway patrol," Burke said, speeding up to close the gap between the SUV and the red sedan.

Kim found her phone and redialed Gaspar. He picked up immediately.

"I'm on it, Sunshine. The car's stolen. Probably from the prison parking lot, although I can't confirm that yet," Gaspar said. "From what I can see, the prisoners that were in the exercise yard when the jetliner hit have been running like cockroaches."

"Can you get an ID on the driver?" Kim asked.

"The helo is keeping an eye on him, but you're closer," Gaspar replied. "I uploaded the best photo I could get off your dash cam. It's running through facial recognition now."

"How about the car?"

"The vehicle is a BMW 6 series sedan with a South Dakota plate. Registered owner is Fern Olson. Licensed to practice law in South Dakota. Lives in Bolton," Gaspar recited from data coming up on one of his screens.

"Anybody headed toward him to intercept?" Kim blinked when she heard the owner's name. Fern Olson was the woman they were on the way to interview in Bolton.

"Doesn't look like it. The helo can't actually stop the guy, and all available units have been mobilized to deal with the prison disaster. If you don't intercept him, he'll probably get away," Gaspar said.

"How'd you do in PIT training?" Kim looked at Burke. She was asking about the precision immobilization techniques. PIT techniques were intermediate force options that could slow a speeding vehicle.

If he executed them well, using the right equipment, and if they had solid backup.

Problem was, they didn't have the right equipment.

They didn't have a second vehicle for backup, either.

Which meant skills would matter.

"PIT? Not so great," Burke replied. "Crashed a couple of training vehicles, but I got the job done."

"Had any field experience since then?"

"Some." Burke shrugged, keeping his attention on the driving. "I'm a SEAL, not a traffic cop."

Kim nodded. There was no time to stop and switch drivers. They'd lose the guy for sure if they slowed down at all.

"We could nudge him. But at these speeds, we might knock him off the road."

Burke said, "He's got nowhere to go, with those deep ditches on both sides of the road. He'd probably try to stay on the pavement rather than go off down the embankment. He might be good enough to do that."

Kim said, "But we'd slow him down, at least."

"As fast as that guy's running, he might spin and slam right into you," Gaspar interjected.

"We'll need another vehicle ourselves if this thing goes south," Burke said, eyes still on the road and the racing BMW, hovering no more than two car lengths behind.

Kim said nothing, watching the red car. She lowered the window. If there were sirens headed this way, she couldn't hear them. She raised the window again.

"If we're gonna do this, we've got to be quick about it," Burke said, speeding up to close the gap again. "He's got a better engine than we do. We're at ninety-two miles an hour now. He's going to leave us in the dust pretty quick. It's your call, boss."

Kim ran through her options.

There were only two real choices, and one was to let the guy go for now. Authorities would find him eventually.

She had no idea why he'd been incarcerated in a federal maximum-security prison.

He could be a serial killer or just a scam artist. Impossible to know.

Should she let him get away?

If she let him go, could she be sure he wouldn't commit depraved crimes against innocent victims while he was free?

"Gaspar, notify the helo to pick him up once we get him stopped." She disconnected the call, took a breath, yanked the alligator clamp from her seatbelt retractor, and cinched her harness tighter. "Do it. And try not to kill us in the process."

"Copy that," Burke said as he pushed the accelerator to the floor, eating the pavement to close the gap.

The driver of the BMW hadn't noticed the SUV coming up fast on his tail all of a sudden. If he had noticed, he'd have shot straight ahead to avoid what came next.

Burke moved out into the passing lane and advanced until the SUV's front wheels were aligned behind the BMW's back wheels.

The red car still had time to speed away.

He didn't.

Burke made contact with the BMW's left rear quarter panel and then accelerated as he steered the Navigator abruptly into the car.

The BMW's tires lost traction and started to skid across the passing lane.

Burke kept moving to the right to get out of the way, letting the BMW spin out.

The red car didn't stop.

It didn't straighten out, either.

The BMW kept moving in the direction Burke had shoved it.

Across the pavement behind the SUV.

Fast and out of control.

When the tires ran off the pavement and hit the grass, the BMW rolled over down the embankment.

Kim counted four complete flips, terminating with the car on its roof in the rushing water.

Burke stopped the SUV and pulled off the road.

Kim jumped out and hurried down the hill toward the red car, struggling to keep upright on the uneven terrain.

Burke parked and followed behind her.

By the time Kim reached the bottom of the embankment, the red car was mostly submerged in the rushing water. The driver had struggled to open the door and pushed his way out of the car.

The orange jumpsuit was wet and plastered to his body. His head was bleeding. His face was covered with grime that looked like black soot.

Burke had slowed his descent about halfway down the hill.

Kim heard the helo approaching, looking for a place to land. She hoped medical personnel were on board.

She reached the edge of the ditch and stepped into the icy water, moving toward the driver. "Hey! Are you okay?"

His mouth split into a wide grin that crinkled his eyes and lit up his whole face. He cackled as he fist-pumped the air with both arms and yelled, "Woo-hoo! What a ride!"

Then he turned, and quicker than a jackrabbit, he jumped up the other side of the ditch and ran.

"Oh, crap," Kim said, as she headed through the cold water and around the submerged BMW and up the other side after him.

CHAPTER 15

Keegan glanced at the clock on the dashboard again. The sun had set and he appreciated the darkness. They had left the kid's Explorer hidden in the woods at the second drop-off point and transferred to a stolen black Land Rover with South Dakota license plates.

The switch severed the last tenuous connection to the hacker. Forensic sciences being what they were, sooner or later the feds might discover Keegan's activities. But that wouldn't happen for a few days, at least. He and Walsh would have escaped to Canada by then.

Walsh was driving along the county road into the mostly vacant, wooded area north of Bolton. Keegan hadn't seen a house or a car for the last thirty miles.

Peering through the windshield, Keegan saw a road sign for the first town north of the prison. Newton Hills. Two miles ahead. Population three hundred and two.

"How are you feeling?" he asked Walsh again, for the tenth time, at least.

"I'm fine," Walsh replied, same as before. Maybe he was.

"Small town up ahead. We'll find a doctor."

"What we need is a gas station and a hamburger. It's been a long time since we ate that crappy mystery meat lunch at Bolton."

"Burgers it is," Keegan said, looking out the side window. "Man, it's *dark* out here. I don't think it's ever this dark in Boston, is it?"

"We picked this road because almost nobody lives out here, and it doesn't get much traffic," Walsh replied as he steered around a pothole. "I've got the high beams on. That's the best I can do." Walsh's words sounded slurred, like he'd been drinking. Even though he hadn't.

"How far are we from the meeting point?" Keegan asked.

The Land Rover's GPS didn't work reliably in no man's land. Keegan had a paper map in the glove compartment, but he didn't want to fish it out and try to read it by the dashboard lights.

"We're still traveling north, the first leg of a wide arc taking us away from and around Bolton. We'll need to turn west and then south to get where we're going," Walsh replied with a glance at the clock. "Maybe another three to four hours' drive time, depending on the roads."

"How's your arm?" Keegan asked.

Walsh shrugged. "It stopped oozing blood a while ago."

Keegan worried Walsh was sluggish, tired. But they'd had an exhausting day. "Can you wiggle your fingers? Make a fist?"

Walsh demonstrated both moves in the glow of the dashboard lights. He pretended not to notice the pain, but Keegan saw the involuntary wince.

"How about your leg?"

"Still there," Walsh replied, wheezing a little bit and definitely slurring his words this time.

Keegan lowered the window and inhaled the fresh night air. It was cool and getting colder. The forecast for tonight was a low of thirty-eight degrees.

He listened to the air whishing across his ears. For the past fifty miles, since they'd jumped into the Suburban with the kid back at the exercise yard, he'd heard nothing but nature.

No helicopters, no sirens, no people.

He pushed the button to raise the window and swiveled his head. Eyes forward.

What was that?

He blinked.

Looked again.

The big creature was still there. Walking on all fours. He turned his head to stare.

Eyes glowed in the headlight beams, five feet above the pavement.

The grizzly bear stopped in his tracks, right in the middle of the two-lane county road.

"Walsh! Look out!" Keegan shouted.

Walsh's chin had dropped to his chest.

When Keegan yelled, Walsh jerked his head up and widened his eyes.

"What the hell is that?" Walsh jerked the wheel to the left to avoid hitting the big creature. Which would have caused serious damage to the Land Rover, at the very least.

But Walsh had oversteered.

The heavy SUV went off the road on the left, bounced hard onto the shoulder, and kept going.

Keegan looked back to see the bear's broad back running in the opposite direction.

"He's gone," Keegan said.

Walsh said nothing, and the Land Rover kept moving off-road.

"Walsh!" Keegan shouted.

Walsh's head had dropped again as if he'd passed out.

Keegan grabbed the steering wheel and leaned across the cabin, over the console, and pushed the button to stop the engine.

Momentum carried the SUV forward, farther into the brush.

Keegan steered as straight as he could from the awkward angle in the passenger seat, avoiding the big trees until the right front tire landed in a hole large enough to swallow the wheel and bring the vehicle to a jerking halt.

The suspension creaked and the springs bounced a couple more times for good measure while Keegan struggled to control his own rapid breathing.

"Walsh? What the hell?" he said, angry now.

Walsh didn't respond.

Keegan reached over and felt Walsh's carotid pulse. He was no doctor, but even he could feel Walsh's heartbeat was weak and rapid.

He rummaged in the glove compartment until he found a flashlight. He lowered the window and shined the beam toward the road.

He'd seen what he suddenly realized must have been a grizzly bear. What he'd read about South Dakota wildlife was that bears still roamed in this part of the state.

The bear's scent wafted on the breeze toward the SUV. No mistaking the stench of a big animal like that.

But Keegan didn't see him now. Perhaps the bear had moved on.

Back in Boston, he'd have called 9-1-1 for a tow and a medic for Walsh. That was impossible out here. He'd never get a cell signal, even if it had been safe to try. Which it wasn't.

The prison break would be all over the news by now. The risk of being recaptured and returned to Bolton was too great.

They were on their own.

Walsh was still unconscious.

Based on the sign Keegan had seen back there, they were still at least a couple of miles from the village of Newton Hills.

No way Keegan could carry Walsh that far.

Walking around outside the SUV seemed like a foolish idea, too, given the rattlesnake debacle earlier. There were bound to be more snakes out there.

Keegan took a deep breath and swiped his palm over his face.

"Now what?" he said aloud. The question was met by dead silence.

He tried restarting the Land Rover. The first time he pushed the button, the engine didn't start, but the dashboard gauges brightened up, so the power had come on.

Walsh had said something about needing gas earlier. He looked at the gas gauge. How much gas was enough?

Keegan didn't even have a driver's license. He'd employed a dedicated driver for decades. And he knew very little about cars. He probably couldn't drive the Land Rover even if he could get it moving again.

The gauge showed the fuel level was below a quarter of a tank. Which might mean there was insufficient fuel to run the heat overnight, even if he could get the damned engine started.

And Walsh was still unconscious. What should Keegan do about that? The gash on Walsh's bicep hadn't looked bad enough to kill him. But he imagined a man could die from rattlesnake bites if he didn't get medical attention soon.

"We can't stay here. We can't walk out. We can't drive out," Keegan said to himself as if ticking off the options on his fingers.

He ran out of alternatives.

CHAPTER 16

Friday, May 13
Bolton, South Dakota
11:05 p.m.

It had been well after ten o'clock by the time they gave up searching in the dark woods for the escaped convict. Another thirty minutes to reach the budget chain hotel in Bolton where the Boss had reserved rooms for the night.

They parked the remarkably undamaged Navigator, lugged their bags inside, and picked up room keys at the desk. Kim was tired and dirty and ready for a shower and food. Her stomach had been complaining for hours.

"How late can we get room service?" she asked the sleepy-eyed teen staffing the desk.

"Sorry. No room service and no restaurant. There's small coffee pots in the rooms, though," he said.

Which was the only good thing about the place, as far as Kim could tell. But she didn't say that. She trudged alongside Burke through the lobby.

At the elevator, Burke said, "I'm going out to find a burger or something after I clean up. Want to come along?"

"Yeah, sure. Meet in the lobby in fifteen?"

Burke grinned. "You're fast for a girl."

Kim nodded. "So I've been told."

They parted when the elevator opened on the third floor and headed in opposite directions. Kim used the keycard to open her room and stepped inside.

The place was basic. Full-sized bed. A small desk and chair. A bathroom smaller than most closets. No closet, either. But she was too tired to care about amenities.

She walked into the bathroom and turned the shower all the way to the hottest setting. She figured this was the kind of place that might be out of hot water at the end of the day. She was right.

She stripped and hopped in. The water wasn't hot, but it was warm enough. She soaped up and quickly removed the travel grime and the mud she'd collected from her run through the woods. A few of the scratches she'd acquired were already crusted over with dried blood. The water ran pink and then clear on the shower floor as she soaped the sting away.

After the five-minute shower, she opened her travel bag and pulled out clean clothes. She dressed quickly, brushed her hair back, and secured it with an elastic at the base on her neck. She was well aware that she might be mistaken for a teenager when the lighting was dim enough.

"Good genes. Thanks, Mom," she muttered.

She picked up her weapon, her badge wallet, the keycard and stowed the few personal items she carried into her pockets.

Kim headed out, closed the door behind her, and took the stairs down to the lobby.

She glanced at the clock. Elapsed time was eleven minutes. Total elapsed time was thirteen minutes.

Burke wasn't there yet. Kim grinned.

She approached the pimply desk clerk, who looked to be about eighteen. "Where's the closest place to get a burger or something right now?"

"Your best bet is probably the chain restaurant next to the gas station on the main road toward the highway." The clerk pointed westward. When she frowned, he looked at the clock and shrugged. "There're other places, but they've already closed for the night."

Kim nodded. She recalled passing the restaurant on the way in. It looked like the kind of local hangout where the food was good, and the ambience was mid-twentieth century. "Thanks."

The elevator pinged, the doors opened, and Burke walked out, exactly fifteen minutes after she'd left him. His eyes widened when he saw her, confirming he hadn't expected her to be there yet.

Kim stifled her grin and tilted her head toward the door. They met up on the sidewalk outside, where the falling temperature made her shiver. She flipped her jacket collar up and stuffed her hands into her pockets. She told him what the kid had said about where to find food.

"Yeah, I saw the place. Maybe ten minutes away," Burke said, as they climbed into the SUV again.

She heard his stomach growling as he pulled out of the angled parking spot and pointed the vehicle westward.

When they got there, the restaurant was empty and looked ready to close up, but the open sign was still on, so they went in anyway. They sat at a table for four. A thirty-six-inch square of laminate had been scoured so many times the flakes in the laminate were faded.

A tired waitress came by wearing a uniform as worn out as she was. She didn't bring a menu. "All we have left is the pot roast."

"Pot roast for two it is," Burke said, flashing her a friendly smile.

"And black coffee, please, if you have it fresh," Kim said.

"Be right back with your food," the waitress replied before she turned and shuffled back toward the kitchen.

Burke folded his hands on the table and leaned forward as if there were other diners prone to eavesdropping. Which there weren't. They were the only people in the place other than the waitress and maybe the cook, assuming there was one.

"Have you heard anything more from Gaspar about what's going on out at the prison?" he asked.

"I haven't had the time to check. Last report was that the county lockup and city jail out at the compound were intact and not involved. It's just the federal facility that got damaged," she replied. "Locals aren't that busy. Between the three facilities, they have enough room to house the inmates until they figure out a better answer."

A television was playing in the corner, running the news. A crawler at the bottom of the screen said the prison was locked down and the remaining prisoners were contained. Which was a lie. But it probably helped the people of Bolton sleep better tonight.

"How many prisoners escaped?" Burke asked.

She shrugged. "All of the men in the exercise yard scattered, but some didn't get very far."

"What about the damaged portions of the building? Any escapees from there?"

"They either don't know or aren't saying. There's still a lot of chaos. Lot of damage to the building." She swiped a hand over her hair and stretched the tension from her neck. "This whole area for twenty miles or more is crawling with law enforcement of one kind or another, I expect."

The waitress approached with the food. Plates were piled high with beef, mashed potatoes and gravy, and green beans.

When she left, Burke said, "So we don't know if the guy we need to interview was one of the escapees or not?"

"Not yet." Kim ate a few of the green beans and pushed the greasy gravy around on the plate looking for the beef.

They ate in silence for a few minutes. The coffee was strong enough to hold a spoon upright. But it was hot and better than nothing.

The front door opened, and a blast of cold air came inside ahead of two uniformed officers from the Bolton Police Department. Kim straightened her shoulders and waved them over. Professional courtesy, as well as curiosity about the prison break, motivated her invitation.

Kim extended her hand to shake as she pulled out her badge wallet and showed it to confirm. "FBI Special Agent Kim Otto. This is my partner, Agent William Burke."

The senior officer replied. He said he was Irwin Mitchell, and he was second in command over at Bolton PD.

The other guy was Sergeant Albert Wood. "People call me Woody," he said.

They sat, the waitress came over with two mugs and a thermos. They ordered the pot roast, and she hurried off again.

"You two are the agents who tried to stop the escapee out on the highway, right?" Mitchell asked. He looked wrung out. Heavy lines etched his face, and his mouth was set into a grim line. He had a thick dark mustache that no longer matched the few wisps of thinning gray hair that remained on his head.

Kim guessed his age at about fifty, give or take. The other guy was a redhead with a scruffy beard, maybe ten years younger. They both had plenty of miles on them.

She nodded. "Sorry we didn't catch him."

"He'll be cold and tired and hungry." Woody shook his head and waved off her half-apology. "We'll get him tomorrow. Unless the bears get him first."

Burke's eyebrows lifted. "You've got grizzlies active in the area?"

"This time of year, they're roaming, looking for food. Rattlesnakes, too. You were smart to come in for the night," Mitchell said, drinking the stale coffee like he was used to it.

Kim shivered. She hated snakes.

"Did you round up the other escapees?" Burke asked. He'd finished his meal but was still working on the coffee.

"We're not done. Got men working out there." Mitchell shook his head. "We just came in for a quick bite before the place closed. Not much open around here so late. After a couple hours' sleep, we'll be back out at dawn."

"Happy to help if you need us," Burke said.

"Thanks." Mitchell sized him up with a glance.

Kim said, "Has Special Agent Smithers arrived yet? We'll liaise with him in the morning."

"Haven't seen him. Been told he's around here somewhere," Woody replied, draining the coffee and pouring more. It came out of the thermos like thick syrup.

CHAPTER 17

Friday, May 13
Bolton, South Dakota
11:30 p.m.

Fern Olson, dressed in her flannel pajamas, belted the matching robe around her waist and stepped carefully around the squeaky floorboards toward her son's room to say goodnight.

Wool slippers kept her feet warm enough and muffled her footsteps as she passed the closed door of her father's room. He'd been asleep for hours, but he rested lightly. She didn't want to wake him.

She crossed her arms against a quick breeze that blew over her from somewhere. Her stomach clenched. She stood still and listened for a closing door or a breaking window. After a moment, she shrugged and walked on.

The old farmhouse had always been drafty. She'd grown up here. She knew what to expect, especially when the weather was still cold outside. But she didn't like the old place. Never had.

One day, her dad would pass, and then she and Noah could move back to Bolton. But since her mother died five years ago, and Dad refused to move in with them, Fern and her son had been living here.

The homestead was old and creaky, but tonight it felt threatening.

"You're imagining things, Fern," she scolded herself, attempting to calm her own uneasiness. "You're twenty miles from the prison. You're safe enough here."

Noah hated the place. Mainly because he was fifteen and he wanted to hang out with his friends. Which was pretty much impossible as long as they were living so far north of town. He begged to stay in Bolton with his father, and during the week, she often gave in.

Like so many other things she wished she could change, Fern should have agreed to let him stay the weekend.

She swiped a stray red curl away from her face and reached out to knock on Noah's door. He didn't answer. Which probably meant he had his headphones on.

Fern turned the knob and opened the squeaky door a few inches to look inside. The lights were off. The blue glow of the laptop screen washed over his face, giving him an otherworldly vibe.

Noah sensed her standing in the doorway. He glanced up and scowled as he pulled off the headphones and demanded, "What?"

Fern sighed. One day, he'd be off to college. Would she miss his attitude after he left? Maybe. She gave him a weak smile. His scowl deepened.

"I've locked up downstairs and turned the alarm on. Grandpa is sleeping. I'm going to bed. Don't go out, Noah. Promise me," she said, hating the pleading tone in her voice.

She'd been frightened today at the prison. And there were inmates still at large. Even though the house was far from the prison break, she didn't feel safe out here alone. But Dad had refused to leave. So they were here. But she didn't have to like it.

"Yeah, yeah. Okay. Like there's anywhere to go. Or anyone to go with," Noah said, surly as ever. He put the headphones on again and returned his attention to the screen.

She glanced briefly at the laptop screen. He played games with friends online, which frightened her, too. But tonight he was safer here than wandering around.

Fern didn't try to hug him. She blew him a kiss, which was met with an eye roll, closed the door softly, and padded back to her room at the other end of the hallway. She climbed into bed and flipped on the TV to catch the late-breaking news before she went to sleep.

The first story was national news. Then the Bolton prison break. The now-familiar video clips showed the jetliner crashing into the prison building. Followed by the black smoke and then the flames. Inmates in orange jumpsuits scattered like bees.

The video moved into a small box at the top of the screen as the anchor read the story from the teleprompter, rehashing what she'd heard earlier.

The fire had been extinguished.

Damage had been mainly to the exercise yard and the back of the building, which was mostly used for storage. Like most buildings designed since nine-eleven, the prison had been engineered and built to withstand terrorist attacks. It seemed to have weathered this event precisely as planned.

The prison was locked down and heavily guarded. Checkpoints were posted on all of the roadways. They'd picked up escaped inmates attempting to flee from the prison. Manhunts would resume and fan out into the uninhabited areas in the morning.

Fern hoped to learn the identities of the escaped inmates, but the names were not released. She assumed they'd tried to balance the public's need to know with an effort to avoid panic.

She assumed there were victims, but they were not identified, either. Even the pilot's name was being withheld until his family could be notified.

When the news report ended, she turned the television off and sat quietly with the bare minimum of information she'd already collected.

Initially, she'd been locked in the prison lobby, mystified by everything about the situation. After Chief Mitchell released her, the confusion was compounded by a thousand questions.

When she'd realized her car was missing, insight dawned. Pieces began to fit together, although gaping holes in the picture remained.

Her car was equipped with strong anti-theft devices. Without the key fob, the only way to steal the car was to tow it. Even then, the thief would need a flatbed tow truck because the wheels wouldn't roll without the signal from the key fob, either.

The little red BMW was a nice car, and she loved it, but what was the likelihood that a flatbed tow truck had hauled it away on the same afternoon a jet crashed into the prison?

Fern said, "If you believe that, Fern, you should buy a lotto ticket. Your luck is just not that good."

No one argued with her. She gave herself a decisive nod. Her conclusion seemed sound.

"So where's your car?" she asked.

A moment later, she replied, "Petey Burns."

The more she considered it, the more certain she became. Fern's last client of the day had stolen her car. Stealing German vehicles was his specialty, Petey Burns had said several times. He'd told her all about how he could clone the signals from a distance using a small device he acquired online.

During their client conference this afternoon, she'd had her key fob in her briefcase the whole time. Petey could have cloned it, and she'd have had no way of knowing.

She recalled how antsy he'd been. How he'd left their meeting early, something he'd never done before.

The more she thought about it, the more convinced she became. Petey must have cloned her key fob and stolen her car.

"A device like that would have been contraband inside the prison," she reminded herself.

Didn't matter. Fern absolutely believed he'd obtained the device, somehow. She talked it through. "All kinds of contraband finds its way into that prison. There must be a thousand ways it could have happened. A visitor brought it. Or another inmate acquired it and gave it to him."

And used it to steal her car when the opportunity presented itself.

But he hadn't been walking around with the cloning device in his pocket for weeks or months, just waiting for the chance to use it. That made zero sense.

Somehow, he'd known that today was the day to clone her fob's signal and steal her car.

"Question is, how did he know to do it today? Petey's a good car thief. But he's no criminal mastermind," she said, head cocked, staring into the distance as if she might find the answer there. Nothing like flashing lights popped up with the answer.

"Come on, Fern. It's not rocket science. You said yourself that Petey's no genius. How'd he know?" she coaxed herself aloud, but it didn't help. She came up with nothing.

She shook her head and tried a different approach.

Fern knew she'd been used. She'd known she was being used all along, just like the partner who'd had this gig before her.

But she hadn't known anything like the prison break would happen. She hadn't expected a jetliner crashing into the building. How could she have?

She'd received cryptic messages from Denny and passed them along on a burner cell phone to a nameless man she'd never met.

That was all. Nothing more. Nothing criminal, certainly.

Surely, she couldn't be held accountable for any of this. Could she?

She reviewed every meeting she'd had with Walsh, Denny, and Petey Burns again. She recalled every message she'd relayed on the disposable cell phones.

She shook her head and wrapped her arms around her body as she watched the television screen, imagining the constantly replayed video as if it was unfolding one frame at a time.

When Chief Mitchell had released her from the lobby earlier, she'd expected him to take her in for questioning. When he didn't, she began to hope that her part in the disaster might stay a secret.

She whispered the disjoined prayers of a terrified lawyer. "Please. Let no one else be dead. If no one dies, if they get away... Maybe they'll never find out. Or I could make a deal. They might let me go..."

Fern switched the television on again and changed to another station to watch the report again. Nothing new. The flicker of hope she held in her heart burned a little brighter, even as she realized how foolish her hope was.

She thought about her dad. About Noah.

The longer the news story droned on, the more her thoughts turned to her own escape.

Canada was not that far away. If they left tonight...or early in the morning.

CHAPTER 18

"We'll find Smithers and let him know we're here." Burke nodded and asked, "Got a headcount on the escaped inmates yet?"

"At least forty tried, as far as we've been able to count. We've already recaptured about half of them," Mitchell replied. "We got the prison locked down to keep the rest of them inside where they belong. It's just a matter of dealing with the damage and the fallout."

Woody said gravely, "Bolton is a maximum-security federal prison. Inmates tend to be violent offenders. Some are confirmed psychopaths. Until we get a handle on who's missing and who's not, keep your wits about you."

"How about prison personnel? Did you lose any?" Kim asked.

Woody shook his head again. "Some injuries, but they were lucky to get out with just broken bones, mostly. The pilot of that cargo plane was not so lucky."

"Any intel on the pilot yet?" Kim asked. "Was this a terrorist attack?"

"Besides the fact that the dude must have been stone cold crazy, you mean?" Mitchell shrugged and shook his head as if he'd seen crazy stuff in his day, but deliberately crashing a jet into a prison might have been the topper. "We've got plenty to worry about on our end. The pilot is someone else's problem."

Burke said, "How about civilians? Any visitors involved?"

"Caught a break there. It was late in the day, so deliveries were already done. No family visits allowed on Friday. Only one civilian was on site that we know about at this point, and she wasn't injured. We'll debrief her later," Mitchell replied. "You'd be smart to stay inside tonight and lock up your vehicle. It's gonna be cold out. Anybody still running around out there will be looking for a warm place to bed down."

They ate in silence for a few minutes after the waitress delivered food and scurried back to the kitchen.

Then Woody asked, "Where were you guys working when you got called out here? You must've been pretty close to Bolton already since you intercepted that BMW."

"That's right," Kim replied. "We were on our way here. From Rapid City."

Mitchell looked up, eyebrows raised, surprised. He swallowed a mouthful of pot roast and asked, "What for?"

"Routine. We're working with the Special Personnel Task Force. Completing a background check on a former army officer who is being considered for a classified assignment," Kim explained, using the official cover story.

"Hard to believe somebody living here in Bolton has indispensable skills," Woody said between big bites of potatoes and gravy.

"Not the job candidate," Kim shook her head. "Our interview subject lives here. A lawyer. Her name is Fern Olson. Know her?"

Woody and Mitchell exchanged glances. Mitchell took a big swig of coffee and swallowed. "Everybody in Bolton knows Olson. She's something of a pain in our ass."

Burke gave him a brothers-in-arms look. "How so?"

"She challenges just about every felony case we put together, and she's damned good at it. We lock 'em up, and she gets 'em out. That's pretty much how it goes. Nobody working the job is happy with that. Olson doesn't have a lot of friends around Bolton PD," Mitchell said before turning his full attention to the food as if he hadn't eaten in weeks.

"If your candidate was one of Olson's clients, it's hard to see how he'd be fit for any kind of special classified assignment, for damned sure. She doesn't represent the choirboys if you know what I mean," Woody concluded as if the matter was resolved. "Who is the guy, anyway?"

"His name is Jack Reacher," Burke said.

This time, Woody and Mitchell exchanged the kind of look Kim had seen before. No one ever had a neutral reaction to Reacher. These two wouldn't be nominating him for sainthood anytime soon.

Mitchell and Woody pointedly returned their attention to their plates without further comment.

"Reacher came through here a few years ago when you were having trouble with methamphetamine trafficking," Kim said. "Did you meet him back then?"

"Yeah, we met him," Mitchell said gruffly, in a menacing tone. "Reacher walked into town, and by the time he was done here, good friends were dead."

"I see," Kim said. That story was familiar. She'd heard it several times before. Different towns, different troubles, but always a trail of violence that lingered long after Reacher moved on.

Mitchell finished his potatoes and cleared his throat. "Straight up? He was like a bad luck charm. Things were bad when he arrived and got worse the longer he stayed. A lot of what happened wasn't his fault. He was actually helpful now and then. But we were glad to see him go and hoping we'd never see him again. You're not telling me he's on his way, are you?"

"If Reacher's coming here," Woody added with a scowl, "five bucks says Olson's right at the center of whatever brought him back."

"Why would you say that?" Burke asked.

"Coply intuition," Mitchell deadpanned as he shoveled the last of his food into his mouth.

"Tell me more about Olson," Kim said, taking a calculated tangent. "When's the last time you talked to her?"

Mitchell looked up from his plate and shrugged. "Few hours ago. She was trapped in the lobby at the prison when they went on lockdown."

"What was she doing there?" Burke asked, eyebrows raised.

"Seeing clients, she said. Three prisoners. She goes in every Friday, I guess," Woody explained.

A familiar frisson ran up Kim's spine and made the small hairs on the back of her neck stand at attention. "Which three prisoners did she meet with today?"

"We haven't had a chance to ask her about that yet." Mitchell turned to look directly into her eyes. "Has Reacher been a guest of the feds lately?"

Kim's first reaction was to answer truthfully, no. First because she'd checked all the federal prison records when she received the assignment. Reacher had never been in prison, according to the databases. He'd been in jail a few times, but not here, as far as she knew.

Beyond that, she believed Reacher had been with her in Carter's Crossing, Mississippi, yesterday.

She hadn't actually seen him there, though.

She hadn't seen him anywhere since that first night in Washington DC, back in November.

But she'd connected with him several times since then.

He'd called. Left her voicemails. He'd texted.

He'd even saved her life once or twice.

Hadn't he?

Kim cleared her throat. "Olson would have arranged those client meetings in advance. The prisoners had to be permitted to meet with her. There must be records. We can find out who she met with pretty easily."

Mitchell nodded. "You offered to help. Why don't you do exactly that? Then we'll see if we can find her clients."

"Because you believe all three men will be on the escaped prisoners list?" Burke asked.

Woody snorted. "And you don't?"

"Well again, they won't get far tonight. Let's table this conversation until the morning," Mitchell said. He stood up, tossed bills on the laminated surface, and handed her a business card. "My cell number's on there."

Kim fished a card out of her pocket and gave it to him. He slipped it into his pocket and left.

She and Burke walked out of the restaurant together a few minutes later. Burke pressed the fob to unlock the SUV and they climbed inside, shivering in the cold. He started the engine and they rode the short distance to the hotel in cold silence.

When he parked out front, Burke said, "You think the lawyer, Olson, was involved in the jailbreak? She took advantage of the crisis situation to get her clients free?"

"Maybe."

"You think Reacher was there?"

She shrugged. Kim didn't think Reacher could have been there. Could he?

She wasn't sure. That was always the problem. She was never sure, where Reacher was concerned.

He turned off the SUV and they trudged through the cold to the hotel. The kid at the desk was staring into the blue glow of a laptop screen. He nodded as they walked past, headed toward the elevator.

"Call you in the morning," Burke said, as the doors dinged open on the third floor.

"Sounds good." She turned toward her room.

When she'd locked the door behind her, she glanced at the clock on the bedside table. It was well after midnight. But Gaspar wouldn't be asleep.

CHAPTER 19

Saturday, May 14
Bolton, South Dakota
12:35 a.m.

Kim opened her laptop and, using the secure encrypted server, located the files Gaspar had sent. While she waited for the download, she flipped the television on and found a twenty-four-hour cable news station. She muted the volume and read through the crawlers at the bottom of the screen.

All the news on the jailbreak was old.

She pulled out the two cell phones she'd been keeping in her pockets and glanced at the screens. Two missed calls from the Boss, spaced two hours apart. The first one came in while they were still in the woods searching for the driver of the red BMW.

She hit the redial.

"Good to hear you're still alive," Cooper said snidely when he picked up on the fourth ring.

She found the mini-bar and pulled a small bottle of cheap red wine from the back, rooting around for a glass. Plastic was the best she could find.

"Nothing new to report. I figured you knew more than I did," she replied, kicking her boots off.

"Which is why I called," he said.

"I'm listening." She poured the wine and settled onto the bed, letting the wine warm up before she drank it. It was late and she was tired. Wine would help her sleep. Maybe.

She closed the lid on the laptop. He'd want to know what she was downloading if he noticed her looking at it while they talked.

This hotel room had equipment he could hack into to spy on her. It was always safer to assume he could see and hear everything. She'd learned not to rely on him, though. He definitely did not always have her back. Which was another reason she needed Gaspar.

The Boss interrupted her thoughts again. "Fern Olson. The lawyer. Did you find her yet?"

"You already know we didn't. We found her car, though. One of the inmates stole it from the parking lot during the prison break."

"Yeah. I saw the video from our satellites. Guy's name is Petey Burns. One of Olson's clients," he said.

Kim narrowed her eyes. "You suppose it was pure coincidence that one of her clients stole her car and made a run for it during the boldest prison break this century?"

"As you would say, what are the odds?" the Boss replied with heavy sarcasm and a snide chuckle.

"Beyond slim," she said just as snidely.

"Indeed."

"Where is Olson now?" Kim asked.

"Unclear. Past few months, she's been living with her father. Out in the country. North of the prison. She has a son who lives with her. Do your homework. Everything even remotely relevant is contained in the files Gaspar sent you," he said, telegraphing that he was well aware of her ongoing connection with Gaspar, and he didn't like it.

Keeping Gaspar in the loop was, of course, a violation of her orders and every protocol on the planet. Her investigation was under the radar. She was allowed to share minimal intel and only when she absolutely couldn't avoid sharing.

Kim didn't bother to argue with the Boss. She hadn't even seen Gaspar's files yet.

But somehow the Boss obviously had.

He was no doubt monitoring Gaspar's every move, just as he monitored hers. Which was illegal as hell, especially since Gaspar became a private citizen.

She'd bet a million dollars that the Boss didn't have a warrant to watch Gaspar and couldn't get one if he tried. Which he wouldn't.

But the rules didn't apply to Charles Cooper. Never had. Never would.

"Get used to it, Sunshine," Gaspar had said back when he was in the field with her.

She shrugged and returned her attention to the Boss. "So why *did* you call?"

"We're getting intel on the pilot. It's looking like a direct hit on the prison rather than an equipment malfunction."

She shook her head. "That's just crazy, though. Was he suicidal?"

"Just the opposite. Solid guy. Family man. Veteran. The whole nine yards," he said, clucking his teeth as if the news baffled him as much as her. "Point is, we haven't found a motive yet. He wouldn't be the first veteran to go berserk. But this doesn't feel like that."

She nodded and sipped the wine, thinking it through. "Usually, a hijacked jet is not a lone wolf operation. Too many moving parts."

"Exactly. We'll find out who was involved. Meanwhile, watch your back." He paused, inhaled deeply, and blew out a long stream of frustration. "Find Fern Olson. Stick with her. Whatever this is, she's right in the middle of it."

"How do you know that?" she asked, not really expecting an answer. But it never hurts to ask.

A couple of moments passed while she watched the news replay of the video view from the helo chasing the red BMW. Nothing she hadn't seen before.

"What does Olson have to do with Reacher?" Kim asked again, but he'd disconnected the call and she was left with nothing but dead air.

She didn't bother to call him back. No point. Asking him wouldn't get her anywhere. If he knew how Reacher and Olson were connected and he'd wanted to tell her, he'd have done it already.

Kim finished the wine, but she was still wide awake. She climbed off the bed and went back to the mini-bar for another four-ounce bottle. This was the last one, and the wine wasn't all that great, either.

She made a mental note to buy a better bottle and bring it back with her tomorrow, if they remained stuck here. She always carried a corkscrew in her travel bag.

Then she resettled on the bed with her laptop open and dialed Gaspar while she paged through the files he'd sent. She didn't see anything with Reacher's name on it.

This intel was mostly about Fern Olson and Burke. There was another file labeled Susan Turner, which was a name she hadn't heard before.

Gaspar had also included a bit about the pilot. Wayne Romone. Employed by an air cargo outfit out of Rapid City. Family man.

Her attention was dragged from the screen when Gaspar answered.

"You're up late," he said with a yawn.

"Sounds like you're the one who's tired." She heard the baby fussing close by.

Gaspar's wife and his four daughters were no doubt abed hours ago. His son was almost six months old now, but he was a noisy baby who seemed to sleep even less than his father.

"Did you read the files?"

"Not yet. Can you give me the highlights?"

"How about I just cut to the chase. There's no mention of Reacher anywhere in Fern Olson's life. If she dealt with him when he went through Bolton seven years ago, there's no mention of that, either."

Kim cocked her head and thought about it. "Huh. I got nothin' brilliant to add."

"Yeah, well, me neither," Gaspar said. "The file labeled Susan Turner is interesting, though."

"Who's Susan Turner?" Kim said, perking up.

"No idea who she is now. But seven years ago, she was the head of the army's 110th Investigative Unit," Gaspar replied, obviously pleased with himself because he finally had something substantive to share. "Based at Rock Creek, Virginia. Reacher talked to her several times while he was in Bolton. She ordered up his personnel file. Held onto it for a while. Then sent it back."

"Really? Why?"

"Good question. She didn't file a report."

Kim cocked her head and considered the options. "Can you chase down the actual conversations?"

"You think they were recorded back then? And more importantly, that the recordings still exist?" His tone was clearly annoyed, and the fussy baby wasn't helping his mood.

She grinned. "This is the army, Chico. They keep everything, don't they?"

"Sometimes. But I've been looking. So far, no luck." He paused to be sure she was paying attention. "You know who you could ask."

"Not in this lifetime," she replied decisively.

"Okay. But Cooper can probably get the recorded conversations from way back then. Hell, he probably has them already."

She nodded, even as she realized he couldn't see her. "I'll think about it."

"While you do that, something else interesting came up."

"I'm all ears," she said with a yawn. Maybe the wine was finally doing its job.

"I sent you the intel. It's classified. So don't let Cooper know you have it."

"Like that's possible," she said. "Okay. What is it?"

He sighed and she heard little Juan crying again. "It's always about the timing, isn't it?"

"What do you mean?"

"There's no paper trail that I can find putting Reacher in Bolton. Ever. But we know he was there. And we can piece together the approximate time frame."

"Yeah, Woody and Mitchell said it was about seven years back."

"Right," he said, inhaling deeply. "No record of Reacher in town. But seven years ago, there was a big explosion near Bolton. I'm still digging, but something of intense interest to Homeland Security and the North American Air Defense Command. Bunch of other official interest, too."

Kim sat straight up on the bed. "Missile launch? Maybe a missile strike?"

"The top brass everywhere denied it."

"Which means nothing."

"They found bodies, weapons. Even the burned-out remains of an airliner. Definitely some kind of underground bunker. There's thousands of pages of documentation and reasonable conclusions drawn by reasonable people," Gaspar said, between cooing noises intended to calm little Juan, who wasn't having it. "Final answer? A refueling accident, they said."

Kim drained the last of the wine and wished for more. "Which means something happened. Something serious and explosive. Figuratively and literally."

"That about sums it up."

"And Reacher was here at the time."

"Timing fits."

"Susan Turner knew all about it?"

"Seems likely."

"How about Fern Olson?"

"That'd be my guess. Yours?" he said, just as Juan started to scream like he was being attacked by wolves. "And I gotta go before the kid wakes up the whole of Miami."

"Okay. Thanks. What about—" she said, but Gaspar had already hung up.

Kim glanced at the clock. It was well after one in the morning. She was still too keyed up to sleep.

She pulled up the Susan Turner file Gaspar had sent and began to read.

Two hours later, she'd finished digesting the files and went to bed. But she didn't sleep. Too much on her mind.

Always where Reacher was concerned, there were too many questions and too few answers.

CHAPTER 20

Saturday, May 14
Near Bolton, South Dakota
5:20 a.m.

Keegan woke up when the sunrise glinting off the Land Rover shot bright rays across his face. He'd slept fitfully in the passenger seat, waking when aches and pains caused by his awkward body position were too sharp to ignore.

He wasn't a young man anymore. His stomach gnawed and rumbled with hunger, and his throat felt like he'd swallowed the Sahara.

Keegan sat up and palmed his hair into place. Sleeping in cars, going without food and water, all of it was beyond his body's limits. He couldn't simply wait here, though. He had to move.

Walsh was still unconscious behind the steering wheel and his breathing was irregular. He smelled like stale vomit and urine, which didn't help Keegan's already queasy stomach.

He leaned across the console and punched the start button on the engine. After the engine caught, he lowered the window and turned his face toward the cool fresh air outside.

"Walsh," he said, hoping a few hours' sleep might have revived him. "Walsh. Can you hear me?"

Walsh did not respond with so much as the flick of an eyelid.

Keegan reached to check Walsh's carotid pulse again. His heartbeat was weak and sluggish, but it was still there.

Walsh wasn't dead.

But he probably would be if Keegan couldn't find a doctor soon.

Newton Hills was probably two miles ahead, give or take. Finally daylight. It was as safe to move as things were likely to get.

Keegan opened the passenger door and looked at the ground around the Land Rover. He didn't see any snakes or smell the big grizzly nearby.

He reached under the seat for the pistol he'd stored there. Carefully, he stepped outside, gun in hand. If he saw a rattlesnake, he'd shoot it. If anybody heard the shots and came running, he'd deal with them, too.

He stood back, looking at the vehicle, shaking his head. "Nothing you can do about that."

The Land Rover's right front wheel had rolled over a rock and off a steep incline. The tire was flat and the wheel was bent. Keegan didn't know much about cars, but he could see the SUV wasn't drivable.

They had traveled about thirty yards off the road through the dense, rocky underbrush. Briefly, he considered trying to carry Walsh to the road and make an effort to flag down a passing farmer.

"Who are you kidding, old man?" he chided himself. "Maybe when you were a young buck. You'd both collapse before you reached the pavement."

He glanced at Walsh again. He probably couldn't walk anyway, even with support.

Which meant Walsh couldn't go anywhere, and Keegan couldn't stay here to wait for help. He shook his head. "How idiotic would that be?"

The kind of help likely to come along was law enforcement personnel searching for escapees.

They'd find themselves right back in prison. He'd come way too far to give up.

"Now what?" Keegan said aloud as if someone might answer. No one did.

He went back to the Land Rover and leaned inside. He pushed the button to start the engine and raised the windows.

He glanced around. The SUV was stolen. Walsh's ID was fake. They'd ditched the orange jumpsuits and anything else remotely connected to Bolton prison a while back.

DNA or fingerprints or even facial recognition software might identify Walsh fairly quickly.

"Maybe they can't process any of that out here in the field, at least for an hour or two," he mumbled under his breath.

He looked around again. They were pretty much concealed by the trees and the bushes. They might be invisible from the road. Maybe even from the air.

"If anyone comes along, they won't find nothing tying me to Walsh right away. Nothing connecting us to the prison break," he shook his head. "This is the best I can do. For now."

He tried to rouse Walsh one last time, but nothing worked.

"I'll be back, soon, Walsh," he said as if the unconscious man could understand him. "Wait here. Don't try to go anywhere. I'll bring help."

If Walsh heard anything Keegan said, he gave no sign.

Keegan backed out of the SUV and closed the passenger door. He had the pistol in one pocket and extra ammo in another pocket. He kept a close eye on the ground as he walked toward the road, avoiding rocks and vines and anything resembling a snake.

Soon, he'd reached the county road. He looked both ways. No cars, no bicycles, no hitchhikers. Just a stretch of blacktop and the sunrise coming up in the distance.

Keegan shoved the pistol into his waistband in the small of his back and covered it with his jacket. It had been a long time since he'd shot a pistol, but he'd been an expert back then. If he needed the weapon, he was sure he could shoot straight enough.

He stepped into the roadway and headed toward Newton Village. He'd kept in shape while he was incarcerated. He was thirsty and hungry and he hadn't slept all that well in the SUV, either. Which meant his pace was slower than it should have been.

But it was still very early. He should make it to the village before too many witnesses were awake to notice where he came from.

He'd been expecting to catch a ride into the village. So far, no passing vehicles of any kind had traveled along this stretch of road in the early dawn. Perhaps there wasn't a roadblock ahead. Which was okay.

But it also meant he had no choice but to put his head down and march forward. He shoved his hands into his pockets for warmth, which was awkward for walking, but at least it was slightly warmer and kept his fingers supple enough.

He walked northward about a mile until he came to a bend in the road. He couldn't see around the bend. He listened for oncoming traffic but heard none.

When he came around the bend, he saw a lone farmhouse on the right at the end of a long unpaved driveway. He was still outside the village limits, which was probably why there were no other homes around.

Smoke rose from the dilapidated chimney, which probably meant it was occupied. The abandoned look the place had made him wonder. Living this far from town, he figured they were probably self-sufficient. They'd have first aid supplies on hand.

Keegan spent about three minutes thinking through the risks before he walked toward the driveway.

At first, he couldn't see any movement inside. The windows in the place were dark. The whole building would probably have been invisible from the road at night.

But as he narrowed his eyes for better vision and peered, he noticed lights shining from the back of the house. Maybe the kitchen was back there. Maybe the owners were having breakfast and coffee. He imagined a hardscrabble old man and a scrawny woman frying eggs and drinking thick, black coffee.

A big "No Trespassing" sign was posted in several places along the road. He wondered how serious the old man was about it.

His stomach growled and he grinned.

"You're at the point where simply thinking about food makes your stomach sit up and take notice, eh?" he said, patting the pistol resting against his back to confirm it was still there.

This far away from civilization, the farmer was likely to have a vehicle. After breakfast, Keegan could use the gun to persuade the farmer to help get Walsh to a doctor.

Mindful of the "No Trespassing" signs and worried about making it all the way to the house without being seen, he stepped off the road before the driveway entrance. He moved into the trees before he advanced toward the house.

He didn't know many farmers. But the ones he'd seen in movies tended to own shotguns. And they knew how to use them.

CHAPTER 21

Saturday, May 14
Near Bolton, South Dakota
6:05 a.m.

Fern Olson opened one eye and looked at the bedside clock. She lay quietly, listening to the old house creak. A strong, cold breeze blew under the door and washed over her bed. Dad probably went outside to collect the newspaper, leaving the back door open long enough to let the heat rush out.

She'd tried to persuade him to read the national papers online. No luck.

"No, thanks." He'd cast a deep scowl toward her at the mere suggestion. "I get more national news than I care to know from the television. It's the local news I care about. I've been reading the *Bolton Eagle* all my life."

Fern had shrugged and moved on. She'd given up arguing with her father years ago. He had always done exactly whatever he wanted. None of his personal habits had changed for decades.

She snuggled further into the warmth under the duvet and closed her eyes. She hadn't slept enough. It was Saturday. Maybe she could get another couple of hours of shuteye.

She'd almost drifted off when a second cold gust blasted over her face like a bucket of ice water.

Dad must have left the back door wide open. Why hadn't he returned and closed the cold out?

She took a deep breath and caught a whiff of bacon frying. She frowned. Did he leave the stove on?

"Are you trying to burn the house down?" she muttered, as ill-tempered as her old man. The apple didn't fall far from the tree, as her ex-husband had always insisted.

Fern threw off the duvet and sat up on the bed. She sucked in a sharp breath as the cold wind assaulted her entire body all at once. She quickly found her robe and her slippers and headed for the kitchen.

Just as she reached the bedroom door, it flew open, slamming back to the wall hard enough to drive a hole in the sheetrock with the doorknob.

Fern gasped.

A big man stood blocking the open doorway.

Her hands flew to cover her mouth as her eyes opened wide with fright.

She looked up into one of the most terrifying faces she'd ever seen.

A face she knew well. One that had invaded her nightmares for years now. Since the first time she'd met him, shackled and locked behind bulletproof plexiglass at Bolton prison.

Even after all these years, she'd never become more at ease around the giant-sized serial killer. She didn't expect she ever would.

Ryan Denny.

What the hell was he doing here?

He looked like he'd been running through the woods all night. Which he probably had. Bolton prison was more than twenty miles south. He must have escaped with the others when the plane destroyed the exercise yard. It had taken him hours, running through the woods and the fields in the dark, to make his way here.

Denny's orange jumpsuit was filthy and torn in several places. His face was smeared with grime. Dried blood streaked along the side of his neck and head. His hands looked as if they'd spent the night digging and shoving and moving obstructions along the way.

When she'd met with him in prison, his dark eyes were always cold and piercing. Now, like the rest of him, they were wild.

He opened his mouth to reveal a mostly toothless smile. Combined with the overpowering stench of body odor, his fetid breath almost knocked her down when he spoke.

"Hello, Fern. I didn't expect to find you here," he said calmly.

"What are you doing here, Denny?" She steadied her tone while frantically searching for a means of escape. His body blocked the doorway, the only possible exit from her room.

"I need the keys to the truck in the barn out back. I asked the old man, but he said his daughter had them. That's you, I assume. Hand them over."

Fern's heart leapt into her throat. She managed to squeak out a question. "The old man?"

"Found him outside, near the back door. He'd come for the newspaper, he said."

"Where is he now?" she asked, holding her breath between short gulps, trying not to vomit.

Denny shrugged. "I need the keys, Fern. Give them to me."

Her mouth opened and closed like a fish. No words escaped, mostly because terror had clamped her vocal cords.

Before she realized it, he'd moved two steps into the room. His arm shot straight out. He closed his big paw around her throat and lifted her off the ground like a toy.

"I don't want to hurt you. But you know I will, Fern." His words were casual, even as his dark eyes narrowed and his grip tightened for emphasis.

Fern inhaled as deeply as possible to stay alert. She'd have screamed, but his big paw blocked her windpipe. She kicked her feet and pulled at his grip with both hands.

He never wavered.

She felt her consciousness fading. The bedroom began to blacken around the edges of her vision.

"Let her go!" A scream from the hallway.

Noah. Her boy.

Denny turned his thick neck to see behind his back. As he shifted his attention, Fern summoned the last of her strength and kicked out with both feet.

She caught Denny with a hard kick in the groin. He barely flinched.

Noah screamed again. "I said, let her go!"

"Go back to bed, kid." Denny squeezed her throat harder. "The keys, Fern. That's all I want."

She barely had enough air to gasp, "Okay."

"See? That wasn't so hard, was it?" Denny said.

Noah yelled like he had as a child when he'd jumped off the high dive at the local pool. A long, loud, piercing screech.

She heard his footfalls as he ran from his room toward Denny.

Fern wiggled harder, kicking forward, trying to loosen Denny's hand from her neck with as much strength as she could muster.

Then, Noah grunted with the effort as he plunged his hunting knife into the muscle of Denny's shoulder. He jerked on the knife after it penetrated.

Denny screamed like a wounded animal and released his grip on Fern's neck.

Blood rushed down Denny's arm and torso, pooling on the floor beside his feet.

He pulled the knife from his deltoid muscle, held it aloft, and charged Noah like a bull, snorting with rage.

Noah fell backward to the floor. He scrabbled backward on all fours toward his room, desperately trying to run from Denny.

Fern steadied her feet on the floor and took great gulps of air, making every effort to oxygenate before she passed out.

Noah pushed to his feet and ran full-out toward his room.

Denny ran after him, with Noah's hunting knife in his fist.

Fern grabbed the first heavy object she could find and threw it at Denny. The lamp hit Denny's head and bounced off, flying over the banister and down to the first floor, where it crashed and scattered.

Noah was almost to his room now. Denny was two steps behind.

Fern ran to her bedside table, yanked it open, and grabbed her pistol. She tried to scream a warning, but her vocal cords were bruised. A weak "Stop!" was all she could manage.

She rushed to the open bedroom door and fired the first shot wide to the right of Denny's retreating body.

The shot was monstrously loud in the enclosed bedroom. Her ears were ringing long before the bullet hit the wall.

Denny slowed and turned toward her, shaking his head like a wounded animal.

Noah dashed into his room and slammed the door.

Fern stood facing Denny.

She held the pistol steady in both hands and aimed it straight at his heartless chest.

Denny stared at her, eyes wide, nostrils flared, red-faced with rage.

She could almost see the gears turning in his head.

If he charged forward, how many times could she shoot him before he grabbed the gun?

They stood like that for a few surreal moments.

Fern tried to speak, to tell Denny to calm down. She didn't intend to kill him. But her throat was too bruised to carry the words through his outrage.

With the percussive damage to her ears from the gunshot, she wasn't sure whether Denny heard her words or cared enough to puzzle out her intent.

Her aim never wavered.

He lowered his head like an animal and screamed as he ran toward her, like a three-hundred-pound offensive lineman.

He was less than a dozen steps away. He'd arrive in a fraction of a second.

If he hit her, he'd kill her for sure.

"Stop!" she tried to scream again.

He was a huge target. From this rapidly closing distance, she couldn't possibly miss him.

Fueled by rage and adrenaline, Denny kept coming, arms wide, faster than a man his size should have been able to move. Each footfall on the old hardwood bounced the floor as he approached.

She actually wondered, briefly, whether he might fall through the boards and land in the kitchen below.

Fern opened fire.

Denny kept coming.

She hit him seven times before he finally fell, less than two feet from where she stood.

She slumped back onto the bed, breathing heavily, staring at his bleeding corpse.

Denny lay face down on the floor. Blood continued to pump from his shoulder wound for a moment. When it stopped pulsing, she knew his heart had stopped.

He was dead.

Fern stared, wide-eyed, but calm enough. *Shock*, she thought.

She had never killed a man before. She'd always said she couldn't kill another person, no matter what. Guess that wasn't true, either.

The list of things she'd been wrong about continued to pile up. She might break under the weight of it all.

But not yet.

After the shooting stopped, Noah opened his bedroom door and peeked out. Half a second later, he rushed toward his mother. They hugged tightly, each attempting to comfort the other through their tears.

Together, they'd killed a man. Both understood that their relationship would never be the same.

After a while, Noah pulled away. He looked into Fern's horrified face.

"Mom?" he said worriedly, sounding like the young boy he once was instead of the sullen teenager he'd become. "What do we do now?"

"We check on Grandpa. And then, I'll call Chief Mitchell. He's got his hands full with the situation at the prison right now. A few more minutes won't matter." She avoided walking through Denny's blood and made her way to the stairs.

Noah followed her lead.

She was already down to the kitchen before she remembered she'd left the gun in her room.

CHAPTER 22

Saturday, May 14
Bolton, South Dakota
6:15 a.m.

A fist pounding on the door of her hotel room jolted Kim awake. She climbed from the warm bed, slipped into her robe, and stood on her toes to put her sleepy eye to the peephole.

After a few attempts, she was able to focus. A huge black man waited, both hands holding hot coffee. FBI Special Agent Reggie Smithers. Her face broke into a grin.

She quickly pulled her hair back and twisted it into a tight bun at the base of her neck. Then she opened the door. "Hey, Smithers. Fancy meeting you here."

"Morning, Agent Otto. Sorry to show up so early, but I thought you'd be ready. Never known you to sleep the day away." He grinned and handed her one of the containers of hot, black coffee. "I've got stuff to tell you and I'm short on time."

"Sure. Come in," she said, accepting the coffee and standing aside. "We were planning to look you up today anyway."

The instant he walked in, the room seemed to shrink a few sizes. Smithers was a big guy. He was also an excellent field agent. Reliable. Steadfast. Competent.

She gave him extra points for being acceptable to Gaspar. They'd teamed up twice before, him official and her off the books, and she trusted him completely.

"Why are you working this prison break?" she asked, waving him to the only chair in the room while she perched on the bed with the coffee, which was way too hot to drink.

He shrugged. "You know how it is. All hands on deck and I was the most experienced agent in the neighborhood. Relatively speaking."

"Right." She imagined he hadn't exactly been hanging out in Bolton. Or even South Dakota. But she was glad to see him, whatever the reason.

"We've been working all night and we've got a meeting to discuss status at oh-eight-hundred. You and Burke should join in."

"Wouldn't miss it." She nodded. "So why are you really here?"

"I'd forgotten how blunt you can be." He grinned. "If you're here, Cooper thinks Reacher's involved. I want to know what Reacher has to do with all of this. So tell me."

"I would if I could, my friend. Trust me on that."

A frown clouded his features. "You're handing me that classified bullshit? You?"

"Not at all." She shook her head. "I meant it literally. I would tell you if I knew. I don't."

He looked at her frankly, sizing up the response. FBI agents were trained to suss out liars. He'd found her explanation credible, she guessed, even if he didn't like the answer.

"Okay. You don't know why or how Reacher's involved. What's your best guess?" he pressed, with a glance at the clock.

"It's always the same. Cooper believes Reacher might be here. Either now, or he'll be arriving soon. Cooper never explains himself. Even when I ask," she replied as she pulled the top off the coffee to allow it to cool enough to drink. "Which I mostly don't do because it's a waste of breath."

"What's your orders? Shoot to kill?" he grinned, swallowing his coffee like it was tepid instead of scalding.

She smiled in response. "Nothing that simple. My mission is to find Reacher. I'm supposed to locate him and call it in. Cooper will take over from there."

Smithers opened his big eyes wider. "And he didn't give you any direction at all beyond that?"

"Not much." Kim shrugged. "He told me to interview a local lawyer. She's got a client I'm supposed to interview, too—an inmate at Bolton Prison. Or at least, he was before yesterday. I assume he's still there. I don't know the inmate's name. I'm supposed to get it from the lawyer."

"Who's the lawyer?" Smithers asked.

"Her name is Fern Olson." She blew on the coffee and managed to take a shallow sip. It was still so hot it scalded her tongue. "I imagine either the inmate or the lawyer is connected to Reacher somehow. Or maybe they both are. I just don't know how. Yet."

He cocked his head and nodded as if considering something puzzling. He reached into his jacket pocket and pulled out a small thumb drive. He held it out to her. "This is a list of all the inmates who escaped yesterday. File materials we grabbed quickly for each one are there, too. Several of the escaped inmates are represented by Fern Olson."

Kim raised her eyebrows. "So you think she's involved in the prison break?"

"Seems likely. But we don't know for sure yet. We got a warrant for a wiretap and phone records when we managed to wake up a local judge. We'll know everything there is to know about Fern Olson in a couple of hours." Smithers paused for a breath and the troubled look returned to his face.

"What's bothering you?"

"You know about the explosion they had out here seven years ago, I assume."

"Gaspar told me." She nodded and took another tentative sip of the coffee, which had finally cooled enough to drink.

He held up two fingers. "Two things. Olson's law partner was killed back then. Shot in the head."

Kim stared at him.

"And one of Olson's clients was involved in whatever went down. He was already an inmate at Bolton. His name's Ryan Denny. He was on death row for a while, but he turned informant on something big and got his sentence reduced to life in prison."

"Okay. Let me guess. He's one of the escaped inmates."

Smithers nodded.

"Have you interviewed Fern Olson?"

"Not yet. We've had our hands full. But we will. This morning, probably." He paused for a deep breath. "Join us for the briefing. We'll hear the rest of the intel. After that, we'll have the phone records, and then we'll go talk to Olson together."

Kim nodded and took a big gulp of the coffee. "Sounds like a plan." Burke's go-to phrase slipped out before she had a chance to squelch it. She wrinkled her nose. Was he rubbing off on her?

"I'll see you in the briefing room," he said before he stood and walked out.

She heard the door latch behind him, but her thoughts were running through the list of Gaspar's files she'd read before bed. Nothing on Ryan Denny, she was sure.

She found her phone and hit the redial. When Gaspar answered, she told him about Smithers and the intel he'd shared.

"Can you find whatever you can on Ryan Denny and send it over? I'm hopping in the shower. I'd like to read it before I go into the briefing," she said then swallowed the last of the coffee.

"Copy that. It should be fairly easy. Inmates generally have a lot of publicly available information in various databases. I can have more than you want to know now, and then more later, probably," Gaspar replied.

"Perfect. Thanks." She thought of something else. "The whole town is crawling with law enforcement personnel by now. And Smithers is here. You don't have to worry so much."

"Right. Wanna buy a couple acres of swampland?" Gaspar grunted and hung up.

CHAPTER 23

Saturday, May 14
Near Bolton, South Dakota
6:35 a.m.

The cold wind gusted across the open ground as he walked along the road, slamming Keegan with a frigid blast every few minutes. He'd experienced weather like this plenty of times back home, but not so late in the spring. He'd begun to wonder how normal humans could live in South Dakota.

By mid-May in Boston, he'd have had blooming annuals in his flowerbeds and maybe a few plants ready for the garden. Here, the ground was bare and the earth hard. Nothing much seemed to grow. At least, not yet.

He welcomed the windbreak when he moved from the road into the trees. When he heard the shots, Keegan had covered about half the distance to the farmhouse, using the trees to conceal his approach.

At first, he didn't identify the quick, sharp explosions.

Then he recognized muffled gunshots inside the house.

One shot followed rapidly by others. He counted six. Maybe seven.

In his experience, return fire should quickly follow, and then the surviving shooter would hightail it away from the scene.

Keegan slipped behind a big tree trunk, thinking things through quickly while he waited for the shooter to flee.

He and Walsh had been extremely careful, stayed on the back roads, and changed vehicles three times.

The plan had worked well. They had not seen another escaped prisoner.

They hadn't run into roadblocks or cops, either.

"So far, so good," he murmured.

Still, there had been more than forty guys in the exercise yard when the fence came down. Most were able to escape.

Some were too stupid to run. Others probably went back, either voluntarily or at gunpoint.

"Where did the rest of them go?"

South, most likely. Because that's where the good roads and easy escape routes were. The bulk of the recovery efforts would be deployed south of the prison, too.

Which was why he and Walsh didn't go south.

But Keegan had the advantage.

He'd known precisely when the jailbreak would occur.

The other prisoners were doing what came naturally, taking advantage of the opportunity when it presented itself.

He shook his head. "They had no plan."

Even so, now that he thought about it, some inmates might have set out north instead.

"They could have walked this far by now. They've been out for ten hours." He paused and stuck his head out from behind the tree like a turtle.

"Yep. They could be inside the farmhouse. Alone. Or not."

Keegan cocked his head. "At least two possible scenarios."

He pressed one finger to the tree trunk. "Perhaps the place is abandoned."

In which case, the inmates could be fighting among themselves inside the farmhouse.

That idea had legs. Various factions had fought often enough in prison. The smallest thing could set one off against the others.

It was no stretch of the imagination to believe escaped prisoners who made it this far could be shooting each other inside the farmhouse now.

Made sense. He nodded.

"Second option. They invaded the house."

Keegan cocked his head to consider it. "Yeah, a few of those guys were dumb enough to try something like that."

He nodded again. "So maybe the homeowner shot them."

Bolton Correctional inmates had displayed extremely poor impulse control. Many were sociopaths. More were stone-cold killers.

Either option meant he was not dealing with harmless farmers.

He turtled his head out again. Still nobody coming.

Now that he understood the situation, Keegan considered moving on.

He couldn't stand here indefinitely.

"Make a decision."

There was no point going back to Walsh because he couldn't move the Land Rover.

He could forget about the farmhouse and go into the village, but he wasn't sure what lay ahead.

He needed a vehicle. He needed to get to Canada. And he wanted to take Walsh with him. Right now, all of those options still seemed viable if he could make it to the farmhouse.

"Better the devil you know," he murmured.

He waited fifteen minutes, which should've been plenty of time for the shooter to get away if he planned to flee.

Seemed like he wasn't running.

Keegan pulled his pistol from his waistband and moved closer, all senses alert. He heard no further gunshots or other problematic noises.

He advanced carefully from one tree to another, approaching the building.

"Front door? No."

He'd seen lights in the back earlier. At least, if there were people inside the kitchen, he should be able to deal with them. It was impossible to handle an enemy he could not see.

Crouched low, he advanced from one concealing point to the next as he made his way around to the back of the house.

The driveway past the farmhouse on the left led to the backyard. He saw an outbuilding twenty-five yards ahead. Probably a garage.

They had to have a vehicle.

"No way they could live out here without one."

He didn't know much about country life, but he assumed the residents would have motor vehicles and not something crazy like a horse and buggy.

He heard voices outside, from behind the house. Two people talked quietly. Keegan strained his ears to understand the conversation.

He couldn't make out the words from this distance.

How could he get closer?

Keegan scanned the immediate area. He could be spotted and picked off by gunfire as he left the cover of the trees.

He paused and checked each window on the side of the house again.

Nothing had changed.

Keegan took a deep breath and ran across the broad driveway to the side of the house. He flattened his back against the peeling paint, breathing heavily with tension.

He waited a bit.

No one called out or tried to shoot at him.

"So far, so good," he murmured again.

He hurried along the side of the house, crouched low, his back close to the building.

The sun was well above the horizon now. Even with the early morning shadows, his line of sight improved when he'd changed positions.

Two minutes later, he made it to the back corner of the farmhouse. He took another deep breath before he turtled out and scanned the backyard.

CHAPTER 24

Saturday, May 14
Near Bolton, South Dakota
7:05 a.m.

The garage door was closed. No windows on this side. He couldn't tell whether a vehicle was parked inside or not.

Opposite the closed garage, beyond a dilapidated wooden porch, an old man was crumpled on the ground. A woman and a teenager were bent over, trying to get him up.

The woman said, "Dad, we can't lift you. You have to help us. Can you stand up?"

The boy tried to leverage a firm grip under the old man's right arm. "Come on, Grandpa. We just need to get inside where it's warmer. Your eggs are getting cold. You know how you hate cold eggs."

He'd heard gunshots from the house, but none of these three had visible bullet wounds. The woman was dressed in pajamas, and so was the boy. The old man had been badly battered. Dried blood had soaked his clothes, and one of his ankles bent oddly.

He managed to shift his weight. The other two, daughter and grandson, lifted him upright. They stood together in an awkward dance, attempting to steady the old man on shaky legs.

While all of their hands were occupied, Keegan tucked his gun into his belt at the small of his back and pulled his jacket down to cover it. He came around the side of the house.

"Oh, my gosh," he said as if he was surprised by the scene. "Can I help you?"

The woman looked up wildly, and the boy's eyes rounded like he'd seen a monster. Both were clearly terrified and barely holding it together.

"Who are you?" the woman screeched at decibels too loud for human ears.

He gestured toward the road as if she wouldn't know where it was. "I heard gunshots. I thought you might need help."

He moved closer and she said, "Stop. Don't come another step. Who are you?"

Keegan recalled the name on the driver's license in his pocket. He put a friendly smile on his face.

"My name is Judd. Thomas Judd. We had car trouble and had to park off the road. About a mile back. My friend is hurt. I was walking to the village when I heard the shots. I thought somebody might need help." The explanation sounded easy and plausible to his own ears.

The woman didn't seem persuaded. "Got any ID?"

"Yeah, sure," he said, reaching for the wallet. He opened it to the plastic window covering the forged driver's license and held it out for her to see.

"Where did you come from?" she asked.

"I don't blame you for being cautious." He tilted his head vaguely southward and gave his words a friendly tone. "We passed through a checkpoint a few miles back. The officer said something about a prison break yesterday. They're apparently checking all the vehicles for escaped inmates.

Just a precaution, I guess. He said they'd already recaptured most of them."

The explanation seemed to calm them a bit. They might have demanded more proof, but they were probably too concerned about the old man's situation. Whatever it was.

"Why didn't you just call for a tow truck?" the boy said.

"We tried. No cell service out there for our carrier, I guess."

The boy nodded, relaxing a bit more. "Yeah, that's a pain. Happens to me all the time."

"What's wrong with your friend?" the woman asked, not quite ready to give up her suspicions.

"Rattlesnake bite. He got out of the car to, uh, urinate and didn't see the nest," Keegan said.

She seemed mildly satisfied or simply just too wrung out to object any further. She handed the wallet back. "Your friend needs antivenom. Soon."

"Antivenom?" Keegan replied.

The boy said, "If he doesn't get it, he could die."

"Right. I'd better get going, then. How much farther is it to the village?" He thought she might offer to drive him. No such luck. She said nothing.

"Couple of miles," the boy replied.

Keegan looked at the old man. He must've been out here for a while because his lips had started to turn blue. Breathing was rapid and shallow. His skin looked cold and clammy, too. Which could have been the frigid weather. But he was probably in shock.

"Is this your dad? Can I help you take him inside?" Keegan said, gesturing toward the back entrance. He smelled burnt bacon wafting through the screen door.

The woman and the boy exchanged glances. Something passed between them that Keegan could not decipher.

They needed a firm nudge to trust him even a little. That much was clear. Briefly, he wondered what the precise problem was. He wouldn't find the answer out here.

For half a moment, he considered killing all three of them here and now. With them out of the way, he could locate the keys to the truck or the station wagon or whatever vehicle was in the garage. Solve the problem and move on.

But how?

Until this moment, driving was a skill he had never once wished he'd learned.

Now was not the time to figure it out.

Too much at stake.

He and Walsh had to put as much distance between them and the prison as possible. Quickly. He'd lied about passing through a checkpoint, but it was likely there were checkpoints along the roads after the cops had had time to organize and get more personnel on the scene.

He needed a vehicle and a driver. And someone who knew the area would be helpful, too.

The old man's injuries prevented him from driving, and the kid was too young. Which would make him unreliable. Uncontrollable, too, probably. He'd made that mistake with the hacker.

Which left the woman. No other options if he wanted to get where he was going. Which he did.

He'd try charm and gentle persuasion first.

Keegan took a deep breath and swiped a palm over his face.

"I've had a few first aid classes," he said. "I think your dad is going into shock. We need to get him warm and see about that leg and his other injuries. Please let me help you."

The boy said, "Come on, Mom. We can't do this alone. We don't want Grandpa to die out here, do we?"

The woman still seemed unsure. But she was smart enough to know that she had no real options. She didn't want her father to die. She shrugged.

He nodded and approached the old man.

Keegan tried to lift him, but the scrawny old dude was heavier than his bony frame suggested.

The boy and the woman joined Keegan's effort. They managed to lift the old guy enough that he could hop on his one good leg.

Awkwardly, they made it up the stairs and into the welcoming kitchen. They seated him at the old-fashioned table. The boy went to the stove and moved the burnt bacon off the burner while the woman rummaged for a first aid kit. Keegan checked the freezer for an ice pack. He found a bag of frozen peas.

Keegan looked the old man over. Then he knelt beside him and laid the peas on the rapidly swelling ankle. The old guy cried out with pain.

Keegan removed the man's flimsy slipper and said, "How about that first aid kit?"

She brought the kit at the same time the kid brought two steaming cups of black coffee. Then she washed her dad's face with a warm cloth and tried to clean the blood off his wounds.

Keegan had no idea what to do with the ankle. But it was already swollen. Every time he touched it, the old man whimpered.

"He's going to need a doctor," Keegan said. "Feels like it could be a bad sprain. But it might be broken."

"Hospitals and clinics down in Bolton," the kid replied. "We got one doc in Newton Hills, but he ain't worth much, and Grandpa hates him. Might be able to help with the antivenom, though. Snakebites are pretty common around here. Just need to get the right antivenom. If you don't still have the snake, he might need a blood test."

"No!" The old man groaned and shook his head wildly when the Newton Hills doctor was mentioned.

"It's okay. Don't worry." Keegan nodded and patted the old guy's shoulder.

Nobody was driving to Bolton while the place was still crawling with law enforcement. No chance in hell Keegan was giving up the truck or station wagon or whatever it was out in the garage, either.

He was in over his head here. All he wanted was a vehicle and a driver. To collect Walsh and get the antivenom and get on their way.

The rest of whatever was going on here was none of his concern.

"You got a sofa or a bed close by? We need to get that leg elevated," Keegan said.

The woman tilted her head toward her right shoulder. "In the living room. This way."

"How about a chair or something with wheels, so we don't risk making matters worse trying to move him?"

The boy and the woman exchanged glances for a long minute. Then the boy said, "Yeah. It's upstairs. I'll get it."

When he'd gone, the woman picked up the hot coffee and stood to stretch her back. "Once we get my dad comfortable, how about we take the truck to pick up your friend and get him to the doc in Newton? Dad doesn't like old Dr. Warner at all, but he's not a bad guy. He'll be able to administer the correct antivenom. And I can drop you at the gas station. They'll have a tow truck and solve the problem with your SUV."

Keegan nodded and smiled as friendly as he could manage. "I'd appreciate that. What will you do about your dad's ankle?"

"He's just upset now. Stubborn. There's no dealing with him when he's like this. He's okay, though. A bad fall off the porch is all. After a while, I'll persuade him to go to the clinic," she grabbed a handful of unruly hair and pulled it back to the nape of her neck. "He's not senile or anything. He's just afraid. We took my mom to Bolton Hospital after a fall, and she never came home again."

"I see. Well, who wouldn't be frightened by that? And yes, I'd be very appreciative if you'd help us." Keegan nodded and drank the coffee, just to be sociable. "What's your name, anyway? You never said."

"Sorry." She wiped her palm on her robe and held her hand out to shake. "Fern Olson. This is my dad, Karl. And my son is Noah."

Keegan nearly spit out his coffee. He coughed a few times to clear his throat and cover his reaction.

Fern Olson. He'd never met the woman before, but he knew who she was. The jailhouse lawyer. Handled work for a lot of the guys, including his cellmate, Denny.

Which had turned out well over the years. Whenever Keegan needed intel passed along, he could count on Denny and Olson to do the job unwittingly. Denny had the IQ of a gnat. But Olson should have known better. Lucky for Keegan that she never seemed to catch on.

She'd had a few Friday afternoon meetings with Walsh, too.

Which could be a problem once they reached the Land Rover and she recognized him.

Fern Olson had been an unwitting tool. Still, she knew too much. He could kill her any time now.

Life's little ironies, as his dad used to say. He shook his head, hiding a smirk.

CHAPTER 25

Saturday, May 14
Near Bolton, South Dakota
7:45 a.m.

The kid came back with the office chair. They lifted the old man into the seat and wheeled him into the other room. He settled on the sofa, with pillows to elevate his leg. By the time all that was accomplished, the old man was exhausted. He closed his eyes and began snoring softly.

Olson covered him with a blanket and stood over him for a few moments. She was worried, but she didn't get emotional. Keegan was glad to see that she was a practical woman.

"I'll just throw on your clothes and then we'll go," Olson said, on her way toward the stairs. She gave the kid a look. "You stay here with Grandpa."

"No problem." Noah turned to Keegan, "Want more coffee?"

"Yeah." He followed the kid back to the kitchen, staying alert.

Something had definitely happened here earlier.

The source of the gunshots had never been explained, and he hadn't asked. He didn't care. His goal was to get on his way without further trouble. The rest of Olson's situation was not relevant.

He watched Noah as the kid refilled the mug. He was too polite. Too helpful. When was the last time a normal teenaged boy behaved like that? Never, in Keegan's experience. He had kids. He knew what a pain in the ass they could be at Noah's age.

His gut said there was more going on here than an old man falling off the porch. Could have been a domestic dispute. Maybe gramps and the kid had a fight and the kid pushed gramps a little too hard. Maybe the kid was feeling guilty.

Or maybe Olson did it. Maybe gramps was abusive. Maybe one of them was abusing gramps.

Hell, it could have been almost anything. Too many variables. No way to guess, even if he wanted to know. Which he didn't.

But he did want to get Olson into the driver's seat and get on the road. Fast.

The easiest way to do that was to ignore the rest unless he had to deal with it. Which he would. Swiftly and permanently.

Might make sense to get a little more info.

"Anybody else here with you guys?" Keegan asked.

Noah's eyes widened and he sucked in a quick breath as he shook his head a little too hard. "Just the three of us."

Uh huh. "Where's your dad?"

"He lives in Bolton. Mom and I moved here after the divorce. Grandpa needed the help. We needed a place to sleep," Noah said with a shrug.

Keegan watched the kid. He'd interrogated plenty of guys back in Boston. Thieves, druggies, thugs. All ages. He could tell when he was being lied to. Like right now. Definitely something going on that young Noah didn't want to talk about.

"You seen any of those escaped prisoners up here, Noah?" Keegan asked.

"N-no. B-but I'm worried about it. W-who wouldn't be?" Noah shook his head again, harder, faster.

Keegan's instinct pinged. Bingo. "He told you not to tell, is that it?"

"N-no. I swear. I haven't talked to anybody. Just Mom and Grandpa. That's all." He was emphatic about it.

Could have been true. Or not.

The kid was a good liar. Most kids his age were. They had a lot of practice.

"Is someone else here, Noah? In the house?"

Noah shook his head wildly.

"In the garage?"

"No, I said!"

Keegan decided to let it go. If he had to guess, whoever the dude was, he'd likely been the recipient of those gunshots anyway. Gave him a new appreciation for Olson. Or maybe the kid or the grandpa.

"Because I'd help you deal with him if he was here. You know that, right?"

Noah nodded and faced the coffee pot, desperate to end the conversation.

Olson returned wearing a jacket that seemed to be hanging a little lower on the left, due to something in the pocket, and carrying the keys.

"I'll be gone about an hour, Noah," She gave him a kiss on the head and patted his shoulder. "Grandpa should sleep until I get back. Keep the doors locked and stay inside, okay?"

Noah turned toward her and nodded. Another meaningful glance passed between them before she headed out the door.

Definitely hiding something. Keegan considered searching the house. He glanced at the clock. He'd spent too much time here already.

"Goodbye, Noah," he said as he left.

He followed Olson across the brown grass to the garage. She punched the code into a keypad, and the big door rolled open.

Parked in the middle of the concrete pad was a beat-up pickup truck. A Ford 150, according to the insignia on the side. The rusty beater had seen better days. But Keegan's instincts had been spot-on. There was no way he'd have been able to drive this beast.

"Sorry it's not a better ride. It'll bounce us all to hell, too. Dad's had this old truck since Methuselah was a pup," she said with a weak smile. "Rusty but trusty, he calls it. I guess the best we can say for it is that it beats walking."

"Absolutely," Keegan replied with a nod.

They climbed inside and she started it up. It was a diesel, and it made quite a racket as the pulsing engine got itself running.

"Gotta let 'er warm up," Olson said. The exhaust filled the garage and smelled to high heaven.

After a few minutes, she pushed in the clutch and put the transmission into reverse. She backed the truck onto the gravel driveway, where she made a three-point turn and rolled slowly down the long distance to the road.

Keegan said, "Turn left here. We're down about a mile or so on the right."

"Will do," Olson replied, applying considerable effort to turning the big stiff steering wheel. "The damned thing has almost no power anything anymore. You've gotta eat your spinach if you want to drive this beast."

The old truck bounced along the road as if shock absorbers and springs in the bench seat were a distant memory. Between the effort of driving and the diesel's noise, they made no further attempt to chat.

He scanned the area repeatedly, alert for every possible danger, looking for the point where the Land Rover went off the road. It had traveled some distance before it came to a stop, hidden in the bushes.

Keegan wasn't sure exactly how to find it. The sun was high enough in the sky to throw off a bright reflection, which would be catastrophic if someone found the Land Rover before he did

CHAPTER 26

Saturday, May 14
Near Bolton, South Dakota
8:00 a.m.

Keegan noticed a misshapen tree trunk on the opposite side of the road. "I passed that tree this morning," he said, pointing. "We're getting close."

"Okay." She slowed her speed to give him time to peer into the high weeds and trees as they passed.

They were almost two miles from the farmhouse when Olson slowed to steer the big diesel around a sharp bend in the road. He remembered that, too.

"Not much farther," he said, just before his sightline cleared.

From his perch high above the road in the bright morning light, he saw the problem ahead clearly.

Every nerve in Keegan's body began to sing.

Stopped on the shoulder was a lone white SUV. The Bolton Police Department logo was emblazoned on the side. Blue lights strobed from the light bar on the roof.

"What the hell?" Olson said.

The driver's door stood open.

The vehicle was empty.

"Where are the cops?" Olson murmured.

Keegan peered down the road and didn't see more vehicles coming. He didn't hear a helicopter overhead, either. The only thing he heard was the diesel, which overwhelmed the breeze rustling in the trees.

He noticed he'd been holding his breath and exhaled.

One lone cruiser. One or two cops. No more. The situation was controllable if he took care of it quickly.

"That's a Bolton PD squad," Olson said.

She seemed apprehensive, which could mean he'd been right about whatever had transpired back at the farmhouse.

Or maybe the habits of her life's work against law enforcement had kicked in.

Whatever her reasons, she wasn't any happier to see the cruiser than he was. Which might be okay. Perhaps this one would be a common enemy.

The heavy object he'd noticed in her left jacket pocket flashed across his mind, too.

As if she was trying to reassure them both, Olson talked loud enough to be heard over the old truck's various noises. "Maybe they can radio ahead for a tow for your SUV. They might have emergency antivenom for your friend, too. There's several different pit vipers around here, but there's probably a standard antivenom for field conditions or something."

She downshifted and slowed the truck onto the shoulder. She stopped in front of the police car and slid the transmission into park. Leaving the diesel running, she struggled out of the seat. Like the cop, she left her door open as if she expected to make a quick getaway.

Keegan climbed down, settling his feet firmly on the earth. The pistol rested against the small of his back, within easy reach.

"I might know the guy," Olson said, as she struck out first, leading the way toward the Land Rover.

From ten yards away, Keegan saw that Walsh remained precisely where Keegan had left him. Still in the driver's seat, slumped over the steering wheel. The same position he'd been in since he'd lost consciousness last night.

The cop had the Land Rover's front door open and was standing near the driver's seat. Bent at the waist, body halfway inside, the cop was probably checking Walsh's vital signs.

As they came within hearing distance, Olson yelled out. "Hey!"

The cop backed away from the vehicle and turned to face them.

He was a young guy, probably new on the job. Looked to be younger than thirty, Keegan guessed.

He didn't seem to recognize them, which might've been a good sign. He was no doubt aware of the prison break. But a couple stopping to help probably seemed harmless enough.

There were no women housed at Bolton Prison and Keegan's mug shot might not be circulating far and wide just yet.

"Stand back, please," the young cop said, holding his palm up. "I've got a man down here. I was just about to call for assistance."

"I'm Fern Olson. I live up the road," Olson said, moving toward the Land Rover and pointing toward Keegan. "This is Thomas Judd. That guy's his friend. He was bitten by a pit viper. He needs antivenom right away."

"I said, stay where you are." The officer pulled his weapon and pointed it purposefully. He stepped away from the Land Rover.

The cop was keyed up. He was young and lacked experience. He was in over his head all of a sudden, and he seemed to know it.

"What's the problem?" Keegan said continuing to advance, holding his hands wide as he walked up level with Olson.

"This guy may have been snake bit, but he's got other injuries, too. Where'd those come from?" His voice wobbled and so did the gun.

Olson lost the last of her patience. "For cripes sake, man. He needs medical attention. Can't you see that? He's in no position to hurt you. Put the gun down."

Maybe he'd had good training, and maybe he hadn't. But he seemed out of his depth. He jabbed the gun forward as if they might not have seen it.

"I said, stay back. I'm calling for help."

With his left hand, he lifted the radio off his belt.

Before he could make the call, Keegan reached behind his back and pulled his pistol. Smoothly, he leveled the barrel, aimed, and pulled the trigger.

The first shot landed squarely in the center of the cop's chest. The force knocked him backward. He landed flat on the ground like a turtle flipped onto its back.

Olson screamed. "What the hell are you doing?"

He might've been wearing a bulletproof vest. Which meant the first shot hadn't killed him.

Keegan walked up to the officer and shot him in the head. Twice. Quickly.

Olson stood by, horrified. Tears sprung to her eyes and slid down both cheeks. "Why'd you do that?"

Keegan ignored her. He walked toward the Land Rover and glanced inside.

Olson's gaze followed. She saw Walsh's face.

He was out of context and wearing civilian clothes instead of the orange jumpsuit. She didn't recognize him immediately.

Half a moment later, she gasped. Her mouth opened wide and both hands flew up to stifle her screams.

"Just relax, Olson," Keegan ordered calmly. "Do what you're told and you'll be fine. Noah will be fine, too. And so will your dad."

"I don't have to listen to you!" Olson yelled. "You killed a police officer. Are you out of your mind?"

Calmly, he pointed the gun directly at her, "I don't want to shoot you. I need you to drive the truck. But you just saw me shoot the cop. You know I will do it."

Olson stood back, eyes wide, mouth still open, shaking her head. Another minute of this, and she'd be hysterical. Or dead.

He said, "Help me get Walsh out of that seat and into your truck."

She didn't move.

He screamed, "Now!"

She still didn't move.

He walked straight up to her and backhanded her hard across the face, knocking her down on top of the cop.

Landing on the dead man seemed to shock her more than anything else. If she'd been a different kind of woman, she might've broken down completely.

While she was disoriented, he pulled her jacket to the front and, pointing the pistol at her head, stuck his free hand into her left pocket. He grabbed her pistol and pulled it out.

"What's this, Fern? You think you're going to shoot me?" Keegan sneered. He backhanded her again, hard enough to knock a couple of her teeth loose.

She barely whimpered this time. She shut her mouth, widened her eyes, and scrambled to her feet. She held both hands high and shook her head. "I-I just wanted to keep the gun away from Noah."

"Why? Did he shoot this gun earlier? Is that what I heard as I was walking up to your house?" Keegan demanded.

She shook her head again. "No. No. Not Noah. It was me. I was defending myself."

"Uh huh. From what?"

She backed out of arm's reach and took a few deep gulps of air. He kept the pistol pointed at her belly while he waited.

Once she'd calmed somewhat, he said, "What were you defending yourself from, Fern?"

"Ryan Denny," she said dully. "He attacked me. I killed him. I had no choice. Self-defense."

Keegan nodded as if he understood why she'd done it. In truth, he did.

He'd wanted to kill Denny a few times himself.

He wasn't sorry Denny was dead. Quite the opposite. Another loose end tied up. One less thing to worry about.

"How did Denny get to your house?"

"He-he said he walked. Took him all night," Olson replied, lifting her chin. The initial shock had begun to wear off. She was more defiant.

Good.

He couldn't stand a sniveling woman.

Besides, Denny had probably been looking for Keegan anyway. It couldn't have been a coincidence that Denny had shown up at Olson's house. Keegan would have killed him, given a chance. Which meant Denny would have been dead even if Olson hadn't shot him first.

Keegan slipped her pistol into his pocket. "Get up. Give me your cell phone."

She was trained now. She didn't want to make him angry. She reached into the pocket of her jeans to retrieve the phone and handed it over.

He held the cell phone like a major league pitcher and threw it far off to the left of the Land Rover. He heard it land with a satisfying thud.

"We need to move Walsh into your truck and get on the road."

Her eyes rounded again. "Where are we going?"

CHAPTER 27

Personnel shuffled through the door, stopped to pick up coffee or a donut, and took their seats. Smithers called the briefing to order precisely on the hour, wasting no time asking for attention. They settled into silent anticipation quickly. There was a job to do. They were here to do it.

The room was small and filled to capacity. Kim and Burke were not officially assigned to the team. They stood together in the back, Burke leaning one shoulder lazily against the wall.

Kim glanced around at the unfamiliar faces. The only agent Kim recognized was Smithers. The rest were highly trained, competent strangers. The kind of people she felt most comfortable with in every situation.

The FBI was here to assist the Bureau of Prisons and the other agencies, local, state, and federal, Smithers reminded them as a brief warm-up.

"We have a list of items they've requested our help with. I've allocated personnel and posted the list next to the door." He gestured toward the exit. "Damage to the building out at the FCI has been contained and is being evaluated now. Looks like we may have dodged a big problem here, but we're still getting our arms around this thing. Personnel is on-site to assess structural issues. A determination will be made on inmate housing and transportation throughout the day."

One agent near the front asked, "Has a motive been determined?"

Smithers shook his head. "At the moment, we're assuming terrorism. It's a precaution until we get more intel. We want all personnel alert at all times. If we find out otherwise, we'll let you know promptly."

A low murmur rippled through the seated agents like a wave washing across them. Nothing was off the table yet.

Smithers droned on about administrative issues that had nothing to do with her, and Kim zoned out for a while. When he cleared his throat and changed to a new topic, she tuned in again.

"We have a list of escapees, complete with names and mug shots. According to the headcount, there were forty-four inmates in the exercise yard at the time the fencing came down. Four of the inmates did not run," Smithers said like a duty sergeant might. "The other forty made a break for it. As of eight o'clock this morning, thirty-two men had been located and recaptured or voluntarily surrendered."

Agents snickered and laughed. Both Burke and Kim grinned. Voluntary surrender was a term of art. It meant the inmates had been found and, with relatively mild persuasion, turned themselves in. The humor died down, and attention focused on Smithers again.

"Which means we have agreed to assist with the recapture of eight inmates still at large." Smithers used a remote to turn on a big screen behind him. He started with a collage of mugshots.

Kim recognized the first photo. Petey Burns. The guy Burke had run off the road and she'd chased into the woods last night.

The other seven men were also strangers to her, but she already knew everything Smithers knew about them.

Smithers identified each man, one by one, and offered a brief description of each. Kim had read the more complete files on the thumb drive Smithers had given her earlier. She'd shared the intel with Burke and Gaspar, too.

When he had finished the presentation, Kim understood that Smithers also had no further information about any of the prisoners who were still at large. He glanced at the clock and a frown creased his normally congenial features.

"Okay. We were expecting a briefing from Bolton PD, but the officer must have been delayed driving in from Newton Hills, a village north of here. So this is all I have to share at the moment. Anybody got anything else?" Smithers asked.

A few questions were asked about equipment and allocation of resources between FBI personnel and other agencies. Smithers answered as succinctly as possible and the questions died down.

He glanced at the clock again and shook his head.

"Our Bolton PD officer still hasn't arrived. So we're going to wrap this up here. We'll pick up with him during the next briefing later today. I'll let you know time and place as soon as I have it," Smithers said. "The long and the short of it is that we do whatever we can to help out. This isn't our show. We're here to assist, like I said, in whatever way we can. No turf squabbles involved. Got it?"

Kim heard murmurs of understanding and no objections from the agents in the room. The meeting broke up, and they began to file out.

Burke straightened up, stretched, and yawned like Kim wasn't the only one who didn't get enough sleep last night.

After the last agent left, Smithers approached and extended his oversized paw. "You must be Will Burke. Reggie Smithers."

Burke was a big guy, but Smithers dwarfed him. Burke nodded. They shook hands. "Good to meet you."

Smithers turned his gaze toward her. "Sorry to waste your time, Otto. I was expecting Officer Miller. He's been working on Ryan Denny's escape. He'd called in an unoccupied vehicle off the shoulder of a county road north of here. Location is between the prison and that lawyer's house, Fern Olson. I had expected him to have new intel for us. Officer Miller knows him. Thought he'd recognize him on sight. No such luck, I guess." Smithers blew out a stream of frustration and swiped a palm over his tired face.

"No problem. We're on our way to meet up with Olson at her office. We'll let you know what we find out," Kim replied.

"You sure she's there?" Smithers asked.

Burke said, "I confirmed that she was expected this morning. We've got a nine o'clock appointment on the books. She hasn't called in sick or anything. Her secretary said she's as reliable as the sunrise. She's got a kid she drops off at school in the morning and then comes directly to work."

Smithers nodded. "Okay. Let me know if you learn anything useful. I'll keep you updated, too."

"Sounds like a plan," Burke said before he nodded and walked out.

"Guy's got great social skills, huh?" Smithers said, annoyed.

"Sorry. He's new." Kim offered an apologetic shrug and turned to follow. She caught up with Burke just outside the station. "What's the problem?"

"Well, that was a waste of time, wasn't it?" he said, moving toward the SUV. He punched the unlock button on the key fob and slipped in behind the wheel.

She settled herself into the passenger seat. She put the address for Olson's office into the GPS and Burke rolled out onto Main Street heading toward town. "Was it a waste of time? I'm not so sure. Why didn't Officer Miller show up?"

CHAPTER 28

Saturday, May 14
Bolton, South Dakota
8:45 a.m.

The law offices of Larson, Hanson, & Olson were three miles from the police station and on the opposite side of the street. Burke pulled into the lot and parked in one of the spaces reserved for clients.

Kim shook her head. Violating such a basic courtesy before they even met Olson didn't seem like the best way to begin. She had no legal leverage to apply here. Kim was a lawyer by training. She understood the ins and outs of lawyer-client confidentiality more thoroughly than most.

She'd get nothing out of Olson unless the lawyer volunteered the intel. And when was the last time a good criminal lawyer had ever volunteered anything remotely useful to the FBI?

Kim approached the glass doors where the name of the firm was stenciled in handsome gold letters. She pulled the door open and walked across the threshold into a comfortably warm reception area.

The quick change in temperature from the frosty outdoors caused a shiver that started in her toes and worked its way up to her scalp.

The young Nordic looking woman behind the Scandinavian-style wood desk looked up. "How may I help you?"

"We're here to see Fern Olson," Kim replied, reaching into her pocket for a business card and handing it over. "We have an appointment."

A troubled look crossed the woman's fair features. She read Kim's card and squinted her icy blue eyes to look at her screen.

"I see your appointment here. You called earlier, didn't you?" She flashed a flirty smile toward Burke and he nodded. She said, "Ms. Olson hasn't arrived yet. I'm sure she'll be here shortly. It's not like her to be late."

Burke flashed a flirty glance back her way and smiled. "No problem. We can wait."

The woman blushed. She cast her gaze to the floor as she stood and pushed her chair back. "Follow me this way."

She led them down a long corridor and into a conference room with a view of Main Street. As she closed the door on her way out, she said, "I'll call Ms. Olson and let her know you've arrived."

After she closed the door, Kim said, "What was that about?"

"Charm works for me," he said, flopping down in one of the chairs opposite the door. "You should try it sometime."

"Why don't you take the lead with Fern Olson then? Squeeze everything out of her she knows about Reacher. Apply your charm. See how that goes." She avoided adding the word *jackass* at the end of her sentence.

Gaspar would have given her a big grin and a snappy comeback. Burke simply replied, "Sounds like a plan."

Seemed like Burke's go-to catch phrase, and she was already sick of it. Kim simply nodded. So far, this guy hadn't displayed much of a sense of humor. Which might be okay, even if it made for long, dreary days.

After thirty minutes, she said, "It's odd that Olson's not here, yet. What school did you say her son attends? The one where she drops him off on time every day?"

"They can't have more than one high school in this town, can they?"

She pulled her phone from her pocket and searched the browser for local high schools. There were three. One public and two private.

Kim knew nothing about Fern Olson except that she was a jailhouse lawyer and her ex-husband was a cop. Which probably meant they couldn't afford private school for the kid.

She punched the number for the public high school and waited while it rang. The recorded message gave her a list of menu options. She chose the administrator's office.

After a few rings, a man answered.

"Bolton High School Administration, Assistant Principal Peterson. How can I help you?" he said, distracted as if he was doing four things at once. Which he probably was.

"FBI Special Agent Kim Otto, Mr. Peterson. I'm helping out with yesterday's prison break. We're trying to find Fern Olson. I'm told that her son, Noah, is a student there. Is he in class right now?"

A long pause followed before he stammered, "I-I'm not at liberty to discuss students without the permission of the parents."

"Mrs. Olson didn't show up for work today. We're worried. In light of the prison break. We're trying to find her. Can you just check on Noah? I'll wait," Kim pressed.

Peterson said, "Noah's one of our best students. I'm sure he's fine."

"All I'm asking you to do is make sure he's in class. If he's not, we've got a problem," she paused meaningfully. "And so do you."

He exhaled loudly, and she could tell she'd worried him. He said, "Okay. I'll look. Hold on."

"Thank you," Kim replied, meaning it.

Burke gave her a smirk and a thumbs-up to show he approved of her initiative. As if he had a right to judge her performance or something. She clenched her fist at her side and turned to look out the window while she waited.

When Peterson came back to the phone, the guy was out of breath. As if he'd run down to the classroom to check for himself and dashed all the way back. "He's not here. I asked the other kids and the teacher. They said Noah didn't show up today."

"I see. And that's unusual?"

"Very. I'm calling his mother as soon as we hang up. If I don't get her, I'll call his dad," Peterson said.

"Okay. Call me back if you find him," Kim said, giving him the number even as her gut said she was wasting her time.

She hung up the phone and pushed Gaspar's speed dial button. She turned to Burke and said, "Let's go."

"Go where?"

"To find Fern Olson."

"Why?"

"You got a better idea? I'm all ears." She hustled toward the exit and pushed her way through the glass doors to the parking lot, Burke trailing behind.

Gaspar picked up. "Good morning, Sunshine."

"Any chance you could find Fern Olson's cell phone for me? She's missing. I'm hoping she's got the phone with her," she said as she hustled toward the SUV. "And find her son's phone, too. Noah Olson. He lives with his mother. Both are probably on the same cell provider's plan since they live together."

"I can do that. Give me a minute," Gaspar replied. She could hear him clicking keys as she climbed into the SUV and fastened her seatbelt.

Burke had started the engine and backed out of the parking space before Gaspar said, "Got them both. North of where you're sitting now. And they're not together. I'll text you the coordinates."

"Great. And then try to get a clear satellite image for both locations, okay?" She paused. "Thanks for the help."

"Anything for you, Suzy Wong," he replied. "And I've sent you a new file. I found a tenuous connection between Reacher and Olson."

"Yeah?"

"An inmate at Bolton. Ryan Denny."

"He's one of Olson's clients. He escaped yesterday and is still at large. What's the connection to Reacher?"

"Denny ordered four murders back when Reacher was in Bolton. Two cops, a lawyer, and an old lady Reacher cared about."

"Seriously?"

"I know, it's hard to believe Reacher cared about an old lady or a lawyer. But two dead cops are another matter entirely," he said before he hung up.

Kim shook her head. Whenever she thought she was beginning to understand Reacher, something threw a wrench in her theories.

"What was that about?" Burke asked from the driver's seat.

"Gaspar says Ryan Denny may be the connection between Olson and Reacher." She paused to wrap her head around it. "Denny might be the inmate Cooper intended us to interview, after Olson."

"How is Reacher connected to Denny?" Burke said with a frown.

"I'm not sure he is. Gaspar sent a file. He says Denny was responsible for four murders while Reacher was in town," Kim replied, still thinking things through.

"What would Cooper expect us to learn from Denny?" Burke shook his head. "Not likely Reacher would come back here just for Denny, is it? And why now? He's had seven years to deal with Denny if he intended to deal with him at all."

Kim shrugged. Gaspar's all-purpose gesture covered everything. "Reacher does what he wants, on his own time. If he was predictable, I'd have found him already."

A few moments later, her cell phone pinged with the text from Gaspar. She entered the location of Fern Olson's phone into the SUV's navigation system as Burke pulled onto Main Street and headed north.

CHAPTER 29

Olson's cell phone was thirty-two miles north of the intersection of Main Street and the county road that led toward Bolton Correctional Facility. According to Gaspar, the phone wasn't moving, which could mean almost anything. But Kim was a realist. A mobile phone found in a static location in the middle of nowhere was rarely a good sign.

Burke drove the big Navigator along the main county road toward the prison. Under normal circumstances, this road led straight into the huge compound. One way in, one way out. Easier to monitor the traffic that way.

Five miles north of town, as they neared the facility, a temporary sign flashed on the shoulder announcing a detour ahead. Burke slowed the SUV, following behind an old Dodge belching smoke from its tailpipe.

Two Bolton PD squad cars, blue light bars pulsing on top, blocked the entrance. On a typical Saturday, busloads of visitors would have traveled from Bolton to and from the three facilities, picking up and dropping off families and friends of inmates.

But not today.

They waited in a short line of traffic as the officers checked each vehicle and its occupants.

This was the first time Kim had been anywhere close to Bolton Correctional Facility. The black smoke from yesterday's fires had dissipated. Clear skies and morning sunshine illuminated the bleak institutional architecture.

The compound looked exactly like the photos she'd seen online. No visible damage had been inflicted on the south side during yesterday's events. From here, the place seemed normal.

But the photographs had not prepared her for the vast size of the facility.

"Land must have been incredibly cheap when this compound was built," she said, turning her head from side to side to take it all in.

"Knowing the government, it was probably public land to start with," Burke replied. "The only reason to build something like this way out here is because a bean counter somewhere said it would be cheap and easy."

"True," Kim said, continuing to scan the massive site before her. "The easy part had to be cheap labor and not much need for security once the place was built."

Burke nodded, inching the SUV ahead behind the belching Dodge. "Because where would an escaped inmate go? No wonder they've rounded up most of the ones who didn't simply come back on their own."

Acres of concrete and blacktop, along with several huge block buildings, occupied the common grounds.

The buildings were not contiguous. They were laid out in a squared U-shape with wide-open spaces between them. The federal prison building was the largest and ran along the back to form the base of the U, opposite the main entrance. The county jail formed the east leg, and the state penitentiary completed the west leg.

At the end of the road, a camera captured images of the vehicles and occupants while the detour sign directed traffic east or west. A Bolton PD officer approached each vehicle and requested identification before passing the vehicle from the checkpoint onto the detour.

When it was his turn, Burke eased into the spot next to the officer and lowered the window. They handed over their badge wallets, and he inspected them. He took a quick snapshot of each using a handheld device created for this purpose.

"We're working with Agent Smithers," Burke said, which was partially true.

"We're glad for the help. Where are you two going?" the officer asked, nodding as he returned the badge wallets.

"Fern Olson's place. We're told it's about thirty miles north of here," Burke replied. "Any trouble out that way?"

The officer shook his head. "Not that I've heard about so far. There's two checkpoints between here and Newton Hills. Nothing's been called in."

Burke thanked him, raised the window, and turned west. After a mile or so, Kim could no longer see the buildings behind the trees and hills surrounding the facility.

The first county road they reached, Burke turned north toward the village of Newton Hills, which was barely a dot on the map.

They passed the next Bolton PD checkpoint a mile along the northbound road. They slowed, showed their credentials, were photographed, and passed through without incident. The facility's crisis plan had laid out the procedure, and Bolton PD seemed to be following it to the letter.

At the checkpoint, Burke asked the officer, "Any news from the roadblocks or checkpoints ahead?"

"No. There's nothing along this road except unoccupied land until you reach the old Olson place. Vehicles going that way have to pass through here. We've got one more checkpoint just south of Newton Hills. After that, we don't have anything set up. But the feds might. I'm not sure," the officer replied.

"Thanks," Burke said, raising the window and picking up speed on the narrow blacktop.

"The coordinates for Fern Olson's cell phone are about twenty-five miles north. Between here and her home," Kim said, looking ahead at the long, lonely county road. "The signal is on the west side, off the road."

"That's a long way for an escapee to run in the dark. Not to mention the threats posed by wild predators," Burke replied.

"Predators?"

"Wolves, grizzlies, pit vipers. Maybe others. All hungry after the long winter. I'm not that up on my native American wildlife," he grinned when an involuntary shiver ran through Kim's body.

"I'll bet it's pitch black out here after sundown. Not much traffic, either," she said, scanning the sides of the road.

Burke nodded. "Yeah. This could have been a viable escape route to anyone who got past the perimeter of the prison before Bolton PD fanned out."

"They probably ran the helos out here last night. Heat signatures from a human body wouldn't be that hard to distinguish from the coyotes and prairie dogs. If they'd found any." Kim saw nothing on either side of the road except trees and tall grasses. "If I were running from a prison break with nothing but an orange jumpsuit on my back, I'd have gone south. Cars, food, people. Harder to find me in even a small crowd and easier to hide, too."

Burke frowned and increased his speed as if her logic annoyed him. She turned her head toward the window and grinned.

After a while, he must have tired of the silence. "Have you been wondering why I accepted this assignment?"

"Somebody's got to do it, right?" Kim shrugged. "You got your orders from the Boss, just like I did. We're not steering the ship."

He nodded, tapping the steering wheel with two fingers nervously. "Truth is, I didn't have a lot of choice. It was either accept the assignment or leave the FBI."

"Was there something you'd rather do instead?" Kim asked.

"I liked the gig I had. I'm well suited to hostage rescue. I didn't want to move on," Burke replied, then inhaled deeply and took more than a minute to empty his lungs.

A habit formed when he was a SEAL, she guessed. SEALs could hold a breath underwater for a long time. "So why didn't you stay with the hostage rescue team? HRT is a much more exciting department than working in the field like this."

He shrugged. "Quite honestly, I'm not sure there's anything else I'm qualified to do other than private mercenary work. So here I am."

"So what happened that got you reassigned?"

"You mean you didn't ask Gaspar to find that out already?" Burke gave her a side-eye and grinned.

"Of course, I did. This is a test." She smiled in return, but the smile did not reach her eyes.

CHAPTER 30

Saturday, May 14
Near Bolton, South Dakota
10:05 a.m.

Kim gave Burke a long, hard look. In profile, he was rugged and all hard edges. Just like his personality. Which didn't make him a liability on her team. Could be just the opposite. She'd wanted a partner and the Boss had sent one. But something about Burke made her more uneasy than she wanted to be.

She'd long passed the point of "trust but verify" where the Boss was concerned. He'd parked Burke here after some sort of problem in his last assignment that should have bounced him from the FBI.

The Boss, true to form, didn't even tell her what the problem had been. Not that it mattered. He'd have stuck Burke on her team regardless.

The file Gaspar had sent proved Burke was a hothead. Maybe he simply got sideways with the wrong guys. Or maybe it was something worse.

Whatever it was, she needed to know. No time like the present to find out.

"My security clearance is higher than yours. So I can't spill the details." Burke gave her a glance to be sure she was listening as if he didn't intend to repeat himself.

"How convenient," she replied.

"Yes. But it's also true."

She shrugged. He'd tell her the whole story, or he wouldn't. No amount of prodding would change things. And she wasn't about to beg, so she waited silently while he made his choice.

"An operation went bad a few weeks ago. People died. Someone had to take the blame, and I was the low man on the team. Next thing I hear, I'm out on my ass," he said, with more concern than she'd expected. "That's all I'm allowed to say. Just know that I took the weight, but it wasn't me. I did what I was meant to do."

She nodded, not persuaded.

"I won't let you down, Otto," Burke said. "You can count on me. You have my word."

He seemed sincere. And maybe he was. But she'd been fooled before, and words were a bankrupt substitute for action.

Before Kim had a chance to reply, she noticed an unoccupied Bolton PD cruiser pulled off the road, up ahead on the shoulder.

"Looks like maybe somebody got here before we did. Let's see what's going on," Kim said.

Burke swiveled his head to scan the desolate area. Nothing but weeds and trees and bushes in every direction. "This is where Olson's cell phone is pinging?"

"About eighty feet off the road and slightly south of that cruiser. Maybe Bolton PD tried to find Olson the same way we did and came up with the same cell signal," Kim replied.

"The officer must be out combing the bushes for the phone," Burke said. "Or looking for Olson's body."

Kim blinked. "Why would you say that? We have no reason to believe Olson's dead."

"Oh, come on. Think about it," Burke said. "Her clients are a bunch of convicted felons. Some are serving long sentences for violent crimes. At least two escaped yesterday that we know about. It's not much of a stretch to assume one of them found her and killed her, is it?"

She said nothing, letting the idea settle in. She hoped he was wrong.

Kim had never met Fern Olson, but she looked okay in her headshots. She had a kid. And she was a lawyer. Whatever she'd done, she didn't deserve to die for it.

Burke pulled off the road onto the shoulder behind the cruiser. He parked, and they both climbed out.

Kim walked around the SUV toward the cruiser and looked inside. Nothing to see.

On the shoulder, slightly ahead of the cruiser, she spied wide, deep tire tracks where a heavy vehicle had left the road.

Maybe the Bolton PD officer had seen the tracks and pulled over to investigate.

Following the tracks, Kim walked ahead of Burke, deeper into the tall grass toward the trees.

Fifty feet into the field, behind thick bushes, they reached an abandoned Land Rover. The front of the vehicle was lower than it should have been.

She walked around the right side. The right front wheel well was crumpled and resting on lower ground.

"Must have been traveling too fast," Burke said, kneeling and pointing toward the rocky surface. "Looks like he bounced over a granite shelf here and blew the tire. Bent the wheel, too. Maybe bent the frame. Probably couldn't go anywhere after that."

"The vehicle isn't drivable. That much is obvious. If this happened last night, he might have tried to call a tow," Kim said.

Burke nodded. "We can check local garages. See if anybody came out to pick him up."

"The driver's door is open." Kim walked around to the other side of the vehicle. She stopped suddenly and held up her hand. "We've got a body here. Shot in the chest and the head."

"Olson?" Burke said as he rounded the back of the Land Rover.

"No." Kim knelt near the male body.

She'd never seen him before. He wore a Bolton PD uniform. There was a nameplate above his left breast pocket.

"It says *Miller*. Isn't that the name of the guy Smithers was expecting at the briefing this morning? The one who didn't show up?" Kim said. "He's holding his service weapon. Maybe he got lucky and wounded his attacker."

Burke scanned the immediate location. "Where is Olson's phone?"

"The coordinates put it fifty feet that way," she pointed, standing up.

"So, what? Olson shot Miller and..." Burke took a few steps in the direction of the cell signal. "It doesn't look like anyone has walked over that way recently."

He came back to the officer's body, thinking aloud. "Bolton PD drove Olson home last night after the jailbreak because her car was stolen from the prison. Maybe she left again. Maybe she was driving this Land Rover. But why did the vehicle leave the road? And why would she kill Miller?"

"Don't disturb anything else. Forensics will have to sort all of this out." Kim fished her phone from her pocket to call Smithers. "I don't think Olson's lying dead over there, though. At least I hope she isn't."

"Make the call. I'll find the phone," Burke said, walking carefully away from the Land Rover. "And don't worry. I won't destroy any evidence in the process."

Kim pulled a pair of latex gloves from her pocket and leaned into the Land Rover, holding the phone with one hand while she scanned the empty spaces inside. She opened the console between the seats, but it was too dark to see inside the compartment.

She put the call on speakerphone and used the flashlight app to illuminate the storage space.

Simultaneously, she spied the pistol, and Smithers finally picked up the call.

"Agent Smithers," he said preoccupied. "What's up, Otto?"

Before she had a chance to reply, Burke screamed like a wounded grizzly from twenty feet behind her. "You son of a bitch!" Followed by a stream of angry curses.

Smithers's booming voice shouted, "What the hell is happening?"

And then three rapid gunshots.

Kim backed out of the Land Rover and stepped carefully around Officer Miller's body. She pulled her service weapon and scanned the field looking for Burke.

CHAPTER 31

Saturday, May 14
Near Bolton, South Dakota
10:20 a.m.

Burke had set off in the direction of the signal from Olson's cell phone. He was standing close to the spot, balancing on one leg, his weapon in his right hand.

"What are you shooting at?" she asked as she ran toward him.

"Wait! Watch your step!" he called out, waving his left arm toward the ground. "Rattlesnakes. They're all over the place. One's clamped onto my boot even though I shot the bastard's tail off."

Kim stopped in her tracks. She looked toward the brown weeds that covered the ground. Pit vipers were native to this area, and they were active now, looking for food after a long winter. She saw a couple of tails slithering away to her right.

"Stand down," she said as she raised the phone to reply to Smithers, breathing normally again but keeping a sharp lookout for snakes. "Burke stepped into a viper's nest. He shot the snakes. That's all."

"Did he get bitten?"

"Don't think so. One tried to strike through his boot but didn't succeed. He should be okay."

"Okay." Smithers exhaled loudly. "Where the hell are you?"

"We're almost thirty miles north of the prison. We were headed to interview Fern Olson. She lives out here. We saw a Bolton PD cruiser and pulled up behind it." She paused for breath. "And we found Officer Miller. He's dead. Shot at least twice. Once in the chest. Can't tell how many shots to the head."

Smithers was quiet for a good long time before he said, "I'll send the helo with backup. Can you wait there until it arrives?"

"Yeah. But we need to get out to Olson's place, just north of here."

"What's the rush?"

Kim paused a moment and then replied, "We've found Olson's cell phone. It's close to Miller's body. But she's not here."

"So you think she shot Wilson and then ran?"

"I don't know what happened out here. As soon as we hang up, I'll try to find out."

"And just how are you planning to do that?" he demanded.

Kim said nothing. Smithers waited a bit so she could change her mind. She didn't.

"One of our teams is ten minutes out. You should see the helo approaching from the south shortly. When they get there, you can head up to Olson's place," Smithers said, in full command mode now. "I'll make some calls. Get more backup. We'll connect later. How's that?"

"Works for me. And there's another abandoned vehicle. A Land Rover. Could be why Miller stopped here. I snapped a photo of the VIN and sent it to you along with a few other photos of the scene," she replied before she disconnected and walked carefully toward Burke, scanning the ground for snakes.

"Okay. I'll get a trace on the Land Rover going now. Need anything else?"

"Not right at the moment."

"Be there as soon as we can," Smithers said before he disconnected the call.

Burke was still balanced on his left leg when she approached. The four-foot-long rattlesnake's wide mouth gripped tightly at his lower calf. Burke's gunshot had blown the snake into two pieces, but the viper wasn't dead.

He was bending to pull the viper off his leg when she rushed up.

"Stand still. And don't touch it. Don't touch any of them," she warned sharply.

"Why not?" he demanded, still bent at the waist, reaching for the head.

She waved her palm toward two more snakes torn apart by his gunshots on the ground near his feet. "Pit vipers can live after you've severed the head. Sometimes for hours. And they can eject a large quantity of venom even after they're dead. Enough to make you seriously ill or even kill you."

"Great. What am I supposed to do? I want this thing off me. And we both need to get out of here before more of their friends come calling. The damned snakes are everywhere."

She scanned the ground around his feet, looking for more snakes. "He may release on his own eventually."

"How long is eventually?" Burke scowled.

Kim ignored his question. Truth was it could be hours before the fangs released. But she didn't think he'd want to hear that. "Can you feel the teeth through your jeans?"

Burke shook his head. "The strike was just a little bit too low. He's grabbed the leather. Not the first time these cowboy boots have saved my life, either."

She found a good-sized stick on the ground and handed it to Burke. "If you see another snake, try scaring it away first. I'd rather not be deafened by another gunshot while we're getting this guy off your leg."

He took the stick in his left hand. "You think I can whack him and he'll go away?"

"Maybe we won't have to test that theory." She reached into her pocket and pulled out a small bottle of hand sanitizer. Keeping her gaze on the ground around Burke's feet, she inched closer.

"Put your foot down on the ground. We don't need you falling over," she said. "I'm going to try to squirt this hand sanitizer into his mouth. According to my old Girl Scout troop leader, if he's alive, the alcohol will burn his mouth and cause him to let go."

Burke grinned. "And what if he's mostly dead? Are his tastebuds still working? What did your old troop leader say about that?"

Kim scowled. "If you've got a better idea, have at it."

"You wouldn't have a quart of vodka in your pocket, would you?" he said, but his tone wasn't at all cheerful.

She grunted. "Thought so. Okay, stand still. And if he starts to let go, use that stick to pry him off, downward and away from your body if you can."

Kim opened the hand sanitizer and gripped it upside down as she moved closer to Burke's right leg.

She bent at the knees, reached out, and squeezed the hand sanitizer bottle, letting the contents spurt.

The clear liquid gel spread over the pit viper's open mouth and oozed inside.

Kim emptied the bottle and tossed it aside. Then she stood back.

They waited a couple of moments and the viper's mouth relaxed, trying to release its grip on the heavy jeans and the leather boots beneath them.

"Now. Use the stick now," Kim instructed.

Burke shoved the stick between the snake's open jaws and his pant leg, leveraging the force away from his body as much as possible, given the awkward angle.

Kim grabbed the stick and applied more weight to force the viper to let go.

When the severed head fell writhing onto the ground, she yelled, "Move away! Move!"

Burke jumped back, half a moment before the viper's head struck again.

This time, it clamped only the space where Burke's leg had been.

When the mutilated body landed again, Burke pointed his weapon and fired, blowing the snake's head away.

"Damned vipers," he said under his breath. "The noise should be enough to chase his buddies to the hills, too."

Kim cocked her head to study him, and she stood. "You know snakes can't hear loud noises, right?"

He turned toward her with his nostrils flared and his lips pressed into a hard line.

He was seriously angry, all traces of humor gone with the dead snake.

That was not good. She needed a partner who kept his anger under control.

"Did you get the phone?" she asked, ignoring his reaction. Now was not the time to handle his issues. But the time would come.

"How the hell do you think I got to be snake bait?" He reached into his pocket and yanked out a cell phone encased in an evidence bag. "The damned snake's nest was right next to it. Who knew the damned snakes blended into the dirt like that?"

Her lips twitched as she tried to control her amusement, but in the end, she just threw back her head and laughed. Which caused him to scowl fiercely in her direction.

"You're sure his fangs didn't break your skin? Because if he did, we'll need to take his head with us to be sure we get the right antivenom."

"I'll take my chances," Burke snarled.

Right at that moment, they heard the helo overhead and looked up.

Kim said, "Come on. It's Smithers's team. We'll brief them and get going."

"Who killed Miller?" Burke asked as they walked along, watching the ground.

"Dunno. I didn't want to disturb the evidence." She shook her head. "Maybe we'll get some solid forensics from the crime techs."

"Or you could just ask Gaspar," he said, snidely. "I'm sure he'll have all the answers."

She said nothing. Even as she wondered why he wanted to curb contact with her former partner. Were his reasons personal? Or had the Boss told him to keep Gaspar out of the way?

Kim fished her phone out of her pocket and dialed Gaspar. When he answered, she told him what she wanted.

Gaspar replied, "Stay by the phone."

CHAPTER 32

Saturday, May 14
Newton Hills, South Dakota
11:15 a.m.

Keegan kept the gun aimed at Olson as she drove. They passed the farmhouse, which seemed unchanged from when they'd left it.

The first challenge was presented by a half-assed checkpoint manned by one Bolton PD cruiser and a single officer. Keegan didn't particularly want to kill the man, but he made Olson understand that he would if the need arose.

She slowed the big diesel and stopped beside the temporary sign. "Morning, Harry," she said friendly-like. "What's going on?"

Harry touched the tip of his hat. "Morning, Fern. We're checking for escapees after that mess yesterday down to Bolton. You haven't seen any on the road, have you?"

Olson widened her eyes and shook her head rather than try to pass off a lie. Which would have made Keegan smile under different circumstances.

"Who you got in the truck there?" Harry asked, coming closer to have a look for himself. "Got any ID?"

Keegan replied, pulling his ID from his pocket and handing it over. "Thomas Judd, Officer. This is my cousin."

"Your cousin got ID?" Harry asked.

"Yeah. He's not feeling well, though. Hang on, and I'll get it out of his pocket," Keegan said, while Olson chatted with Harry about his family and the local high school football team.

As he pulled the ID from Walsh's pocket, he took a quick look because he had no idea what name was on the driver's license. He opened the wallets to display the IDs and handed them over to Olson, who passed them through the Harry's window.

"This looks fine. Hope Mr. LeRoy gets to feeling better," he said, barely glancing at the fake IDs before returning the wallets and waving them through. "See you later, Fern."

Slowly, she rolled the truck past the cruiser and sped up once more on the open road.

"Very smart, Fern. Keep up the good work, and you'll be home with your boy before nightfall," Keegan said, resting the gun in his hand on his lap.

Olson said nothing.

She drove through the village of Newton Hills. The main street was not even two blocks long. It had a gas station and an independent grocer. The rest of the shops handled outdoor gear of one kind or another.

Keegan noticed that the crisp air was clean and pure and smelled like nothing he'd ever experienced in Boston. But the land was rugged here, and the people were rugged, too. They enjoyed outdoor activities, some as a hobby and others by necessity. Hunting, fishing, hiking, and the like, Keegan figured, based on the shops he saw.

Olson drove within the speed limit to Dr. Warner's office on the northeast side of Newton Hills, which turned out to be attached to his home. She turned onto the driveway and parked around back, where the old truck couldn't be seen from the road.

"Who lives here with the doc?" Keegan asked, looking around for problems of any kind.

"He's single since his wife died last year. If he had other patients inside, their cars would be parked here. Since there're no cars, we've got a better than ninety percent chance that if he's home, he's alone." Olson shifted the truck into park and shut off the engine. The roar of the diesel stopped, leaving a strange empty quiet.

Keegan held his palm out and she gave him the keys. He stuffed them into his pocket. "I don't need to remind you to cooperate if you want your kid and the old man to live, do I?"

She shook her head. "Let's get Walsh inside. See if Doc can fix him up so you can be on your way. I need to get back to my dad."

After a lot of struggle, they managed to get Walsh out of the truck to the back door. Olson had Walsh's left arm draped around her shoulders. Walsh's right arm was draped around Keegan, leaving his gun hand free.

The deep gash on his left arm had reopened during all this rough handling. Fresh blood soaked through his sleeve. Olson noticed it, but she made no comment. The extent of Walsh's injuries wasn't the only thing Keegan had lied to her about. She must have figured that out by now.

Olson used her free left hand to open the storm and then the interior door. When the second door opened, Keegan heard a doorbell chime somewhere in the house.

They heaved Walsh across the threshold. Olson pushed the door closed behind them with her butt.

The first thing Keegan noticed was how hot it was inside the small frame building. Doc Warner must have been sending all of his profits to the gas company to pay for heat. The scent of baked bread wafted from the kitchen.

There was a small desk and two straight-backed chairs in the tiny reception room, which was probably a foyer or a mudroom of some sort before the medical office occupied it. No one sat at the desk and no one came to greet the new patient.

"Doc will show up in a minute if he's here. Let's get Walsh into the exam room." Olson tilted her head toward a doorway to the right of the entrance.

They continued to drag him into the small room and plopped him onto the exam table on his back. It was the first time Keegan got a good look at Walsh's face since yesterday. His complexion was gray and cold, but Keegan could still feel a weak carotid pulse.

"Behave yourself," he said sternly to Olson, showing her the gun as if she might have forgotten it. "No reason for anyone to get hurt here."

When he heard slow, heavy footsteps heading toward them, Keegan slipped the gun into his front pocket where he could retrieve it quickly.

The footsteps reached the doorway. A stooped old man wearing a white coat over a plaid flannel shirt and a pair of brown corduroys filled the frame. "Hello, Fern."

"Hey, Micah. This is Tomas Judd and his cousin, Dave LeRoy. They were hiking near my place, and Dave got snake bit. He needs antivenom," Fern said as if to forestall as many questions as possible.

Dr. Warner took one look at Walsh and moved over to the table to examine him. "Do you have the snake?"

"No, we don't," Keegan replied.

"When did this happen? I'd say hours ago, from the look of him," Warner said, using the stethoscope to listen to Walsh's weak heartbeat and shallow breathing. "Show me the bites."

Keegan pointed to Walsh's right leg.

He must have seen the bloody sleeve of Walsh's shirt, but he turned his attention to the snakebites first. He pulled off Walsh's shoe and used a pair of scissors to cut up the pant leg all the way to the knee. Then he pulled off Walsh's sock and dropped it on the floor.

Walsh never moved. He didn't groan or make noise of any kind.

Keegan saw eight oozing puncture wounds in Walsh's calf.

The doctor took one look and shook his head. He found a blood pressure cuff, wrapped it on Walsh's arm, and pushed the button to let it pump up.

Warner said, "I've got antivenom here. But it's not likely to help. Too much venom from these bites and the poison has been circulating in his body too long."

"Is he going to be okay, Micah?" Olson asked.

"I don't know." Warner shook his head. He looked directly at Keegan. "He needs immediate emergency care in a hospital. The closest place is Bolton General. We can get him airlifted. Maybe they can save his life. I'm not sure whether they can save that leg."

Keegan stuck his hand into his pocket to grip the pistol, just in case.

"What about the arm?" Dr. Warner asked, moving toward the bloody sleeve with the scissors.

Olson's eyes widened. "Give him the antivenom, Micah. Then we can call the medivac."

The blood pressure cuff on Walsh's left arm beeped, and Dr. Warner looked at the readout briefly. "I'll see how much antivenom I have. He needs several vials. Might be better to wait until we get him to Bolton."

Keegan pulled the gun and aimed it at Warner. Gruffly, he ordered, "Give him the antivenom. Then we'll leave."

Warner looked at the gun as if he didn't care about it at all.

He'd lived here in rugged country for many years. Guns were second nature to him. He probably owned a few, too. Something else to keep in mind.

Warner replied, "You'll want to wait until I give him the injections before you shoot me. This stuff is tricky. You can't do it yourself."

"Let's get it going. Time is of the essence, right?" Keegan said.

"You understand it's probably too late already, right?" Warner replied.

"Get on with it," Keegan growled and brandished the pistol. "We'll wait to see how it works. He gets better, we're all good. He doesn't…"

"This all okay with you, is it, Fern?" Warner said, looking into Olson's flat gaze, like her dad might have done when her friends used to misbehave.

"Just do what he says, Micah," she replied wearily.

Warner gave them both another hard look before he left the room.

"Walsh may die here. If Micah says it's bad, you can believe him," Fern said from the corner where she leaned against the wall as if she was too exhausted to stand.

Keegan said nothing, but he was revising his plans silently. He glanced at the clock. The Gulfstream would be ready for the final leg of his escape to Canada Sunday morning. He could wait for a while. If Walsh recovered, he'd kill these two and leave the bodies here.

Otherwise, he'd need Olson.

Dr. Walker came back with a small plastic tray filled with several vials. "There are side effects to this antivenom. Particularly with administering large quantities. He really needs to be in a hospital. The antivenom alone can kill him."

Keegan narrowed his eyes and his nostrils flared. He clenched his fist at his side and held the gun steady. "He dies, you die. Simple as that."

Walker shrugged and prepared to administer the medication. "This will take a while. You might want to find a chair."

CHAPTER 33

Saturday, May 14
Near Bolton, South Dakota
11:45 a.m.

The roaring helo set down on the road near the Navigator, so loud even the dead couldn't possibly fail to notice. The rotors pushed a powerful wash across the air, kicking up dust and a strong breeze in all directions.

Kim and Burke waited near the Navigator while the team emerged from the helo, carrying crime scene equipment, and wearing white suits to protect the evidence. Which seemed a bit silly out here in the fields. But proper protocol was always worth observing if they wanted to get admissible evidence.

Two guys in street clothes came out behind them. Chief Mitchell and his second in command, the guy everyone called Woody. Briefly, Kim wondered why the Bolton PD high command was on the scene, but maybe it was just the allocation of manpower. They had to be spread thin.

The last one to exit the helo was Smithers, and Kim was glad to see him. He was a good man to have around in a crisis. Which this wasn't. At least, not anymore. The facts on the ground were a puzzle. But the crime was done. All that remained here was to decipher the evidence.

Smithers smacked the helo with the flat of his hand to signal all clear, and the big bird lifted off the pavement. Its body rose high above the tree line and turned back south toward Bolton.

The group made their way across the pavement toward Kim and Burke.

"Guys, watch where you're stepping. Rattlesnakes are all over this place. The helo's vibrations may have chased them off. But nobody needs a trip to the doctor at the moment," Burke said with a smirk, pointing his thumb over his shoulder. "Don't ask me how I know."

The techs laughed and the ice was broken. Burke was good at putting others at ease, Kim noticed. So why did he set off her internal radar so often?

Once Smithers joined the group, Kim gave them all a quick report.

"Officer Miller's body is on the ground ten feet from the open front door of the Land Rover," she pointed. "There's a pistol in the console compartment between the front seats. We didn't disturb anything."

"Is that pistol the murder weapon?" one of the techs asked.

"I guess we'll need forensics to say for sure. I didn't touch it. When you lift it out, you may be able to tell if it's been fired recently," Kim replied. "But it would be odd to shoot Miller with that pistol and then put it back in the console, wouldn't it?"

Burke nodded. "Yeah, but everything about this is odd."

Smithers raised his eyebrows. "How do you mean?"

"We came out here because we knew Olson's cell phone was pinging from this location. We expected to find her here. We didn't. Instead, we discovered the phone had been tossed into the weeds away from the Land Rover. The Bolton PD cruiser was parked at the road. The Land Rover was disabled right there," Burke said, pointing and ticking off the oddities on his fingers as he spoke.

"What about Miller?" Chief Mitchell asked.

"Officer Miller was already dead," Kim responded. "But there's blood on the front door of the Land Rover that looks old and dried, so it's probably not Miller's."

"Suggests someone else was hurt. Maybe by Miller before he died." Burke picked up with his list of questions. "But where is he? And what happened to Olson? Why was her cell phone off in the weeds? And Miller's sidearm is still in his hand. If the gun in the console hasn't been fired, then where's the murder weapon?"

Smithers nodded, considering the questions. "So you think Olson was here. She shot Miller."

Burke replied, "That's one possibility. There are others."

"There usually are," Smithers said, as the team filed out toward the Land Rover, keeping a close look at the ground along the way. Mitchell and Woody went with them to get a firsthand look at the scene.

When they had moved out of hearing range, Smithers turned to Kim. "We got a preliminary on the Land Rover off the VIN you sent. It was reported stolen last week."

She nodded. "Figured. Stolen from where?"

"That's the interesting part. The owner lives in Minneapolis. The local field office followed up. The owner is a normal citizen. Claims he hasn't been out of state for months. Works for a bank. Says the Land Rover was stolen from the bank's parking lot. He reported it at the time. We confirmed the report," Smithers said.

"You're checking out the whole story, though," Kim replied. Vehicles were stolen from parking lots every day. They didn't usually end up abandoned in a field next to a dead cop.

"What are you thinking?" Smithers cocked his head.

"Minneapolis is a four-hour drive from here. The tire tracks leading from the road to the Land Rover looks like they were driving north, away from Bolton. If the vehicle was stolen north of here last week..." Kim said, letting her voice trail off as the possibilities ran through her mind.

Burke scowled. "Normal tourists driving from Minneapolis to Mount Rushmore don't steal a Land Rover to make the trip and then go home."

Smithers nodded, following along.

"Something caused the vehicle to leave the road," Kim said, thinking aloud. "Once it hit those rocks in the field and damaged the tire, the wheel, and possibly the frame, they couldn't drive the Land Rover at all. They were stuck."

"Makes sense." Smithers nodded and picked up her train of thought. "So the driver was still here, in the vehicle when Miller came along. But why kill him and then leave both the body and the police cruiser here?"

"The driver didn't need to take Miller's cruiser to get away," Burke said. "Which means someone else was involved. A team or an accomplice or even a rescue vehicle. Because nobody can drive two vehicles at once."

"You think it was Olson?" Smithers asked, raising his eyebrows. "There's no history to suggest she'd kill a police officer. Her ex-husband works for Bolton PD. By all accounts we've gathered so far, she's a law-abiding citizen. Maybe on the wrong side sometimes, people say. They don't like that she works for the bad guys instead of the good guys. But still, her criminal record is clean. We checked."

One of the crime techs came up from behind. He was carrying a pistol in a plastic evidence bag. "Agent Smithers, here's the weapon from the console. Doesn't seem like it's been recently fired, but we'll need ballistics to confirm it wasn't the murder weapon."

"Thanks," Smithers said. "We can check that off the list of open questions."

The tech said, "Thing is, Chief Mitchell said you'd want to know that this Glock has a history."

"Yeah?" Smithers asked without touching the gun.

"It was tied to a murder in Sioux Falls last year," the tech said. "Dead guy was a member of the Irish mob out of Boston."

"Who killed him?" Burke asked.

"Case is still open. Unsolved," the tech replied.

CHAPTER 34

Saturday, May 14
Near Bolton, South Dakota
12:45 p.m.

The crime tech wasn't finished. "Somebody who knew what they were doing cleaned the Land Rover. Very little trace evidence left in it at all. What there is so far is all in the front seat area. We've called a flatbed to tow it out of here when we're done. We'll give it a thorough exam. But it doesn't look like the rest of the processing will tell us much."

Kim felt her phone vibrating in her pocket. She glanced at the screen to confirm. "I need to take this."

Burke frowned, and Smithers nodded. Woody and Chief Mitchell walked up as she left. They could question the tech and catch up on whatever facts they'd gathered thus far. She wouldn't be long.

She walked away for privacy as she picked up the call. "What have you got?"

"Let me tell you what we don't have. Satellite images." Gaspar replied, sounding annoyed. "I've checked all the possibilities. Even the classified satellites that roam around aren't focused on that area often enough to help you out."

She felt the disappointment and realized how much she still depended on Gaspar. She'd expected him to have more. "Is there good news?"

"Not much. I've got Olson's cell phone logs. No calls this morning. No texts, either. The phone was pinging from that location for well over an hour before you found it. Maybe two hours."

"But?"

She imagined his smile, which she heard in his voice when he said, "Before that, the phone was located at her home. A farmhouse not far from where you're standing."

"Can you trace it?"

"Great minds think alike. The phone moved from the farmhouse to where you're standing. That's all. Took about fifteen minutes to get there. And then it never left," Gaspar said. "And from your questions, I'm guessing you didn't find Olson there holding the phone."

"Give that man a cigar," Kim replied sourly.

"The other good news is about Olson's kid, Noah. His phone is still at the farmhouse. No way to know whether he's there with it, but the phone has been used in the past hour."

"Yeah? Used for what?"

"You know kids. Text messages. He's chatting with his friends. Last text was five minutes ago." Gaspar paused. "A couple of his buddies want him to play hoops this afternoon. Noah says he can't because he has to stay home with his grandpa until his mom gets back. Says she should be back shortly."

Kim grinned. "You're a genius, Chico, you know that?"

"So I've been told," he deadpanned before he hung up.

Kim dropped the phone back into her pocket and rejoined Burke and Smithers. "We need to get going."

"Where?" Smithers asked.

"Olson's place is a few miles from here. We were on our way there when we found all of this," Kim said. "We've got our own work to accomplish."

"Uh, huh." Smithers cocked his head. "How is Reacher involved in all of this? You're still conducting his background check, I assume? What knowledge does Olson have on the subject?"

Burke replied, "We won't know until we ask her. But it has something to do with one of her clients. An inmate at Bolton prison. And before you ask, we don't know which one."

"It's possible that either she shot Miller or whoever did is there with her. Could be the same guy you're interested in." Smithers narrowed his gaze as if he didn't like the logic but couldn't come up with a better answer. "I'll call for another team to come out in the helo. You'll need backup."

Just as he said it, Bolton Police Chief Mitchell came back. "Where are you going that you need backup? Miller was my officer. If you have a lead on his murder, I'm coming along. I've got guys driving in from Bolton. They should be here in another twenty minutes."

"Can you get your team to the Olson farmhouse?" Smithers asked. "My guys won't have ground transportation. Take too long to wait for that."

Mitchell nodded. "Let me tell Woody what's happening. Be right back."

Kim walked toward the Navigator and Smithers joined her. Burke followed behind. When they reached the vehicle, Smithers said, "Was that Gaspar on the phone?"

She nodded. "Yeah. He says there's no satellite imagery that can help us with Miller's murder."

Smithers said, "I won't ask how he knows that."

Kim didn't respond. Gaspar's access to intel she couldn't get any other way was more valuable to her than Smithers's approval. She had no guilt about asking Gaspar. He was a big boy. He knew his own limits. The Boss could have helped her out, but he never did. So what choice did she have?

"What else did Gaspar say?" Burke asked, frowning as he opened the driver's door.

"He said Olson hasn't used her phone today, but he thinks Olson's kid is still at the farmhouse because he's been on his phone with his friends," she said, climbing into the passenger seat.

Smithers settled into the backseat. His booming voice filled the cabin. "Who else is at the farmhouse with young Noah? Reacher? And where's Noah's mother? Gaspar have any intel on that?"

"He's working on it," Kim replied as Mitchell stepped into the backseat and Burke started the engine.

Before Burke pulled away, he scanned a text on his phone. He read it quickly and shut the screen off.

"What's up?" Kim asked.

"Just one of my old SEAL buddies. He's in DC for the night. Wanted to meet up for a drink," Burke said and rolled onto the pavement.

Something raised the hair on the back of Kim's neck and knotted her stomach. She hadn't read the text. Still, a big part of her job was spotting liars. She was damned good at it. And she didn't believe him.

CHAPTER 35

Saturday, May 14
Olson Farmhouse, South Dakota
1:10 p.m.

Burke drove north along the deserted road about two miles to a big bend in the road. As the Navigator came around the bend, Kim saw a lone farmhouse ahead at the end of a long gravel driveway.

The silence inside the SUV deepened. The only sound was deep breathing while five law enforcement professionals evaluated the scene.

The farmhouse was an old-fashioned, two-story wood building. At one time, it might have been painted white. The clapboards had weathered over the years to a lifeless gray. A few scattered trees obscured the view on either side of the driveway. The expanse of weeds covering the ground from the road to the house had been mowed, but no one would have called it a lawn.

"Looks abandoned, doesn't it?" Smithers said from the backseat in his deep, rumbling voice. "I suppose we know that people actually live here, right, Mitchell?"

"Yeah," Mitchell replied. "Olson's old man has lived here more than eighty years. His wife died a few years ago. Fern got divorced and moved back home with her boy when the old man got too frail to take care of himself."

"The boy's father is Ned Turner. He's one of our Bolton PD detectives. Fern kept her maiden name through the marriage and after," Woody added. "I called Ned, and he's on his way. He was on the other side of Bolton. He's about an hour away."

"If there's been trouble here today, there's no sign of it that I can see," Burke said, slowing at the entrance to the driveway. "We don't know how many people are in the house or whether they're armed and dangerous."

"Even if Olson killed Officer Miller, it would have been fairly stupid to come back here," Kim said. "It's more likely the shooter wants to put as much space between himself and the crime as he can. He's probably on the way to Canada by now."

After a brief pause, Burke said, "Should we go in or wait for backup?"

"I know the kid. Noah is in school with my son," Woody replied. "We're all armed. We can take care of ourselves if it comes to that. I say we drive up to the front door and I'll knock. We can take it from there."

The question was probably directed to Chief Mitchell, Woody's boss. Professional courtesy, if nothing else, meant the decision was one Mitchell should make. If things went south, his would be the head on the chopping block.

They gave him a few moments to make the right decision.

Mitchell opened his phone and hit the redial to talk with his backup team. "How far out are you?"

He listened to the answers and offered a couple of "uh-huhs" before he hung up. He asked Woody, "What's back there behind the house?"

"I've only been here a couple of times to pick up Noah," Woody replied as if searching his memory and reporting what he could recall. "The driveway goes around on the left of the house. There's a big barn back there for farm equipment, and it doubles as a garage. Old man Olson has a truck parked in there. There's a back exit off the kitchen. A big open field behind the house."

A long pause followed before Mitchell said, "Okay, Burke. Let's do it Woody's way. Slowly up the driveway all the way to the front of the house. But be careful about it and everybody keep your wits about you."

"Copy that," Burke said and drove as instructed.

"My sergeant just confirmed," Chief Mitchell said. "We still have eight escaped inmates at large. Haven't been able to find them at the roadblocks or using the helos. Three were clients of Fern Olson's law firm for sure. We're checking on the other five."

Smithers cleared his throat. "Are you saying Olson was involved in the prison break and is harboring the fugitives now? Here in her home?"

"It's possible. At the moment, we can't rule it out," Mitchell replied. "It's more likely they're on the way to Canada, like Otto said."

"So we could be heading straight into a firefight," Smithers said. "Or we could wait until we get backup. Go in the right way."

Burke continued to roll the big Navigator toward the farmhouse.

Kim said, "Woody, how well do you know the boy?"

"He's stayed overnight with my son and his buddies a couple of times. Seems like a good kid, but he's rebellious, like a lot of teens. I know his dad very well," Woody replied.

"Noah's been texting with his friends all morning, planning to go hang out with them later. Doesn't seem like a kid who is being held hostage in his own home to me. Does it to you?" Kim said. "So why doesn't Woody just call Noah? See if you can find out what's going on."

Smithers shook his head. "I don't like it. Officer Miller's killer could be inside. A phone call might push him to do something desperate."

"Anybody else want to weigh in?" Burke asked, still driving toward the house. They were about a hundred feet away now. Chances were high that they'd been seen already.

Mitchell said, "Woody? What do you think?"

"I think Otto's right. I'm game to try," Woody replied.

"You've got your vest on?" Mitchell asked, referring to the Kevlar that might save Woody's life if he was unlucky enough to take a bullet.

"Yeah."

Burke pulled up close to the house, and Woody climbed out of the backseat. He made the call to Noah on his cell phone, nonchalantly, as if his visit was entirely normal.

Kim opened the door and stepped out behind Woody.

The others left the Navigator and positioned themselves behind the vehicle, weapons ready.

Kim and Woody walked side by side up the steps and onto the decrepit front porch.

CHAPTER 36

Saturday, May 14
Olson Farmhouse
2:30 p.m.

Woody persuaded Noah Olson to allow the five of them to come inside. They'd filed in and fanned out and now the farmhouse was abnormally crowded. The place smelled old and musty. Kim noticed a faint whiff of something unpleasant in the air.

The kid was fidgety and scared. He'd already chewed his fingernails to the quick and Kim noticed dried blood at the edges of his cuticles.

Noah should have been comfortable around cops. He knew Woody. His father was a Bolton PD detective and his mother was no stranger to law enforcement. But he was unusually nervous all the same. More nervous than he would have been under normal circumstances, Kim felt sure.

At first, Noah seemed uneasy about his grandfather, who was sleeping fitfully on the couch. His face was bruised and scraped and he groaned a few times as if in pain. Noah said he'd fallen off the back porch this morning. Which sounded plausible enough, Kim supposed.

"When Mom gets back, we'll take him to the hospital for X-rays on his ankle. Probably a bad sprain. Let's not wake him," Noah said as he herded them into the kitchen.

Which meant his mother wasn't here. Where was she?

The kitchen was like the rest of the house—ancient, decrepit, unkempt. The scent of old grease lingered. A few slices of burnt bacon and congealed eggs rested on a plate on the table along with cold coffee in three chipped stoneware mugs.

Woody sat at the table and gestured toward another chair for the boy. He glanced at the others filling his kitchen with authority. Perhaps he realized he had few alternatives. He plopped into the seat.

Chief Mitchell took the seat at the head of the table. Smithers stood off to the side. Kim and Burke waited near the doorway.

"Noah, we need to find your mom," Woody said. "Do you know where she is?"

Noah's eyes widened and he bounced his leg nervously. He shook his head.

"She's not home, right?" Woody asked.

Noah shook his head again.

"How long has she been gone?"

Noah shrugged.

"You've got to help us out here, Noah. We need to find your mom. It's really important," Chief Mitchell said. "We're very worried about her."

"Why? Why are you worried?" Noah asked, gnawing his lip.

Mitchell replied, "You know we had a prison break yesterday. There are prisoners still at large."

"You think my mom is with them?" Noah's mouth formed a perfect circle, and he inhaled sharply.

"We don't know. We're working on that. Did she leave here alone?"

Noah said nothing, but the level of his concern had set his hands to trembling. He clasped them together under the table.

"Who was with her?" Woody asked. "You need to tell us, Noah."

Noah shook his head.

Woody said, "What are you afraid of?"

"What makes you think I'm afraid?" Noah said, jutting his chin forward defensively.

"I know you love your mom and you wouldn't want anything bad to happen to her," Woody said. "Did someone threaten her?"

The kitchen probably felt crowded and threatening to Noah. It seemed like Woody and Mitchell might get further if they could establish more intimacy. At the moment, there was nothing for Kim to do here.

She backed through the doorway and left the kitchen. Burke followed behind her into the narrow hallway.

"The kid's hiding something," Burke said quietly.

"Yes, but what?"

"For starters, the old man didn't fall off a porch. He looks like he landed on his face. Pretty impossible to sprain your ankle with your face in the dirt," Burke replied. "Someone worked him over."

"Probably not Fern, but it's possible," Kim said. "Maybe she's strong enough to best a frail old man in a fight. But that answer doesn't feel right to me."

Burke nodded. "You think Fern might be hiding here in the house?"

"Possibly. Let's take a look around." Kim pulled her weapon and pointed toward the rooms on either side of the hallway. "I'll take this half of the downstairs. You take that half. Meet at the staircase and we'll go up to the second floor."

"Copy that," Burke said, following her lead.

Kim wandered through rooms on the south side of the house. Grandpa Olson was still sleeping on the couch in the living room. She got a better look at the damage to his face and flipped the covers back to see his battered ankle. He grimaced and moaned, but he didn't awaken. He might have internal injuries as well. He needed a doctor. And soon.

Quickly, she opened each door and looked inside. A dining room, a TV room, a bathroom. Fern Olson wasn't hiding in any of them.

Kim moved to the base of the stairs, arriving a moment before Burke. A broken lamp lay in pieces on the floor, probably thrown down from the second floor.

"What do you suppose that's about?" Burke said.

Kim shook her head. "No clue."

She climbed the treads slowly, with Burke close behind.

Just before she reached the landing at the top, Kim gestured Burke toward the right. She would take the left side. She stuck her neck out past the corner and scanned the open corridor.

There were four closed doors that she could see from her vantage point. One at each end and two in the middle. Bedrooms, probably. An old house like this was likely to have four bedrooms upstairs, she figured. Maybe more. At least one bathroom, too.

Kim took a breath and snugged her back to the wall as she edged around the corner.

The first thing she saw was a big man on his back on the floor. Blood had pooled under him. His lifeless eyes were wide open. No need to check his pulse.

From this angle, she counted two visible bullet wounds in his torso. Well placed at center mass, she noted. Probably fired at close range, given the limits of the space.

She turned to Burke and gestured toward the man. Burke nodded.

"Take the rooms on the right. I'll do the others," she said quietly.

She approached the body carefully. Now that she had an unobstructed view, she recognized him. She'd committed the photos of the prison escapees to memory. This one was the scariest of the eight. No one was likely to forget his face.

The corpse was Ryan Denny.

No doubt.

She stepped around the body, careful to avoid the congealing blood, and checked the two closest bedrooms. The first was probably Old Man Olson's room.

It was furnished with an unmade dark pine bed and a chest of drawers across from it. A television rested on the top of the chest. A recliner poised in the corner opposite the door provided a clear view of the television.

Kim closed the door and moved to the room at the end of the hallway. The door was open, and she glanced inside. The furnishings were similarly spare and disheveled, but more feminine. Brighter colors, Makeup on the dresser. The bed was unmade. Night clothes had been dropped on the floor.

The room was most likely Fern's since no other women lived here. She holstered her gun and returned to the body.

Burke joined her. "All clear. Nobody here. The kid's room is at the end of the hall. Has its own bathroom. The other one is a guestroom. Bathroom across the hall."

"Fern's room." Kim gestured with her left hand. "The old man's room. Both unoccupied."

Burke looked at the body. "So who shot this guy?"

"Four options, I'd say. Fern, Noah, the grandpa, or whoever assaulted the grandpa."

"My money's on Fern."

"Why?"

"The second inmate probably wouldn't have killed his buddy. And if gramps killed this guy, the buddy would have killed him instead of just knocking the crap out of him," Burke said.

Kim nodded as he confirmed her conclusions.

"And the kid's too scrawny. Did you see the knife over there?" Burke tilted his head in that general direction.

"Looks like something a hiker would carry. Probably belonged to the kid."

"Could belong to the grandpa and Noah grabbed it," she said. "But I'm not sure it matters who owns the knife. That knife wound didn't kill Denny. The gunshots killed him."

Burke said, "Fern was more likely to own a gun or know where to find one. And she'd know how to use it."

"Let's go with that for now. I'll take a better look around in Fern's room. You check out the others. Take photos. Video, too. Might be helpful later," Kim said. "Then we'll head downstairs and hand this situation over to Mitchell and Smithers."

"Why hand it off?" Burke cocked his head.

"It's not our case. We don't want to hang around here or come back to deal with the fallout," Kim replied. "And we've got our own work to do."

"Copy that," Burke replied, already moving toward Noah's room.

CHAPTER 37

Saturday, May 14
Olson Farmhouse
4:30 p.m.

When Kim and Burke returned to the farmhouse kitchen, she caught Mitchell's eye and continued outside onto the back porch. Burke and Smithers followed. The porch was protected from the wind, and afternoon sun had warmed the air enough to stand around without a heavy coat.

The view from the back of the farmhouse was acres of open land, empty fields on all sides. If this had been an active farm at some point in its history, it must have been in the last century.

A line of mature hardwood trees beginning to leaf out established the property line. In mid-summer, the trees would provide a thick privacy wall, protecting the property from nosey travelers.

"Any luck with Noah?" Kim asked when Smithers closed the kitchen door to keep the conversation outside.

"He's afraid," Mitchell replied. "He's also protecting his mother and his grandpa."

"Protecting them from what?" Burke asked. "Did he say?"

Mitchell shook his head. "His dad's still thirty minutes out, give or take. When he arrives, maybe we'll get somewhere."

"Kid has good reason to be scared." Kim pulled her phone out and located the headshots Smithers had given her earlier, thumbing through to find the one she wanted. She showed the image to Smithers first, then Mitchell. "Ryan Denny. He's dead on the floor upstairs."

She found the photos of the body and showed them. "Shot seven times in the torso. Before that, stabbed with a hunting knife in the shoulder."

Mitchell narrowed his eyes and frowned as he swiped through the photos and then handed the phone to Smithers. "Now we know what's got the kid so freaked out."

Smithers thumbed through the photos and returned the phone to Kim.

"Who was Denny's cellmate at Bolton?" Kim asked.

Smithers replied, "Duff Keegan. He's still at large, too. Possible he killed Denny?"

Burke shook his head. "We think it was Fern."

Mitchell cleared his throat and listened to Burke's theory. Smithers nodded as Burke laid it out, same as he'd done upstairs.

Smithers swiped a flat palm across his face as if attempting to erase the fatigue. "Okay. Let's show Keegan's photo to Noah. Get him to tell us the whole story. Shake him up a bit. Maybe he'll tell us where Keegan went and how his mother figures into all of this."

Mitchell shook his head. "If Fern shot Denny, we've got to be careful here. The kid's a minor. I don't have to tell you that if we push him too hard before his dad gets here, the judge won't like it. We'll lose all of our evidence and have no chance of a conviction."

"Let me try," Kim said. Mitchell flashed her a questioning glance. "This isn't my case. I'll never need to testify at the trial. I have no official role here. I know how far I can push a young witness. I won't cross the line."

Mitchell frowned, his lips pursed. He didn't like the idea.

Kim played her ace in the hole. "I'm closer to his age as well as his size. Usually gives me an advantage with kids because they think I'm not as scary as you big guys."

Smithers snorted, "Colossal mistake if the kid thinks that."

Kim shot him a glare. "Noah might volunteer as much intel as we need if I play it right."

"And get lucky," Smithers said.

"Exactly," Kim replied.

After a moment's thought, Mitchell shrugged. "Don't cross the line."

"While we're questioning Noah, maybe you want to take a walk. Stretch your legs," she said to Burke.

"You think?" he replied, eyebrows arched.

"We can't search the garage," Smithers said. "We asked for permission. Kid said no. We couldn't get gramps awake enough to understand the question."

Burke frowned. "Did he say why?"

"The question alone freaked him out. But no probable cause," Smithers replied. "We decided to circle back to the issue later."

"Don't go inside the garage," Kim said, to cover their butts.

Burke didn't reply as he took the six porch steps down to the worn dirt at the bottom. He turned around. "Do we know where the old man supposedly fell off this porch?"

Mitchell said, "Not yet."

When they went back into the kitchen, Woody and Noah were still sitting across from each other at the farmhouse table. The uneaten congealed breakfast was more unappetizing than before.

Kim said, "Noah, any chance you could help me make coffee while we wait for your dad?"

The kid seemed relieved to have an excuse to move. "Sure. The coffee maker's over here."

He pulled the plug from the stainless steel percolator and rinsed out the old coffee. He put the grounds into the disposal and flipped the switch for a couple of seconds. While he worked, he pointed his chin toward a stainless steel canister set on the counter beside the stove. "The coffee's in the middle one."

Kim grabbed the canister and brought it to Noah, who scooped the coffee into the basket. She put the canister back while he replaced the top of the percolator and plugged it into the wall.

"Do you want milk? Sugar?" Noah asked.

"Black is good for me," Kim replied. She looked up toward the others crowding the kitchen. "You guys?"

They shook their heads, and Smithers said with a grin, "Black's good for me, too."

The comment caused Noah to crack a smile. The first time Kim had seen him relax at all since they'd arrived. The kid had finally begun to loosen up. Which could be helpful.

The coffee finished perking. Noah poured it into chipped stoneware, handed the first cup to Kim. and then passed the others to Woody, Mitchell, and Smithers.

While he was busy with his tasks, Kim leaned her back casually against the counter. "I want to find your mom, Noah. Do you have any idea where she is?"

His face pinched up again and he shook his head.

"Your mom's a good person, Noah. She's a lawyer, right? I'm a lawyer, too. I understand how hard her job is, even if other people don't." Kim spoke quietly as if she didn't want the others to hear the kind words. "She got locked up in the prison last night. I'm sure that must have been terrifying."

Noah nodded. As much as he wanted to be an adult, he was a boy, not a man. Not yet. And he was worried about his mother. For good reasons he knew about and believed that they didn't. Kim's kindness was unexpected. He squeezed his eyes closed in an effort to keep the glassy tears from rolling.

"Some of the men who escaped yesterday, men we haven't been able to find, were your mom's clients. She tried to help them before. We think they might come here," Kim said, observing Noah.

He kept his head down, and one of his tears dropped onto his lap. But he listened.

So far, Kim had simply said what she knew to be true in the most sympathetic way possible. Moving on into the realm of speculation would be trickier.

"These men might think your mom would help them get away. Because she's a lawyer, and she represents them."

He shook his head slowly.

She realized she was on the wrong track. "None of her clients came for help? Are you sure, Noah?" Kim asked, placing a hand on his arm.

He nodded again.

"But someone came here. Tell me about him, okay?"

CHAPTER 38

Saturday, May 14
Newton Hills, South Dakota
5:30 p.m.

Noah shrugged. Another tear fell. The fidgety nervousness returned, but he replied this time. "He helped us with Grandpa. After he f-fell off the porch. He wasn't a client, though."

"Did he take your mom away with him?"

He shook his head. "No. She offered. She wanted to help."

"How could she help him?"

"Not him. His friend. His friend was hurt. Got snakebit. He needed a doctor. Mom offered to drive him to get help," Noah whispered.

Kim glanced toward Mitchell. He nodded and said, "Rattlesnakes are all over this area in the spring. Easy to get bit. He'd need treatment right away. Best hospital is down in Bolton."

"Have you heard from your mom since she left?"

Noah shook his head.

"Did he tell you his name?"

"Thomas Judd," Noah said quietly. Calmly. Neither the name nor the man seemed to frighten him.

Kim pulled her phone out and found Denny's headshot photo again. She showed it to Noah. "Is this him? Thomas Judd?"

Noah looked at the photo. His eyes widened, and he gasped. His entire body began to shake. "No. No. Not him. No. Definitely not."

Kim frowned and slid the images across her screen. Eight headshots. The prisoners who remained at large. "Was it one of these men?"

Noah looked at each one and shook his head.

Until she showed the photo of a man he recognized.

"That's him," Noah said, clearly terrified now. He burst into tears. "That's Judd. He's got my mom."

Kim showed the image of Duff Keegan to Smithers, Mitchell, and Woody. "Okay, Noah. We're going to find your mom. I promise."

Noah nodded, wiping tears with the back of his hand.

"But to help me find her, you have to tell me everything that happened," Kim said.

Noah shook his head violently. "No. No."

Frissons ran up Kim's spine and tingled the hair on her neck. The kid knew more than he was telling, but he was trying desperately to conceal whatever he knew. "I can't help your mom if I don't know what happened to the man upstairs, Noah."

Noah gasped, then clamped his lips together and refused to say anything more. His entire body quivered. He looked down at the floor and refused to make eye contact.

Burke came in from the cold through the back door just as Noah stopped talking. "There's no truck in the garage."

"I gave him the code to open the garage door," said a man following close behind Burke.

Bolton PD Detective Ned Turner. Had to be. His son Noah looked just like him.

"That truck's ancient and the springs are shot. It runs on diesel, which isn't easy to find around here. And it's not all that easy to drive, either. Shouldn't be hard to find. I issued a BOLO on Fern and the truck," Detective Turner said before he asked, "What happened here?"

"Looks like two inmates, Ryan Denny and Duff Keegan were here. They were cellmates at Bolton. Fern left with Keegan," Chief Mitchell said. "And Denny's lying dead upstairs. Looks like Fern shot him."

"Fern?" Turner asked bewildered. "Fern killed Denny?"

Noah jumped up from his seat, looking wildly at Kim before he announced, "Dad, she had to! He attacked her!"

"Slow down, Noah," Turner said, placing a calming hand on his son's shoulder. "Tell me what happened. Don't leave anything out."

The kid started talking, and it took him quite a while to get the story told. Kim listened to his tale with a practiced ear. She'd heard countless stories from crime victims and perpetrators before. This one sounded basically true.

Noah admitted that he'd stabbed Denny after the inmate attacked Fern. And then she'd shot him in self-defense.

Noah's report made sense based on the evidence Kim had seen upstairs. But his tale didn't answer all of her questions.

Smithers asked a few follow-ups, mostly trying to tease out memories the kid probably didn't realize he had until Kim heard a helo landing out front.

"That'll be my guys," Smithers said. "I'll get them started upstairs."

Mitchell's backup teams began to arrive and tightly controlled chaos reigned. Various law enforcement and crime scene personnel deployed throughout the house and grounds, collecting data and evidence. The process unfolded slowly and meticulously and would continue for hours. Maybe longer.

After a while, an ambulance arrived to collect old man Olson, and Woody volunteered to take charge of Noah.

Smithers, Mitchell, and their teams were fully occupied with handling what had become the never-ending fallout from the prison break.

Kim walked out onto the back porch. She needed to think things through. And she wanted to talk to Gaspar. Hours ago, she'd asked him to gather the intel from Fern's phone and anything else he thought relevant. He should have something to report by now.

Her muscles felt knotted and stiff from inactivity as well as the constant tension. She missed her daily run and the yoga routine she'd recently adopted. She stretched in the late sunlight like a sleek Siamese cat, reaching high and then bending low from the waist to touch the floor.

She glanced at her watch. It would be dark in a few hours. The season of longer days and shorter nights was upon South Dakota along with the rest of the country. Sunset tonight was forecast shortly after eight o'clock. Searching for Olson and Keegan in the dark wouldn't be an easy task. They needed to get going.

Burke came outside to join her. "They've still got a lot of work to do in there."

Kim nodded.

"Think we still need to locate Fern Olson?" he asked. "Or are we looking for Keegan now?"

Olson's files hadn't painted her as particularly threatening. The files were wrong about that point. What else were they missing?

Fern Olson was no longer simply a witness to be interviewed.

Whether she'd acted in self-defense or in defense of her family or not, Fern Olson had killed a man three times her size.

Shot him seven times in the chest.

Olson was much more dangerous than she had at first appeared. Which meant Kim needed a new plan. Simply making an appointment with Olson and walking in to discuss Reacher was no longer an option.

"I haven't heard from the Boss that our assignment has changed," Kim said.

"Our assignment is to find Reacher. In pursuit of that assignment, our task was to interview Olson and then move on to the unnamed inmate who has an unknown tenuous connection with Reacher. It seems clear that inmate was Keegan," Burke replied, as if he was lecturing a new recruit on matters even a newbie should already know.

Kim frowned and narrowed her eyes. This guy had a high opinion of himself, for damned sure. Before she had a chance to reply, the Boss's phone vibrated in her pocket.

As always, Cooper's timing was impeccable. Which probably meant he was eavesdropping on their conversation.

As she reached to answer the phone, Burke said, "I called Cooper when I discovered the farm truck was missing from the garage. He's probably calling to say he's located it."

"That would be a first. He's never that helpful," Kim said, noticing the gnawing in her belly, probably caused by Burke's easy relationship with Cooper.

Given a choice, she wouldn't have told Cooper about the truck, and she was annoyed that Burke had done so. Asking Cooper for help was never a good plan. He'd made it plain that he expected her to work independently, anyway.

"I've got ten bucks that says you're wrong," she said.

Burke lifted his eyebrows and nodded to accept the wager.

The cell phone continued vibrating insistently.

Before she could hit the green button to answer, Smithers joined them on the porch. "We've found the truck parked at a local doctor's office. Back parking lot. I've got a team on the way. Probably ten minutes out."

"Keegan and Olson?" Burke asked.

Smithers shrugged.

The Boss must have grown tired of waiting and the phone stopped vibrating.

CHAPTER 39

Saturday, May 14
Newton Hills, South Dakota
6:25 p.m.

Fern Olson wiped her sweaty palms down her jeans again. Sweat soaked her bra under her breasts. Her breathing became rapid and shallow and nothing she had tried to do had calmed her nerves since Judd shot that cop.

She had been frightened before in her life. Doing the work she did, living out in the country with Noah and her dad, being afraid was normal. Hell, it was almost her regular state of existence. She'd learned to handle it, most days, and carry on.

But the level of terror she felt now was almost beyond enduring.

She wondered how much adrenaline her body could produce and absorb. At some point, wouldn't she collapse from the overload? Perhaps her heart would simply stop the painful, rapid pounding.

Wasn't that what the doctors called sudden cardiac death? She thought it was. All of a sudden. The heart just stops. The end.

What would that feel like? Another long shudder ran through her body.

When Micah had said Walsh might die with or without the antivenom, Fern's tension had ramped up to a level beyond her endurance. She'd had to sit down and try to calm herself. No success. Her heart pounded harder than a frenzied rock band.

She'd suspected that Judd was not the guy's real name the moment she'd seen Walsh unconscious in that Land Rover. Then Judd shot that cop, and she'd been too freaked out to think clearly at all.

Her suspicions were confirmed when Judd gave the cop at the roadblock two fake IDs, one for Walsh and one for himself. Whoever he was, his name was not Thomas Judd.

But she didn't know who he was or what else to call him, even in her head. Judd would have to suffice for now.

Micah had come back into the exam room with a plastic tray containing several vials of antivenom. He administered the drugs and then monitored Walsh closely while Fern and Judd watched.

Nothing happened at first. After an hour, Judd had demanded, "How much longer before he revives?"

"I don't know. I've never had a patient like this before." Micah snapped his reply and slammed his palm down hard on the counter. "I'm not God. I'm just a country doctor. My resources here are limited. He needs hospital care. I've told you that already."

"You did." Judd leveled the gun at Micah's chest. Steadily, coldly, without a trace of doubt, he said, "And if you want to live until supper time, you won't say that again."

Fern's breath sucked in of its own accord. It felt like her heart had stopped beating in her chest at that point. Intense pain doubled her over.

Her vision darkened at the edges. Her entire body trembled uncontrollably.

She'd never had a full-on anxiety attack before, but she hoped she was having one now instead of a massive heart attack.

"What is your problem?" Judd turned his gaze, and the gun, toward her. "Go get coffee and something to eat. Dr. Warner and I need to talk."

Fern somehow stood on wobbly legs and took a few steps toward the doorway, holding onto the wall to keep her balance.

"Fern!" Judd said sharply. "Do anything stupid and the doc dies. And your kid. Your dad, too. Got that?"

She didn't trust herself to speak. She simply nodded and kept moving toward the kitchen. With every step away from Judd, her anxiety lessened. She didn't normally suffer from extreme emotional reactions. But she'd never been faced with circumstances like this, either.

In the kitchen, she found the coffee maker and the coffee and got the pot brewing while keeping one ear trained toward the exam room. Inside the small house, Fern would hear the gunshots if Judd made good on his threats. Which she absolutely knew he was capable of doing.

She went to the bathroom and washed her face with cool water. When she returned to the kitchen, she glanced toward the back door.

A pegged board held Micah's coats but not the keys to his two vehicles parked in the garage. He'd probably left them in his Jeep and his truck. She looked out the window. Dad's old beater was parked out there on the driveway where she'd left it, too.

She had options. She could run out the back and get away before Judd noticed, maybe. He could flee in Micah's Jeep. It was newer and easier to drive.

If he could get away, maybe that would be enough for him.

For half a moment, she considered the option seriously.

And then she shook her head.

If she ran now, Judd would make good on his threat to shoot and kill Micah, for sure. She'd known Micah Warner all her life. He was a few years older, but they'd always been friends. They'd even dated a few times when she was in college. Before she'd fallen in love with Ned Turner.

"No," she murmured aloud, rejecting the brief plan.

It was her fault Micah was in this position. She'd brought Judd and Walsh here. Micah's fate rested squarely on her conscience.

She couldn't give Judd an excuse to kill Micah, either.

Not only was Micah a good friend, but the community also needed a physician, and not many were willing to live way out here. He didn't deserve to die.

Fern watched the coffee drip into the pot and inhaled its life-affirming aroma. Which steadied her breathing and calmed her anxiety a bit. Her heart rate slowed, no longer thumping like a giant jackrabbit.

When she'd managed to peel herself off the ceiling, she admitted that things with Micah could go either way. If the antivenom worked and they could get Walsh away from here…

She searched the kitchen until she found cheese and crackers and an opened package of salami. She grabbed a few napkins, too, and put everything on a tray.

When the last of the coffee dripped into the pot, she collected three empty mugs from the cupboard. She noticed that her hands didn't shake as she carried the tray toward the exam room. Progress.

She'd left the exam room door open in case she needed to run back quickly. No alarming noises had reached her while she'd been gone, and she heard no conversation of any sort as she returned.

Perhaps the quiet was a good sign, too. She hoped.

CHAPTER 40

Fern walked into the exam room and set everything down on the counter next to a small stainless steel tray containing a suture holder and the remnants of suture materials. She'd seen her son get stitches enough times to recognize the equipment.

She hoped it was a good sign that Micah had bothered to treat Walsh's wound. Surely he wouldn't have done that if he'd thought Walsh would die, would he?

She poured coffee into the three mugs, inhaling the comforting aroma, which helped steady her resolve and cover the antiseptic odors that overwhelmed the place.

"Bring mine over here, Fern." Judd was leaning against the wall. He had an unobstructed view of Walsh on the table and the doctor standing eight feet away.

Judd still held the pistol in his right hand. It would be easy for him to raise it and shoot. No one could possibly miss a target from such a short distance.

Fern's hands began to shake again as she carried the mug and the snacks across the small room, passing the food to Judd. "Micah, your coffee is on the counter there."

"Thanks," the doctor said, without looking up.

He had inserted an IV into Walsh's right arm while she'd been in the kitchen. He'd also cleaned the wound on Walsh's left arm. He must have stitched the gash before he'd applied the clean dressing. He'd cleaned the grime from his patient's face, too.

Micah checked Walsh's vital signs again as Fern moved to sit in the visitor's chair in the corner. She wanted to ask how Walsh was responding to the antivenom, but she was afraid to hear the answer.

Instead, she watched as Micah worked without pause. Her mind wandered. She'd lost track of how much time had passed. It felt like she'd been sitting in the same chair for days.

Her mind began to wander. Walsh. The dapper, friendly man Fern had enjoyed chatting with at the prison just yesterday. Walsh had been one of her easier clients. She'd genuinely liked him.

He'd made no demands, which was unusual and distinguished him from the other inmates she'd inherited. Every now and then, he'd asked for a favor. Small things. Make a phone call or send a text to his family. Confirm flight times so he could arrange visitation. Stuff like that.

When she'd caught that first glimpse of him slumped over the Land Rover's steering wheel out in the field, his face had been grimy and contorted with pain. She could have been mistaken about his identity, given the panic and hysteria of the moment. But she wasn't.

Walsh had an oxygen cannula in his nose that hadn't been there before she left the room. His breathing was ragged and labored. In a hospital, he might have been intubated right away, Micah had said.

The automatic cuff on his arm continued to monitor Walsh's blood pressure. When it completed the current cycle, the machine flashed a seriously low blood pressure warning.

Judd didn't seem to notice. But Micah did.

Micah pulled an old-fashioned blood pressure cuff from the drawer and applied it to Walsh's right arm. He put the stethoscope in his ears and pumped the bulb to inflate the cuff.

The ragged breathing became more pronounced. Walsh began to wheeze as if his windpipe was blocked.

Fern noticed his lips looked blue. So did his fingertips.

"Can I help?" she asked.

"Just stay out of the way," Micah said, attention fully focused on Walsh.

The tension in the room changed from taut to frantic.

Judd stood up straight, no longer slouching against the wall, watching intently. His eyes narrowed and his nostrils flared. He said nothing. But his hand gripped the pistol tighter at his side.

The doctor began working furiously, moving around the small room, pulling and setting equipment, and applying it to Walsh's body.

One thing after another.

Time and again.

Each effort failed.

Fern glanced at the clock. Micah had been working a long time, making every effort to save Walsh.

Dr. Warner refused to give up.

Sweat broke out on his forehead.

He worked until he was exhausted, and still he tried.

Until his patient wheezed a final, tortured breath.

Micah exhaled at the same time.

His shoulders slumped, and he hung his head for a few seconds. Then he raised his face and gazed directly into Judd's eyes. "I'm so sorry, but—"

Before the defeated doctor finished his sentence, Judd pointed the Glock directly at his chest and fired three times.

Fern jumped from the chair, dropping the coffee mug to the floor, and screamed as she rushed toward her friend, the good doctor. "Micah! Micah!"

Dr. Warner crumpled onto the floor. Fern bent down beside him.

Judd calmly fired one more shot, directly into Dr. Warner's head. Then he grabbed Fern's bicep and yanked her to her feet.

He shoved her through the doorway and poked hard in the center of her back with the gun, growling like a wounded animal. "Move it. Now. Let's go."

"Go where?" Fern said, sobbing as she stumbled toward the back door.

CHAPTER 41

Saturday, May 14
Newton Hills, South Dakota
7:45 p.m.

After Smithers said they'd located Olson's farm truck and teams were on the way to Dr. Warner's office, Kim asked, "Have you recaptured all of the inmates except Keegan?"

"Chief Mitchell just told me we've got three still at large," Smithers replied.

"Who are they?" Burke asked.

"Petey Burns, the kid you ran off the road after he stole Fern Olson's car. Keegan. And Keegan's pal Liam Walsh," Smithers said ticking them off on his fingers. "With Denny dead, that's all of them, according to the intel we have from the prison."

"And Walsh was one of Olson's clients, too. She met with those three yesterday afternoon. Just before the jetliner crashed into the prison," Kim said slowly.

Burke nodded. "Which makes Olson the link between them."

"Seems like it," Smithers said. "We've been all over her background, along with her clients. She seems to be the weak tie, at least. At this point, we can't say whether or not she played a bigger role."

"Got anything that's stronger tying these three guys together?" Kim asked.

Smithers raised his eyebrows. "Like Reacher, you mean? We haven't been focused on that question. Possible, I guess."

Kim shook her head. "I was thinking about Keegan. Can you tie Petey Burns to Keegan?"

Burke said, "Burns is a geeky car thief. He's good at his job but not good enough to stay out of prison. Keegan's a mob boss. An old fashioned gangster. Savage as they come. Walsh was one of his captains. What would Petey Burns have to do with Boston's Irish mob?"

Kim shrugged, the all-purpose gesture she'd learned from Gaspar. "It feels like Burns was a distraction, doesn't it? He just *happened* to steal Olson's car. Which, early on, led Mitchell and the others toward Rapid City instead of north toward Newton Hills."

"Very early on. Before Bolton PD could get enough backup in the field." Smithers nodded slowly, considering the implications. "When Keegan and Walsh and Denny were headed north."

Burke said, "And while Olson was stuck inside the prison lobby. Which is looking a little too convenient at this point, isn't it?"

"Right," Kim said, working things through in her head. "How long had Keegan, Walsh, Denny, and Burns been locked up at Bolton?"

Burke said, "Keegan and Denny were inside the longest. More than ten years. Walsh arrived two years ago. And Burns has maybe been a guest of the feds a few months, at most."

"What are you thinking, Otto?" Smithers asked.

"It's just a theory." She took a deep breath and shoved her hands into her pockets. "We've been assuming this prison break was a crime of opportunity."

"Reasonable assumption. Not exactly the kind of thing it would be easy to orchestrate." Burke shook his head. "A jetliner crashing into the prison instead of hitting the runway seems like a once in a lifetime lucky break, sure. But the inmates in the exercise yard seizing the chance and hightailing it out of there in the chaos that follows seems like a no-brainer."

"What if it wasn't?" Kim asked.

"What if the crash itself wasn't a fluke?" Smithers replied.

"Right. What if the crash was engineered that way? Then some of the prisoners take advantage of the chance," Kim said, thinking aloud. "But others already had an escape plan in place."

"And Olson was facilitating all of it?" Burke asked.

Kim went quiet, considering the implications. Smithers and Burke did the same.

Smithers was the first to break the silence. "So Keegan is the mastermind. Olson's the facilitator. Let's go with that. Where does that leave us now?"

"Logically, there must be a rendezvous point," Burke said, head cocked. "They must have had a plan to connect somewhere."

"And then what?" Smithers said.

Kim had watched them catch up with her thinking. Three logical FBI special agents trained in criminal analysis should reach the same conclusions.

Burke finally said, "Canada. They could drive from here. It's not that far."

"Harder to drive across the border when there's a manhunt going on," Smithers said. "All the crossing checkpoints have been blocked since the prison break happened."

In the silence that followed they were all thinking the same thing. The border between the U.S. and Canada was the longest land border in the world. It was watched by the governments of both countries more carefully than most people knew. Which didn't mean the surveillance was perfect. No government project ever is.

Which meant that Keegan and the others could cross it without being caught.

"Right," Kim said, nodding. "So they'd fly deeper into Canada. In a private plane."

No one suggested flying a private plane undetected into Canada was impossible. Because they all knew it could be done. Traffickers of all sorts of contraband had done it many times before. All the pilot had to do was avoid the air traffic control radar.

It was as simple as turning off the transponder and flying low. Probably two thousand feet above terrain would do the job. Which would burn more fuel. But easy enough in a private jet. Something like a Gulfstream G4 had enough range to fly low for a long time. Certainly long enough for Keegan's needs.

Burke nodded and said, "Makes sense."

"They'd need a specific point to meet up. Somewhere a private jet could land and take off again without drawing too much attention," Kim said. "Is there someplace like that around here?"

Smithers shook his head. "There's not much of anything around here. That's why the prison facility was built here in the first place."

"Okay," Kim said. "But somewhere close by. Close enough to drive to. Something old and unused, preferably."

"There was a place like that back when Reacher was here. An abandoned military airstrip, I think?" Burke said. "But it was destroyed back then, wasn't it?"

Kim nodded. "Yeah. So that's not it."

Smithers said, "How would Keegan know about a place like that?"

"He probably wouldn't," Kim replied, breathing a long sigh. She straightened her posture and stretched her neck. "But Olson would. Or she'd know how to find such a place. Because she's lived here all her life."

"I can't go chasing around the countryside looking for abandoned airstrips. I'll ask Mitchell about it. He'll follow up," Smithers said, pushing off the porch rail.

"What about her cell phone? Did you get the records yet?" Kim asked.

"Still waiting. We have the warrant. The phone company is dragging its feet," Smithers said, swiping a big palm over his head and cupping the back of his neck. "The phone is locked, too. We haven't been able to break the security yet."

"But you will," Kim said, smiling.

Smithers nodded and headed toward the back door. "For now, we've found Olson's old truck. We'll find her. And then Olson will tell us the rest. She killed Denny. Even if it was self-defense, she's going to want to be cooperative."

Burke said, "Sounds like a plan."

"Keep in touch," Smithers said before he went inside and closed the door behind him.

Kim said nothing. All theories had flaws and there were several in this one.

Would Olson flee to Canada and leave her son behind? Not likely.

So would she circle back to collect Noah first, before she met up with the others? Maybe.

What was Olson's motivation here, anyway? Kim didn't know enough about her to divine a solid incentive.

And where did Reacher fit in?

"We're not needed here. They've got plenty of hands on deck now," Kim said, pulling the Boss's phone out on her way down the porch stairs. She pushed the redial and listened to the incessant ringing for a while before she hung up and slid the phone back into her pocket.

"He'll call when he can." Burke followed, easily catching up with her shorter stride about halfway to the Navigator. "Where are we going?"

CHAPTER 42

Saturday, May 14
South Dakota
8:20 p.m.

Fern didn't notice the beauty of the spring evening. Driving north, about thirty miles from Newton Hills, the sun dipped low in the western sky casting a warm glow over the South Dakota hills.

She loved her home state. She'd been born here, married, and raised her son here. There were easier places to live. More hospitable climates. States with convenient services. But for Fern, rugged South Dakota would always be home.

She'd never thought much about death or dying until she'd lost her mother. Even then, her busy law practice and taking care of Noah and her dad had been enough to keep her thoughts from darkness.

Until today.

Since Judd shot Officer Miller this morning, Fern had been terrified.

She was barely holding it together, and she knew it.

He probably knew it, too.

Judd opened the glove box and rooted through the papers stuffed inside. "We need a map."

"I've lived in South Dakota all my life. We don't have a lot of roads and I know most of the main ones. Where do you want to go?" Fern hated the tremor in her voice. She'd tried to control it but failed.

Judd was crazy. Until she could get away from him, every cell in her body would remain taut with fear.

He ignored the question and continued to shuffle through the stuff Micah had shoved into the glove box.

After a while, Judd found a paper map. It was creased and grimy and torn in places.

Micah had probably used it to find remote, unspoiled hiking and fishing spots and stuffed it into his pockets for easy reference. The map looked about thirty years old. But an old map of South Dakota was just about as good as a new one.

Judd jammed all the junk back into the glove box and refolded the map to study nearby roads.

Fern's mind turned to practical matters to cope with her constant fear. Judd had already displayed a terrifying lack of patience with any show of emotion. Pushing his patience was a bad idea.

If she wanted to stay alive, she had to keep her wits about her. She knew that.

First things first.

Where the hell were they going?

He'd be smart to head to Canada. Get out of the country.

Canada was a big, wide-open place. And if he should be discovered there, the Canadian government probably wouldn't extradite him because he'd be facing the death penalty here in the U.S.

With a fake passport, Judd might live in the U.S. undetected for years. But it would be easier to do in Canada. From there, he could travel to other places in the world, too.

So if Judd made it to Canada, he'd feel safe. If she helped him get there, maybe he wouldn't kill her. Or hurt her family. She hoped.

Fern had been to Canada several times in her life. Beautiful country. Nice people. Living in Canada would be no hardship for a guy like Judd.

She and Noah had driven to Winnipeg once on vacation years ago. The drive time was about ten hours from Bolton on the interstates.

But the highways were better and faster than the county roads they were traveling on now. It would take longer to get to the border if they stayed on the secondary roads.

They were probably headed toward a closer crossing point at one of the small Canadian towns across the border from North Dakota. Judd would probably have a better chance of slipping through law enforcement.

But all the border crossing checkpoints would require a passport. Judd probably had a counterfeit with a false identity. Fern didn't carry her passport in her purse. Which meant she didn't have it with her. They wouldn't let her cross.

How would Judd deal with that? Not well, probably.

Fern kept both hands on the steering wheel, mostly to prevent shaking as she considered her limited options.

Before his Land Rover was damaged, Judd's plan might have been to cross over to Canada in the dark through the forest. The Land Rover probably would have handled the drive along a dirt road somewhere near the border. This Jeep didn't seem up to the task.

Dr. Warner's SUV was a serviceable but battered ten-year-old Cherokee with more than one hundred thousand miles on the odometer. The green body paint had dulled and faded over the years.

He'd been an all-around sportsman, so the cargo area was filled with hiking, hunting, and fishing equipment, which kept knocking around back there whenever she hit a pothole or made a sharp turn.

Judd sat silently in the passenger seat with the folded map and the pistol, which didn't settle Fern's nerves at all. He wouldn't hesitate to use the gun. She'd seen him kill twice today, shooting at point-blank range. No reason to believe he wouldn't do the same to her.

But probably not until they reached his destination, since he couldn't drive. He'd need her until then.

She needed an escape plan before they reached Canada. Because at that point, she'd be utterly dispensable.

Fern noticed a road sign on the right. Mission River was three miles ahead.

She glanced at the fuel gauge. "We need to get gas. After Mission River, we won't find another station for a long time."

"Okay," Judd replied. "We'll pay with cash. You'll stay with the Jeep. You'll speak to no one. Understand?"

She nodded. The town, and the gas station, were located on the other side of the old Mission River Bridge. She'd crossed it many times.

It was a standard steel girder concrete deck design, built about 1960. A quarter-mile long and two lanes wide, each with a narrow shoulder. Nothing fancy. The point was to carry limited traffic from one side of the river to the other.

As they approached the bridge, Fern noticed a sidewalk running beside the water. A few sport fishing boats were docked along the river banks, twenty feet below the bridge.

When she looked ahead again to the end of the bridge, her heart skipped a beat. Sweat popped out on her forehead. She gripped the steering wheel tighter.

Four police squad cars, lights flashing, blocked the road, checking vehicles heading to and from the town.

For half a moment, she considered flooring the accelerator. She could get onto the bridge, and there would be nowhere else to go except straight into the roadblock. Directly into the arms of law enforcement.

She might get away.

Judd might be captured.

Almost as soon as the crazy plan popped into her head, she discarded it. Before the police reached the Jeep, Judd would kill her. No doubt in her mind.

Wildly, she ran through as many other options as she could muster.

She had talked her way through the roadblock at Newton Hills, but that was a single cop. She'd known him, and he'd known her. He'd trusted her. So they had passed without incident.

This was different.

CHAPTER 43

Saturday, May 14
South Dakota
9:00 p.m.

Before Fern could come up with a plan, Judd noticed the roadblock.

He grabbed her forearm and squeezed like a vise. "There's a parking lot on the right of the bridge. Pull off. Park the Jeep."

Fern said, "We have to get across the river. There's no place else to go."

Faster than she could process his intent or move out of the way, Judd fisted his left hand and punched her right bicep. Hard. Shoving her sideways into the door. Her head hit the closed window.

Pain, instant and intense, shot through her body. Tears sprang to her eyes and welled there.

She bit her tongue to hold back the screams and felt the iron taste of blood in her mouth.

Without another word, Fern pulled off the road on the right and drove down the paved driveway to the parking spot Judd had pointed out.

"Turn off the ignition," Judd instructed.

Fern twisted the key to the off position. Her arm was throbbing, but she swallowed the hurt and said nothing.

Judd said, "Get out of the Jeep. Now."

She did as she was told.

Once she was free of the Jeep, she scanned the area for a place to run. The parking lot abutted a wide strip of green space beside the river. Picnic tables, benches, and a walking trail completed the idyllic park.

For half a moment, she considered running. She saw no reliable cover that would protect her from a gunshot to the back. How far would she get?

"Come on." Judd grabbed her arm and dragged her along toward the pillars of the bridge close to the water. They hurried to the shadows and then made their way to the riverbank.

The fishing boats were uncovered. Fishing was a popular pastime in the Mission River during the springtime. The boats were littered with rods and reels and tackle boxes. They reeked of dead fish, too. A few of these boat owners had had fresh fish for dinner.

The largest boat was about eighteen feet long. They had outboard motors mounted on the back.

Judd scanned all of the boats and chose a smaller one near the end of the row. He pushed Fern toward the boat. "Get it."

She climbed in from the dock and sat on the front bench. Judd untied the boat and gave it a shove into the river. He sat in the back and pull-started the motor. He gave it some gas and steered the boat westward.

From her vantage point in the front, looking backward, she didn't see anyone coming after them. The squad units didn't abandon the roadblock to give chase.

Perhaps no one had seen them. Or maybe their actions seemed normal. They could look like two people going fishing, she supposed.

Fern turned and looked forward toward the last of the sunset. The open air was cold as it washed across her body. She wrapped her arms around her torso in an attempt to avoid hypothermia as the river widened.

The wind across the water caused choppy waves. The boat bounced hard a few times as it crossed, sending hits of icy cold spray across her face. She felt her teeth chattering in the increasing cold.

The boat was small and the outboard motor pushed it along at full throttle, but they were probably traveling only ten miles an hour.

Progress was slow.

She had no idea where they were headed. But it would take a long time to get there at this rate, and the twilight had faded into near-total darkness. She was wet and cold and scared out of her mind.

What did Judd plan to do?

The Mission River was a tributary. It ended a few miles from the point where they'd stolen the boat. Which meant he couldn't take this boat all the way to Canada. Did he realize that?

Her arm was still throbbing, and the lump on her head didn't feel great, either.

If he struck her again out here, she'd fall into the cold river and drown.

The last time she'd tried to help him, he'd reacted by punching her so hard she'd banged her head against the Jeep's window.

So she said nothing.

As they traveled farther along the river, they'd passed a few decrepit homes. The population out here was sparse, for sure. She couldn't remember the geography well enough to predict where the next town might be, but she knew the elevations would start to rise the further west they traveled.

When they'd been running west for about an hour, she saw a building ahead on the right, ablaze with lights.

A church.

Floodlights illuminated the spire at the top. The parking lot was also well lit and about half full of empty parked vehicles.

Judd saw the church, too. He steered the boat toward the shore. He slowed and ran parallel to the riverbank until they passed the parking lot. Then he nosed the bow of the boat into the weeds and beached it.

"Come on," he said as he stepped onto the ground. "We need a new vehicle."

Fern scrambled to the bow, struggling to keep her balance as the boat tilted side to side in the water. She held onto the boat, swung one leg over and then the other to climb out. It took her a moment to steady herself again on solid ground.

She scanned the area. She didn't know where they were exactly. But they'd traveled far enough from her farmhouse. Judd wouldn't be able to make good on his threat to her family before she could protect them.

Judd grabbed her arm and pulled her toward the parking lot. He peered into a dozen windows before he found a late model Chevy Impala sedan with the keys in the ignition. He opened the door and shoved her into the driver's seat.

He pointed the gun at her head. "Try anything and you'll die right here."

Fern nodded. He left her door open and walked around the front of the car, pointing the pistol toward her as he hurried to the passenger seat.

He jerked the door open and jumped inside. "Let's go."

She closed her door and turned the key. The engine started up instantly. She turned the headlights on. She drove slowly toward the exit.

"Which way?" she asked when they reached the county road.

"West," he replied.

She turned onto the westbound lane and accelerated to the speed limit, looking for an opportunity to escape.

CHAPTER 44

Saturday, May 14
Newton Hills, South Dakota
9:10 p.m.

"Let's get a bite to eat," Kim had said when they left the Olson farmhouse. Newton Hills was only a few miles up the road. The village had a diner.

Burke was driving. He parked the Navigator in the lot and they hurried inside against the cold wind blowing in from Canada.

The diner was the usual setup. Long and narrow. Windows on one side, counter and grill on the other. Booths upholstered in red vinyl placed in a row alongside the windows. How many of these ubiquitous diners had she patronized since she started hunting Reacher? Too many.

A burly guy in a denim shirt, sleeves rolled up above his hairy forearms, stood behind the counter. "We're closing up, but I can get you a burger and fries. Will that do it for you?"

"Coffee?" Kim asked.

"I'll make a fresh pot," he replied.

"Perfect," Kim said as Burke settled into an empty booth. "I'll be right back."

She walked to the restroom and washed her hands. She looked at herself in the stainless steel tray that served as a mirror. The dark circles under her eyes were vivid enough to reflect back.

She straightened her hair into its bun at the back of her head and splashed a bit of water on her face. She pulled a couple of paper towels to dry off and then returned to the booth.

"Your turn," she said. Burke nodded and headed toward the back.

While he was gone, she called Gaspar.

"Good evening, Suzie Wong."

His easy humor always made her grin. But the silly nicknames they'd adopted early on had become a sort of code, too. They meant each had permission to speak freely.

"I feel like I'm running in circles here, Chico. Got anything you'd like to tell me?"

"Since I don't listen in on your life every moment of every day like Cooper does, I'm gonna need a bit more meat on that question," he said. She could hear him chewing something, which was not unusual. Gaspar ate whenever he had the chance. He ate more calories in a day than she consumed in a week.

"Start with Fern Olson's phone. What can you tell me about that?" Kim asked.

"Reams of data over the past few years. But what you probably want to know is whether she was involved with this prison break in any way."

"Was she?"

"Inconclusive. She's got a lot of odd random calls and texts. Quite a few with a Rapid City phone number belonging to the dead pilot of that cargo jet," Gaspar said. "Not likely that's a coincidence."

Kim's gut did a somersault. Partly due to hunger, perhaps. The rest was due to the usual anxiety. "Nothing overt in the texts or the voice messages, I'm guessing?"

"You mean, like did he say he was on his way to crash into a prison in Bolton where Olson represented about thirty inmates?" Gaspar's smile traveled across the miles with his words.

She grinned. "Yeah, like that."

"Nope. But there was a lot of talk about landing to pick up a package. And how he'd get paid for the work," Gaspar said. "I can send you the transcripts."

"Please do." She nodded when the cook silently gestured with a coffee thermos and two plastic mugs. He left them on the table and went back to making the burgers. "Turns out they've recaptured all but four of the inmates."

"And they're all connected to Olson," he deadpanned. "What a shock."

"Right. One is dead. Ryan Denny. Her son says Olson shot him when he attacked her." She heard his keyboard clacking as she talked. "The other three are still at large. We think two are with Olson now. The locals are on it, along with Smithers and his team."

"And those two are?"

"Duff Keegan and Liam Walsh," she said. "The other one, Petey Burns, was the car thief we chased down. He escaped into the woods and they haven't found him yet."

"Got it. You do know that prison inmates have escaped and stayed at large for decades, right?" Gaspar said. "Remember Archuleta? He was out there for something like forty-six years before they found him."

"Yeah, that's not helpful," she replied. "The point of that story is that the FBI finally did get him. We always get our man. Haven't you heard?"

Gaspar chuckled. "What do you need to know?"

"We could keep chasing Olson, I guess. But it's smarter to figure out where she's headed and get there before she does."

"How do you plan to do that?"

"I think they may have a meeting point set up to catch a private plane. The final destination is probably Canada."

"They could drive there. It's not that far," Gaspar said, keys still clacking. "Eight to ten hours by car from Bolton.

There's gotta be places they could cross over the border undetected."

"Yeah, and if they do that, Smithers and his team have all the gear they need to catch them first," Kim said. "I'm thinking that's not what they'll do, though. I think they want to get deeper into Canada. Gives them more breathing room."

"Okay. What do you want from me?"

"Anything in Olson's phone records that might mean she'd set up a meeting point? Somewhere they could fly out from?"

"Why?"

"A private jet just makes more sense. Road vehicles are slow. They're clumsy. They're easily traced." She paused a few moments. "I don't know. Just a hunch, I guess."

Gaspar's heavy breathing came through the earpiece as he searched through the records. "It's going to take me a bit to find something like that."

"If you find it, look for an airstrip they could use, too. It's likely to be abandoned. That would be the safest option. The second safest would be a private airport. I guess there was an old abandoned military airstrip around here when Reacher came through seven years ago. But it was destroyed."

"So we need another one. Probably smaller than a military base. Say within a four-hour drive radius from the prison," Gaspar said, thinking aloud. "Runway about a mile long would be enough for a Gulfstream that could fly deeper into Canada."

"Makes sense. Can you look? And call me back?" Kim said.

"Copy that, Sunshine. Stand by," Gaspar said as he hung up.

She smiled and disconnected just as Burke returned. "Talking to Cooper?"

"No." She placed the phone on the table where she could grab it easily. "Gaspar."

Burke frowned. "So you're working with Gaspar against Cooper's orders? Sharing intel with him that's classified?"

"Gaspar knows more about this assignment than you do. His clearance level is higher than mine." Kim shrugged.

"Yeah, well, don't expect me to visit you in Leavenworth when you're caught," Burke said.

"Noted," she snapped. And then she relented. "Look, I tried to call Cooper. He didn't pick up. We need help now, not when he gets around to it."

The cook walked up with two plates piled high. The cheeseburger and fries were perfect. They looked like a television food commercial. Kim inhaled the aroma and her stomach growled with anticipation.

"Here you go. Take your time. I've got plenty of cleanup to do," he said, like a business owner who couldn't afford to turn away hungry customers. Which he probably was.

Kim put dill pickles and mustard on the burger and squirted a puddle on her plate. Her first bite confirmed the cook's skill on the griddle. The burger was perfect.

"You put mustard on fries?" Burke asked with a mock frown as he slathered everything with ketchup. "Such a heathen. I don't know how we're ever going to work together."

She swallowed the burger and dunked one of the fries into the mustard with her fingers. She licked her fingers after she ate it, too. She didn't need to impress Burke. He needed to impress her. Whether he knew it or not.

But she understood that he was offering an olive branch, so she teased, "Gaspar liked ketchup, too, and he turned out all right. Maybe there's hope for you yet."

"Oh, well, if Gaspar does it, it must be okay," he mocked as he gobbled his food, exactly the way Gaspar always did.

Kim grinned. It was the first time she'd felt any kinship to Burke. Maybe this partnership would work out better than she'd feared after all.

"Tell me why you're so sure the Boss will help us out here," she said, taking a break to let her food settle while she thought about Gaspar's intel.

Burke raised his eyebrows. "Why wouldn't Cooper do everything he can? This is his black op. We're following orders. His ass is on the line. It's to his advantage if we get the job done."

Kim sat back in the booth with the coffee. She cocked her head. Could he possibly be that naïve? Of course, he could. She had been, back when she got that first four o'clock phone call in November.

She was seven months smarter now. Burke would catch up. But she couldn't give him seven months to do it.

The phone danced on the table. She glanced at the caller ID before she picked it up. "Smithers. What's up?"

"Just got word. Olson's not at the doctor's office. Keegan's gone too. The doc and Walsh are both dead," Smithers said wearily.

Kim closed her eyes and kneaded the pain at the bridge of her nose as she listened to his brief report. When he finished, she said, "Okay. Now what?"

"Looks like Olson and Keegan took the doc's Jeep. I'll text you the details. Mitchell's got roadblocks and BOLOs out. We've put the helos to bed for the night. Unless we find them before daylight, there's not much we can do from the air."

"What do you need from us?" Kim asked, shaking her head to let Burke know they'd hit a wall.

"Nothing tonight. We're still working at the farmhouse. We have another crime scene here at the doc's office. We're gonna be here until mid-day tomorrow, at least." Smithers was as matter-of-fact as always, but she knew he had to be exhausted. "We'll work in shifts. Get some sleep. Recon at daylight, unless Mitchell finds the Jeep before then."

"Copy that. I'll let you know if we turn up anything," Kim said as she signed off.

Burke had eaten every morsel of his food. Half of Kim's cheeseburger had congealed on the plate. She pushed it aside and poured more coffee as she relayed Smithers's report to Burke.

Adrenaline, anxiety, and plenty of caffeine would keep her going another night.

"Now what?" Burke asked.

"You call Cooper," she replied.

CHAPTER 45

Saturday, May 14
South Dakota
10:00 p.m.

Burke had relaxed into the booth with his coffee. He frowned as if he were perplexed. Maybe he was. "You want me to call Cooper now? Why?"

"He's got access to satellites that can track the Jeep. Those satellites are constantly recording everything," Kim replied.

"Satellites like that have long been rumored. But whether or not they exist is classified," Burke said, nodding as if he was following along but not making the same leap of logic that she'd made.

"The Boss can pull up the video footage of Dr. Warner's house and confirm that Olson and Keegan left there together. He can follow the Jeep and find out where they are." Kim knew the satellites existed and she was betting Burke knew, too. It was one of those not so well kept secrets about which only the gullible public remained doubtful. "Should take about ten minutes of his time."

Her request was a test. Burke knew it. The Boss, who was always listening, would know it, too. If he gave Burke the intel, they could find Olson within the next couple of hours.

If he withheld the intel, Kim would find Olson anyway.

But Burke would know exactly how helpful Cooper was or wasn't. The knowledge might save his life.

Or both of their lives.

Because right now, Burke held the crazy idea that the Boss was on their side. He wasn't. Never had been.

Kim knew she was expendable. Burke had a right to know that, too.

He cocked his head and took another swig of coffee. He spent a few seconds pondering whatever was on his mind. Then he fished the burner phone he'd received from the Boss out of his pocket and pressed the redial button.

The phone rang several times. But the Boss never picked up and Burke finally disconnected.

"He's busy. He'll call back," Burke said.

Kim said nothing. She drained the last of her coffee and collected her cell phone from the table. She scooted across the bench and stood in the aisle.

"I'll pay the bill and meet you outside," Burke said, making his way to the cash register to settle up.

At the Navigator, Kim rooted around in her bag and found a fresh burner phone. She fired it up and moved toward the trees on the other side of the parking lot. She dialed a number she'd memorized weeks ago. A number limited to her alone.

Lamont Finlay, Ph.D., Special Assistant to the President for Strategy, picked up. "Agent Otto. Always good to hear from you. How can I be of service?"

She relayed the facts and the request, adding as many details as she knew. Anything the Boss could do, Finlay could do, too. Hell, Finlay might even have more options.

"Faster to ask Cooper. He has the video at his fingertips, and it'll take me a few minutes to get it," Finlay's deep, rumbly voice with the Boston accent was still as terrifying as always.

When she said nothing, he chuckled a little under his breath. "Never mind. I'll call you back."

"Thanks," she said. She dropped the phone into her pocket and waited. Asking Finlay for anything was always a risk. But he'd been a better source than her boss, by a long shot.

She glanced toward the diner. Burke was coming out now. He took the steps two at a time and strode toward the Navigator. He was a confident man. Capable. Experienced. She had asked the Boss for a solid partner, and at least on paper, Burke was all that.

He made her uneasy though she didn't know exactly why. He hadn't done anything wrong. Not overtly anyway. Still, her instincts had served her well for a long time. She wouldn't abandon them now.

When Burke opened the driver's door, and the overhead light came on, he saw she wasn't in the vehicle. He scanned the parking lot and didn't notice her hidden by the shadows.

Her feet were cold, and her teeth had begun to chatter. Still, she waited. Finlay had never let her down. She kept a tight rein on her anxiety about his motives, but she didn't give up. She never gave up. Never.

Gaspar thought Finlay shouldn't be trusted. He was probably right.

Plausible deniability was a big part of Kim's survival strategy. Someday, Cooper would throw her to the wolves. She'd be asked to testify about the hunt for Reacher. Her career with the FBI would be over.

When the time came, she had three objectives. To lie as little as possible. To avoid prison. And to come out alive. Not necessarily in that order.

"Otto!" Burke called out. He'd left the door of the Navigator open and walked a few feet away from it, scanning the darkness. "Otto!"

The burner phone finally vibrated. She pushed the talk button.

Finlay said, "Olson and Keegan left the doctor's home in a green Jeep. They drove north until they hit a snag. At that point, they evaded a roadblock, abandoned the Jeep, and stole a fishing boat. They traveled west on the Mission River. Beached the boat at a church and stole an Impala sedan. I'll text you the details on the Chevy."

She appreciated his no-nonsense approach and took a moment to metabolize the intel. "Great. Where are they now?"

"Headed west toward Sardis on a county road."

"West? Not north? Are you sure?"

"Absolutely certain."

"Thanks," she said slowly, digesting the data. "Did you get any audio inside the vehicles?"

"Very little, and it's garbled. They're not talking much," Finlay said. "For what it's worth, I did get the sense that she's a hostage, not a willing participant."

"What made you think so?"

"He's been pretty rough with her a couple of times." Finlay paused as if he had to think about the gut feeling before he could explain it. "Something else. She was driving. Both the Jeep and the Chevy. Could mean that he's incapacitated."

"Can you keep an eye on them in real-time?" she asked.

"That's problematic," he replied. "For one thing, the satellites don't see as well out there in no man's land. For another, I've already got a job."

She nodded although he couldn't see her.

He asked, "Why does Cooper think you'll find Reacher in the wilds of South Dakota?"

Finlay was always two steps ahead of her. Which meant he was more likely to know the answer to that question than she was.

"You tell me. I'd really love to know," she said sourly.

"You're asking the wrong man," he replied. Which only meant that he wouldn't say.

She shrugged, alone in the dark. "Thank you. I'll call back if I need anything else."

Finlay chuckled wryly. "Now that Gaspar's not there telling you to avoid me like the plague you mean?"

"Something like that." She grinned, too. Then she disconnected and dropped the phone into her pocket.

She couldn't help it. She liked the guy. He was dangerous, for sure. But Finlay hadn't double-crossed her yet. Which was more than she could say for the Boss.

As she walked out of the trees toward Burke, she pretended to be zipping her jeans. "Over here. Sorry. Call of nature."

"I thought maybe a grizzly had grabbed you or something," Burke said, sounding genuinely concerned. Maybe he was. "Come on. It's freezing out here."

They climbed into the Navigator. Burke started the engine and turned the heat on full blast, rubbing his hands together like a frostbitten munchkin.

Kim fastened her seatbelt and put her alligator clamp at the shoulder harness retractor. Otherwise, the seatbelt would cut off her head in a crash.

What was it with men and big vehicles, anyway?

"Did Cooper call you back?" she asked.

"Not yet. But he will." Burke scowled.

"I wouldn't hold your breath," she replied with a smirk he couldn't see in the dark.

Burke didn't argue. He simply asked, "Where to?"

"Let's see if the GPS on this beast will work out here," she said, turning it on. After a few moments, it showed a pulsing blue dot at the Navigator's location.

A system of more than thirty satellites circled the earth. GPS needed a signal from three or four satellites to triangulate properly and find things. The satellites could, theoretically, find anything, anytime and anywhere.

In the real world, sometimes GPS worked well and sometimes it didn't. Anybody who carried a cell phone in Manhattan could confirm. At the moment, the GPS in the

Navigator seemed to be performing as intended. Whether it would work throughout the state of South Dakota, up through North Dakota, and on into Canada was bound to be hit or miss.

"What are you looking for?" Burke asked.

"Not sure yet."

On the screen, she expanded the map of the immediate area. "There's one paved road through Newton Hills. It runs due north until it reaches the Mission River Bridge."

Which was where Finlay had told her that Olson and Keegan had headed west in the fishing boat, but she didn't say that.

Burke said, "Chief Mitchell's a smart guy. Smithers said he had BOLOs and checkpoints set up. He probably had a checkpoint at that bridge."

Of course he did. She nodded.

"Okay. Look here. A county road runs alongside the river," she said, tracing it with her finger.

She found the church where Olson and Keegan had stolen the Chevy, but she didn't mention that yet.

Burke said, "That road runs west for miles."

"It does. It connects with a highway, here, just past a small town called Sardis." Kim tapped the screen. "That interstate runs south all the way past Nebraska."

"Yeah, and north to Canada," Burke said. "They could get across the border before Smithers gets the helos out there in the morning."

Which was true.

But it didn't make sense to Kim.

Keegan had been clever and resourceful so far. He'd spent a long time setting up his escape. He wouldn't try to bluster his way across the border. Not if he had a better option.

She believed he did. Keegan was the kind of guy who left nothing to chance. What she needed to do was figure out the plan. And stop it.

CHAPTER 46

Saturday, May 14
South Dakota
10:30 p.m.

Fern drove the Chevy westward in the darkness, northeast of Rapid City. The terrain had become more rugged as they'd moved toward the Black Hills. The Impala's high beam headlights illuminated the roadway ahead creating a tunnel of light inside the black emptiness.

South Dakota was an outdoorsman's paradise. It was nine times larger than the state of New Jersey. But the total population was less than Austin, Texas. Which meant very few people occupied a vast, rugged landscape.

They could travel for hours and never see another soul. The chance of coming upon a hitchhiker out here was probably lower than winning the Powerball lottery.

Judd, or whatever his real name was, didn't talk much, and his silence was nerve-wracking. The silence left her too much time to wonder how he'd kill her when they reached his destination.

She tried not to focus on her family. Fern hoped that Judd would keep his word and leave Noah and her dad alone because she'd done everything he'd demanded. She was willing to sacrifice her life for theirs, even as her mind worked furiously to devise a plan to keep them all alive.

For many miles, she'd expected Judd to direct a north turn toward Canada. Instead, they'd kept traveling west.

He must be headed toward a rendezvous. Nothing else made sense.

Which meant she had to find a way to escape before they reached the rendezvous.

The Chevy was equipped with a GPS system. Judd had turned it on shortly after they left the Church. Every few minutes, he looked at the blinking blue light marking their position.

The farther they drove from Mission River, the weaker and more intermittent the signal became. There was little else depicted on the screen. At this point, the road they were traveling was surrounded by emptiness on all sides.

Fern was surprised the GPS worked at all. In theory, GPS would operate wherever she could see the sky. But not always. She knew that sometimes the signal was blocked by trees or hills or buildings.

"How's the fuel?" Judd asked, punching a couple of buttons directing the GPS to find the nearest services. The GPS returned nothing but an empty screen.

"Less than a quarter tank left," she said. The Chevy probably had an eighteen-gallon tank and could get maybe twenty-five miles to the gallon.

"Do you know where we are?" Judd asked.

"Roughly. North and east of Rapid City would be my guess. Which would mean there's an interstate we could reach."

"No," he said.

Her heart thumped a little faster as she realized this might be her chance. "We're more likely to find a gas station closer to the highway."

"No," he repeated.

A gas station would have an attendant, at least. Perhaps other travelers. Long-haul truckers, maybe. Someone who could help her.

"We've got enough gas to go maybe another fifty miles," Fern said, leaving him to reach his own conclusions.

She slowed her speed in an effort to conserve fuel. He didn't object. Which suggested they were in no hurry to get wherever they were going.

The GPS continued to operate intermittently, showing their location but nothing else nearby. No gas station, no fast food joints, no homes or vehicles. Nothing but nature, and lots of it.

Fern watched the fuel gauge nervously as it moved toward empty. If they ran out of gas here...

She noticed a decrepit sign on the side of the road. It was the first sign of any kind she'd seen for hours. The poles were bent and the sign had been battered by weather for a long time. But the faint letters on it were barely visible.

The sign said: Sardis 5.

Did that mean a town five miles ahead? She'd never heard of Sardis. But that didn't necessarily mean anything. There were plenty of wide spaces out here with names she didn't know.

Judd saw the sign, too. He said, "We'll get gas in Sardis."

Fern had a thousand objections. But she didn't raise them. No point.

They traveled five miles, and Sardis came into view at the edge of the Chevy's headlights' beam. An intersection and four buildings. One of which was a gas station. The others were a general store and two homes.

The gas station was a shack off to the right and two pumps, one for gas and one for diesel. Fern pulled up and stopped next to the gas pump.

Judd reached over and grabbed the keys from the ignition. "I'll go inside and pay. Fill up the tank. And remember what I said about your son and the old man. I can reach them any time."

Fern nodded. She opened the door and stepped out into the cold darkness. Her plans to attract attention or scream for help were all useless. She could scream all she wanted. There was no one around to hear. The general store and the two homes were already dark. The owners had gone to bed for the night.

Her shoulders slumped as she accepted the inevitable. She couldn't escape here. But she would. They would find a busier road eventually. Fern had loved the South Dakota landscape all her life. She'd never expected the remote beauty to become her enemy.

She took a deep breath and turned her face into the cold wind to dry her tears. She remembered an old joke and smiled.

"Everything will be all right in the end, Fern," she said aloud. "If it's not all right, it's not the end."

Police would be watching, looking for Judd and the other escapees. She couldn't escape at this station, but she'd have another chance. They would come to another roadblock. And this time, she'd be prepared.

She filled the gas tank and replaced the cap. She'd pumped seventeen gallons into the almost empty tank.

"God watches over fools and children," she murmured when she realized how close she'd come to running dry. It was something her mother used to say. She hoped her mother's faith would carry her back home to Noah and her dad.

As she replaced the pump, Judd emerged from the station carrying two bottles of water and two packages of peanut butter cheese crackers. "Let's go. The guy says we're about ten miles from the interstate."

Fern's heartbeat quickened. The interstate beckoned like a life raft in a raging sea. Her chance to escape might come sooner than she'd expected.

They settled into the Chevy again, and Fern pulled onto the dark county road. With a full gas tank, she felt confident increasing her speed. The Impala covered the miles with ease.

A newer sign on the roadside said the interstate was two miles ahead.

There were no services at the north and southbound entrances. Not even an exit ramp.

The intersection was as deserted as the rest of the drive had been. It felt like everyone in South Dakota was asleep except Fern and Judd.

"Which way?" she asked as they approached the northbound ramp.

"Straight ahead," Judd said. "I'll tell you when to turn."

Her best means of escape zoomed past her periphery. Tears sprang to Fern's eyes, and she blinked them away furiously in the dark.

She considered entering the southbound lanes and speeding along the highway for as long as she could before Judd did something to stop her.

He must have read her mind. Before they reached the ramp, she felt the cold barrel of the pistol jab against her right temple.

"From this distance, I won't miss," Judd growled.

She kept the Chevy pointed west and the speed level as they passed the cloverleaf and under the overpass. No cars traveled across on the interstate above. She hadn't seen another vehicle since they'd stolen this one in the church parking lot.

It seemed that all of South Dakota had tucked in for the night. The only things alive and awake out there in the cold were wild creatures, a few of which were deadly. Unless she could get Judd out of the car, there was no way she could escape until daylight.

When they'd driven ten miles past the cloverleaf, Judd said, "There's an intersection coming up. A county road. Turn left."

She put her turn signal on out of habit. A glimmer of hope lifted her spirits, and she smiled to herself.

They were heading south.

Toward Mount Rushmore.

The busiest tourist attraction in South Dakota.

One of the most heavily watched places on earth.

CHAPTER 47

Saturday, May 14
South Dakota
10:45 p.m.

While they were still sitting in the diner's parking lot, Kim opened her laptop and connected it to her secure satellite.

"What are you doing?" Burke asked.

"Downloading files while I have a strong signal," she said as she retrieved the data Gaspar had placed there. One file was labeled simply "runways."

"Hello. We're supposed to be partners here. You're gonna need to start trusting me. What've you got?" Burke asked.

"Sorry. I've been working solo too long," she said with a shrug. "I don't believe Keegan was planning to drive that Land Rover to Canada."

"Based on what? Coply intuition?" Burke said, mocking Mitchell without cracking a smile. Maybe Burke wasn't totally humorless after all.

"Logic, wiseass. The longer Keegan and Walsh stayed on the road, the more likely they were to get caught. Keegan would have understood the risk of a long drive like that using the same vehicle," she explained, holding her patience. Burke was a new partner. She'd give him time to get used to her methods. "So it makes sense that they'd want to drive that Land Rover as little as possible."

Burke nodded, as he grasped her point and extended the analysis. "But they also needed to get out of the country as quickly possible. So you think they planned to fly?"

"Makes sense to me," Kim said. "Got a better theory?"

He shook his head. "Let's go with yours. Say Keegan's plan was to fly into Canada. Smithers and the locals are stretched thin, but I'm sure he has the airports on alert. They'll find him."

"They probably would if he tried to take a commercial flight. Keegan is smart enough to know that, too." She opened Gaspar's file and scanned it quickly. "So I'm guessing he made an alternative plan."

"A private jet? Every phone call Keegan ever had, incoming or outgoing, while he was inside Bolton prison would have been recorded and monitored. Every piece of mail, too. How would he have set up a private jet while he was inside?" Burke asked, and then answered his own question half a moment later. "Through his lawyer. Fern Olson."

Kim nodded. "Most likely."

"So what are you looking at in those files?" Burke asked as if she'd convinced him.

She didn't mention that Gaspar was the source of her intel. No point in getting Burke's panties in a wad about that again.

"We've located four runways within a four-hour drive from Bolton prison. All are at least a mile long."

"Why four hours?"

Kim shrugged. "Just a guess. But closer to Bolton would mean a greater chance of getting caught. And farther from Bolton would have meant more drive time in the Land Rover. Four hours seemed like a reasonable distance."

"So a four-hour drive to a runway that's a mile long. Means it could be used for takeoff by a private jet with enough flight range to reach deep into Canada," Burke said, head cocked as if he was thinking things through. "Four runways, four hours. That's a lot of ground for us to cover. We'll need help."

"Not all four are viable options, though. Keegan is smart. He'd have figured out the best choice," Kim said.

"What's wrong with them?"

"One of the runways is the abandoned military facility destroyed seven years ago when Reacher was there. The runway shows on the maps, but the satellite images reveal only charred and buckled tarmac."

"Any idea what happened there?" Burke asked.

"Not really. Lots of investigation, but ultimately? No real answers." She paused and then added, "The usual result where Reacher is concerned."

Burke nodded again. "So that runway isn't usable. What about the other three?"

Kim replied, "The second one is an executive airport in Rapid City near the commercial aviation terminals."

"Too public. Keegan wouldn't use it if he wants to remain undiscovered," Burke guessed.

Kim nodded. "And Smithers's team would apprehend him if he tried."

"What about the third one?"

"A private airport near Mount Rushmore," Kim replied.

"Sounds promising."

She shook her head. "It's used by a civilian tour company to ferry tourists. Private jets land and depart several times a day during high traffic tourist seasons. Which means FAA and flight plans and communications with towers and all that."

"Is this the high tourist season?"

"No. But it's still too risky," Kim replied. "The more people coming and going, the more likely someone will recognize Keegan and Olson. Their photos are all over the news now.

And flights in and out of that airport will be monitored just like the others."

"You've narrowed it down to the fourth runway, then?"

"It's promising." She turned her laptop screen toward Burke. "An abandoned hangar about ten miles south and east of Mount Rushmore. Built by a now defunct mining company. Hasn't been used for years."

Gaspar had flagged it as the most likely option for Keegan's escape plan, too. Which meant he agreed with her analysis.

Looking at the terrain and the satellite images Gaspar had included, Kim thought getting into the runway on the old roads would be difficult, at best. Which Keegan would probably have seen as a virtue because it meant few people were likely to try.

The land on the east side of Mount Rushmore, around Bolton and the prison, was flat. But closer to the monument, the Black Hills area provided greater challenges.

Kim nodded, poking the screen with her index finger. This one, for sure, was the best option Keegan would have if he'd planned to escape on a private jet.

"How does Keegan plan to stay undercover and out of sight at Mount Rushmore?" Burke asked. "That's probably the one place in South Dakota that's actually crowded every day. Someone is likely to recognize him there, too."

"It's early in the season, but yes." Kim nodded. "I think he's counting on the small crowds for camouflage. He'll blend in with the tourists. With a little bit of air traffic, he could get lucky. The FAA might not see his plane as too odd. Private pilots have been known not to file flight plans. With other jets coming and going, his might not trigger any alarm bells."

"Sounds risky to me," Burke said, shaking his head.

"It is risky. Lots of things could go wrong. And maybe Keegan's pilot will file a flight plan and communicate with towers. It's hard to say."

"But?" Burke arched his eyebrows to reinforce his question.

"But Keegan is the guy who engineered the first large-scale federal prison break in U.S. history. And he's one of two escapees still out there when the rest have already been caught," Kim reminded Burke. "He's smart. He's clever. He's got resources. And he's cocky. This feels like the sort of thing he'd absolutely do."

Burke didn't reply.

"It's not smart to underestimate any opponent, Burke. You know that as well as I do. If we give him too much credit and try to outwit him, we have a chance to win. If we assume he's stupid…" She didn't finish the sentence. She shouldn't have to. If Burke didn't understand the basics, he'd never last in the job.

"Okay," Burke said slowly, studying the images and thinking things through. "So let's get Smithers over there. He's got to have a team closer than we are. Better equipped, too."

Kim talked through the facts as she saw them for Burke's benefit. "Keegan would have built breathing room into his plans. He'd have assumed a few problems along the way. The runway looks like a treacherous location, in a canyon. There's probably no runway lights."

"So you think Keegan's plan is to leave tomorrow. In the morning, probably. What time does the park open?"

"Eight o'clock, although a few hardy souls may arrive on the grounds earlier."

"Which means he might bed down somewhere for the night," Burke said slowly. "Maybe inside that hangar at the runway site."

"If we're lucky," she nodded. "And even if we're unlucky, we should get there before he flies out. If he doesn't show up and we're wrong, we haven't really lost anything, and we don't look like idiots. If he does show up, there's two of us and one of him…"

"I'm game if you are," Burke said. "But call Smithers anyway. Let him know where we're going and why. Keegan might have reinforcements on the way. We may need backup."

Kim already had the phone in her hand. After several rings, Smithers's phone went to voicemail. She left a long message and hoped he'd get it before he turned in for the night.

She didn't bother calling the Boss. No need. He'd been listening anyway. He always did.

"Let's head toward the hangar. We'll want to be there before daylight," Kim said. "If Keegan tries to leave tomorrow, we don't want to miss him."

Burke nodded. "You think he won't try to fly out during the night because he loses the camouflage effect of the tourists and other flight traffic."

"That, and the terrain. There're no runway lights out there. Getting a private jet in and out in the dark wouldn't be simple. Why risk it?"

He put the Navigator into gear and pulled out of the parking lot as Kim entered the coordinates for the old runway into the GPS to get him headed in the right direction.

Then she downloaded the maps Gaspar had sent to her phone. Inevitably, the GPS would lose its signal at precisely the wrong time. When that happened, she'd be ready.

CHAPTER 48

Sunday, May 15
South Dakota
12:45 a.m.

Aside from Olson in the driver's seat, Keegan had not seen another living soul along the dark country highway. They had been driving southbound for about a hundred miles.

The GPS system was still functioning off and on. It had lost the signal several times. As they passed behind the monument at Mount Rushmore, signals would fail more often. Which was fine. In fact, he'd been counting on it.

They were passing through the forest on a narrow winding road. Often, he could not see the sky. Which meant the satellites probably couldn't see him, either. Perfect.

The last bit of civilization they had passed was at the Sardis gas station.

The peanut butter crackers he'd bought there were long gone. So was the water. Olson's stomach growled repeatedly, which he didn't care about. But Keegan was hungry, too. Not that it mattered. He had no food.

The emergency provisions he'd stocked for this leg of the trip were still in the back of the damaged Land Rover unless a cop had found them already. Keegan hadn't actually touched anything, so there was no chance he'd left DNA or other biometrics they could use to confirm he'd shot that cop.

Not that it mattered now. They wouldn't find him before he left the country, and he'd be in Canada tomorrow before noon.

The thought made him smile in the dark. Things had gone wrong right from the start. But he'd adjusted on the fly and he was almost there.

His stomach complained of hunger. Too bad.

Fasting a while longer wouldn't kill him.

But dehydration was another issue altogether. He needed water.

He'd chosen this route precisely to avoid other people. At the time, the decision had made sense. He had provisions in the Land Rover to get them through the journey. No point in thinking about that now.

There would be food and water on the Gulfstream. All he had to do was get to it.

Even without the GPS, Olson must have realized they were driving toward Mount Rushmore. The park had opened a few weeks ago and tourists had already started to show up, even in early spring when the weather was still cold.

The forecast tonight called for snow. He hated snow. Always had. But he'd be okay inside the Chevy for the night.

During the planning, Walsh had argued that Rushmore would be busier during the summer months, and thus a better rendezvous point. Not only because of better weather. It was also easier to get lost in a sea of people than a few dozen sightseers and outdoor nuts.

But Keegan hadn't wanted to wait. The cargo pilot was the critical piece of the prison break plan. Once they'd found him and confirmed that he could be bought, Keegan wouldn't risk losing that advantage.

He'd spent way too many nights in prison. He vowed he'd never find himself a guest of Uncle Sam, or any other government, ever again.

The South Dakota wilderness had almost defeated him. He'd lost Walsh, which was a blow, to be sure.

But Keegan had integrated redundancies into his plans every step of the way. He'd deployed another second in command who was already on his way. Former U.S. army major. He'd said his name was Leon Garber, which was an alias. The real Leon Garber had died years ago.

Still, this Garber had training and skills. His résumé was perfect, right from the start. He understood the chain of command. He'd know his place.

Garber was set to meet Keegan at the hangar and fly to Canada in the Gulfstream.

Garber had been hired to back up Walsh when Keegan was creating his plans. Now, with Walsh dead, Garber would be handling security solo going forward. He'd come highly recommended.

Although Walsh would always be his sentimental favorite, Keegan knew the new guy would probably do a better job. He was younger and better qualified, among other things.

The Impala was west and north of the monument now. Terrain between here and the south side of the park was treacherous. If they had a flat tire or any other difficulty out here, their bodies might not be found for days.

Which was fine.

Keegan didn't expect to die tonight. Cold and hunger for one night wouldn't kill him. But he simply couldn't live confined in prison. Never again.

"Where are we going?" Olson asked in a whiney tone that grated on Keegan's last nerve.

The woman had become increasingly difficult as the journey had progressed. He itched to kill her and be done with it.

He would have done it, too. But he needed her to drive the Chevy.

For now.

Once they reached the rendezvous point, he would happily dispense with her.

In fact, he was looking forward to it.

The GPS pinged again when the Chevy took a bend in the road to the east, no longer in the shadow of the monument. As Keegan recalled the map, they were less than twenty miles from the abandoned hangar and still covering ground.

The final approach from the west side was across an old dirt trail. The mining company had used it to ferry passengers to and from the runway. But that was long ago. When the company abandoned the mine and the hangar, they also abandoned the roads.

Keegan squinted into the darkness, peering out, seeking to find what had been no more than a faint line on the old map.

He saw the turnoff after Olson drove past.

"Stop," he demanded, holding his free hand up in the air to emphasize the order.

Olson was so terrified of him that she no longer objected or attempted to argue with his commands. She braked hard, and the Chevy slowed to a full stop in the center of the paved road.

"Back up. Our turnoff is fifty feet back," Keegan said.

Olson put the transmission into reverse and drove slowly backward until Keegan pointed out the abandoned dirt road.

"Turn here," he said.

Again, she did as she was told without objection. But he could feel the fear radiating from her in waves across the cabin. He smirked in the darkness.

She probably thought he planned to kill her here.

He said nothing to disabuse her of the idea.

The more frightened she stayed, the better.

Less energy required to manage her that way.

The trees had grown together overhead, making the gravel drive a tunnel of near-total darkness. The Chevy's headlights illuminated the way ahead as the Impala crawled along.

Twice, Olson had reduced speed to roll the tires slowly over a downed tree across the lane.

When they'd traveled a couple of bumpy miles, the high beams illuminated a problem they couldn't roll over.

Olson stomped hard on the brakes mere feet before hitting the scrap lumber blocking the trail.

"What the hell?" she said, almost involuntarily, breathing hard. "We can't drive over that. Flat tires would be the least of the damage if we tried."

Keegan stared ahead where the high beams floodlighted the problem.

A one-lane wooden bridge had once crossed the road here. Years ago, it had rotted away, and the gushing stream of icy snowmelt flowed at a rapid pace in the crevasse and over the sides of the trail.

From inside the vehicle, Keegan couldn't judge the depth of the water. But safe to assume it was too deep to drive through, even if they could move the lumber out of the way. Otherwise, the wooden bridge wouldn't have been constructed at all.

The first order of business was to assess the situation. And then to figure out another way to get across. Going back was not an option.

"Wait here," he said as he opened the door and stepped out into the darkness.

The dirt under his feet was hard-packed and flat, but the last thing he needed was a sprained ankle. He made his way carefully to the old lumber blocking the road.

Most of it was rotted and crumbled. A few larger blocks were piled together in the middle of the trail. The two of them could move the boards aside with a little bit of effort.

The bigger problem was the stream.

The headlight beams were partially blocked by the debris pile, but he could see the stream was too deep and moving too swiftly to drive through.

Could they walk across?

He looked around for a tree branch long enough to test the stream's depth. When he found one, he used it as a walking stick to test the ground as he climbed over the debris and moved toward the running water.

On the other side of the debris pile, he heard the door slam and the Chevy's engine change pitch. He whipped around to stare into the bright lights.

It took him a moment to realize that Olson had thrown the transmission into reverse and punched the accelerator. The Chevy retreated along the dirt road, as quickly as Olson could drive.

Keegan couldn't possibly run fast enough to catch her.

He whipped the pistol into the air and shot at the retreating vehicle. The headlights shined into his eyes, blinding his aim.

He fired three times in the general direction of the retreating windshield.

Two shots were deflected by bad angles. He heard the ricochet.

One of his bullets penetrated the safety glass.

Olson screamed, but she kept driving.

Had he missed his target?

Keegan fired off three more shots, this time aiming between the headlights. He heard the bullets hit the Chevy, for sure.

Somehow, Olson kept going.

The Chevy backed around a bend, and the headlights no longer aimed straight toward him.

But he no longer had a clear sightline.

He couldn't hit her from here.

He couldn't run her down on foot, either.

Those last shots had hit the Chevy. Maybe damaged it enough.

She'd be stuck somewhere soon. No way would she make it out tonight. Especially if he'd wounded her well enough. With any luck at all, her wound would prove fatal within the hour.

As the illumination from the Chevy's headlights faded and total darkness descended upon him, Keegan considered his options.

He was only about three miles from the hangar, give or take. Four miles at the most. He could walk that far. All he had to do was cross the stream and then stay on what was left of the old road until he reached his destination.

The Gulfstream was scheduled to arrive before nine o'clock in the morning. The pilot was reliable because he'd been on Keegan's payroll for years. No worries there.

Keegan's backup security man would arrive by four o'clock, he'd said. He would signal from the ground to let the pilot know it was safe to land.

The Gulfstream would touch down to pick up two passengers and then take off again.

A quick turnaround. Not more than fifteen minutes on the ground. The jet probably wouldn't even come to a full stop. The engines wouldn't be shut down at all.

The plan had been solid when Keegan had originally conceived it, and despite a few necessary adjustments, it still was.

This was a temporary setback. Nothing more.

He couldn't worry about Olson sounding the alarm. Even if she survived, she didn't have a cell phone or any other way of communicating out here.

Eventually, someone would find her.

Maybe she'd still be alive. Hopefully, not.

But by then, he'd be gone.

Right now, Keegan needed another plan for the rest of the night. He didn't have a flashlight or anything else to illuminate the pitch blackness.

Even if he could safely cross the stream in the dark, the road might be washed out or blocked again farther along.

Reluctantly, he accepted that he couldn't reach the hangar tonight.

"Okay. No problem," he said aloud. "You'll have plenty of time to get there after sunrise."

First light would come early. All he had to do was find a safe place to wait for it.

CHAPTER 49

Sunday, May 15
South Dakota
7:35 a.m.

The specialized GPS system Kim had connected to the government satellite routed them through the South Dakota backcountry toward an old airstrip that no longer appeared on any map. The airstrip was just over ten miles south and east of the Mount Rushmore monument.

Older maps showed two entrances, both long closed. The main entrance, on the east side of the runway. And a smaller service road that exited on the west side.

The east entrance was the most accessible and closest to Bolton, which was why Kim had chosen it. It had been much slower going than the distance alone warranted. But they'd finally found the road and slowly advanced toward the hangar.

"We should have been out here at the crack of dawn," Burke said, stating the obvious.

"We tried," Kim replied. "If Keegan is already gone, we've lost. But if he waited until the park opens, we still have a chance to pick him up before he's gone for good."

The abandoned gravel roadway had last been graded across uneven hilly terrain, maybe back when the sculpture at Mount Rushmore was created during the Roosevelt administration.

The road wasn't much more than a trail now. A single lane with steep drop-offs on either side was designed for a heavy truck or tractor, Kim supposed. A slow, heavy vehicle with sturdy tires and a dirt-proof engine.

The oversized Lincoln Navigator was none of that. It was a full-sized luxury SUV meant for soccer moms and weekend warriors.

"How far do we need to go before we reach the runway?" Burke asked.

"Fifteen miles, maybe?" Kim replied. "But it looks like this road was well-traveled back in the day."

Eleven miles off the main road, a tree had fallen across the road. Burke stopped the SUV and put the transmission into park.

"I'll move the tree out of the way. You drive through," he said, climbing out of the Navigator.

Kim changed to the driver's seat. She pushed the lever to move it all the way forward toward the steering wheel and securely fastened her seat belt.

She was as stable as she could get to drive the ridiculously mammoth-sized Lincoln along the treacherous strip of dirt. If they slipped off and rolled down the hillside, she wouldn't fall out of the vehicle, at least.

Burke struggled to move the tree aside. When he finally shoved it off the road, Kim drove through. Burke grabbed a backpack from the rear and then opened the passenger door and settled into the passenger seat.

"Can you drive the rest of the way? In case we come to another problem?" he asked.

"Yeah. This beast has four-wheel drive, doesn't it?" Kim asked. "We may need it further ahead, so we should engage it now."

"Yeah." Burke adjusted the dials.

The SUV's heavy suspension bounced along the rough gravel road, lifting her from her seat every time she hit a hole. Which was often. This old road hadn't been graded since the last century, for sure.

Progress was slow. She kept both hands on the steering wheel and pressed the accelerator with her toes to increase speed as much as she dared along the few straight stretches, raising her foot to take the curves.

She stole a glance across the vast cabin toward Burke, organizing equipment he'd retrieved from his backpack. "What is it with men and big cars, anyway? Compensating?"

"Size matters. Bigger is better." Burke grinned. "I miss my aircraft carrier. I like room to move. Sue me."

"No ocean around here. An aircraft carrier would be useless," Kim quipped and then laughed when he wiped away a fake tear. "Once a SEAL always a SEAL, eh?"

"That's the Marines. We're both Navy, but not the same," Burke shot back. "Now that we're actively trying to locate this place, I'm wondering how Keegan knew it existed?"

"He'd have had no access to old maps while he was in prison," Kim replied. "Someone on the outside told him about it."

"Had to be Olson, right? She was his connection to the outside world. Through Walsh or Denny," Burke said, as he attached the sight to the rifle he was assembling.

"What are you planning to do with that?" Kim asked, slowing to take another treacherous switchback without rolling down the embankment.

"Be prepared. That's what I learned back in Boy Scouts," Burke replied.

She scowled at him.

He grinned again. "Hey, you weren't the only one who got early training."

Before she had a chance to slay him with a snappy comeback, she rounded the next bend, and the view opened up ahead.

Which was when she saw the low, decrepit building across an open expanse of landscape.

Between her and the building was the runway.

Precisely where the old maps indicated she'd find it.

She stopped the Navigator to get a better look.

The runway's origins were uncertain. It might have been built during the construction of the monument, same as the road. Somehow, building supplies and equipment had to be shipped in, and there were no real roads and no trains out here back then. Cargo planes were the most likely method for delivering freight.

Or maybe it had been a part of an old defense system built during the Cold War. The mining company bought it and used it for a while after the Cold War ended.

Regardless of its origins, at some point in the last century, mining operations had ceased.

The runway was more than a mile long and in decent shape for its age, all things considered. Better than she'd expected. Which meant it had been used for something in the not too distant past.

Perhaps another owner had bought it from the mining company and used it to fly tourists over the parks for a while. Or maybe it had been used for drug trafficking. Which, now that she thought about it, was much more likely.

Whatever the reason for the runway's existence, two things were obvious now.

The runway had been abandoned.

And it was still usable.

Which explained why the sleek white Gulfstream was parked at the far end, both engines running, the sound echoing off the Black Hills that surrounded them.

Kim glanced at her watch. It was nine-fifteen. The park had been open for an hour. Tourists were likely arriving and departing. Probably a few of them were on private planes.

Just as she'd thought.

"Well, look at that," Burke said as if he hadn't expected Kim's hunch to pay off.

She might have gloated, but in truth, this was a long shot. The odds were against her, and she knew it.

But there it was.

Keegan's getaway vehicle.

Fueled up and ready to fly out of the country. The Gulfstream had a flight range of about five hundred miles. Which meant there were other places Keegan could go from here. But she was a betting woman, and she'd put her chips on Canada.

Kim picked up her phone to call Smithers.

She still couldn't get a cell signal here.

There was plenty of open sky, though, which meant two things.

First, a satellite phone would work if she'd had one. Which she didn't.

And second, the Boss could see and hear them if he tried. Gaspar and Finlay could see and hear them, too.

Whether any of the three were paying attention or not was another question entirely.

The Gulfstream's jet stairs were down, leading from the door behind the cockpit to the pavement. From this vantage point, Kim could see the pilot in his seat and two men at the stairs.

"Burke. Look," Kim said, pointing, when the first man trudged up the last few steps, ducked his head, and entered the jet. "Keegan."

The second was a bigger man. He was dressed in jeans and work boots. He wore a brown leather jacket.

He waited on the pavement until Keegan was inside.

She guessed him to be about six feet four or five, maybe two-fifty. Longish fair hair blowing in the breeze.

Burke confirmed her thoughts quietly. "Jack Reacher."

Kim exhaled slowly. She'd never seen Reacher in daylight. Before now, she'd seen only photos and video and shadows.

Many times, she'd doubted Reacher's very existence.

Jack Reacher had become a mythic creature in her head.

Could the second man really be him?

She raised her phone and pushed the zoom lens to get as close as she could and recorded video as the big man bounded up the jet stairs.

CHAPTER 50

Sunday, May 15
South Dakota
8:30 a.m.

At the top step, the big man paused a moment, glanced around, and then doubled over to enter the plane behind Keegan.

As he pulled the stairs in and snugged the door closed, Kim enlarged the video on her phone. It was grainy and unfocused.

Was it him? After all this time? Had she finally found Reacher?

The sound and vibration from the Gulfstream's engines changed. The jet began to move toward the opposite end of the runway. In no time at all, the plane would be in the air.

Unless she stopped it.

Kim knew a lot about planes of all sorts. She'd made a point of learning every conceivable way a plane could fail and how she could survive if it did.

Which was how she knew the only way she might be able to prevent takeoff now, with the jet on the runway and already moving, was to damage the plane.

A damaged jet could crash.

No pilot would take such a deliberate risk.

She hoped.

"Hang on," she said to Burke as she slid forward and stomped on the accelerator with as much force as she could muster.

The big Navigator's engine growled as it revved up and began to move. The SUV was pointed straight at the jet, but both were moving.

The apron where the aircraft must have once parked before heading through to the runway was wide.

She used the full width of the apron, sweeping the SUV around while keeping her foot down on the gas pedal.

The tires squealed.

Burke held onto the grab handle, hefting the rifle with the other hand.

The Gulfstream was moving faster now, its twin engines leaving heat trails in the air and stirring a storm of debris from the rarely used runway surface.

The Navigator's wheels thumped over the expansion joint and they were on the runway.

Kim pushed the pedal to the floor, chasing the jet. She had to reach it before takeoff. This was her last chance to get Keegan and Reacher into custody.

The runway debris hammered the SUV, joining the roar of the engine, although they were quite a ways back. Damage to the Navigator would be extensive. She didn't care.

"Go to the left side," Burke said, lowering his window. "There's more room to move over there."

Kim eased the vehicle to the left of the plane's path as Burke leveled the gun out of the window.

"What the hell are you doing?" Kim said, speeding ahead. "We want to arrest Keegan and Reacher, not kill them."

"I'm aware of our mission," Burke replied, attempting to aim out the open window.

Kim had no time to argue now. She turned her full attention to stopping the jet.

The Navigator was gaining ground, reducing the distance between them, but the roar of the air and stones and the Gulfstream's jets was deafening.

A few moments later, Burke brought the gun back in. "The ride is too rough. Can't line up to shoot the tires."

That settled the matter.

The Navigator was a hundred feet back but still gaining fast. Soon, the jet would speed out of range.

Burke didn't need to disable the Gulfstream's tires. That had been a crazy plan. So crazy, she wondered for a brief moment why he'd even tried. But she couldn't puzzle that now.

All Kim had to do was damage the plane, which wouldn't take much. She could impair the jet seriously enough to persuade the pilot not to take off.

"Hang on!" she gripped the steering wheel tightly and yelled toward Burke into the overwhelming noise. The stink of jet fuel filled the Navigator's cabin making it difficult to breathe.

The big SUV sped past the Gulfstream's tail and engines with ease. She kept her focus forward on her driving.

Stone chips would be the least of the damage to the Navigator now, but she wasn't letting Reacher get away. She'd come too far, tried too hard, endured too much to let him slip from her grasp now.

She stared ahead, judging the distance.

In the high riding SUV the jet's wingtips looked to be at head level.

She could hit the wing or damage the hydraulics, which would interfere with the pilot's ability to steer and to land.

He'd still have the second engine. Maybe he was good enough to fly to Canada and land with one functioning engine. But she had to try to stop him.

Burke must have realized what she planned to do. They would feel the impact with the jet's wing inside the SUV. He hunkered down, still holding the rife.

Briefly, Kim considered easing off the accelerator to just tap the wing, do less damage. But she didn't, and the Lincoln covered the distance before she made the conscious decision.

"Hang on!" she yelled again, a split second before the SUV's roof smacked into the jet's left wing, maybe three feet from the tip.

Metal crunched at ear-piercing volume.

The Navigator rocked.

The Gulfstream did too.

The jet's tires skipped on the pavement, kicking projectiles against the Navigator like bullets.

Kim backed off the accelerator.

The Lincoln lurched hard.

The SUV had connected to the aircraft and stayed locked to the wing.

"Roof rack," Burke said, pointing up to demonstrate the problem. The roof rack had wedged onto the wing and stuck there.

She had to get loose. She tapped the brakes.

The SUV jolted, bouncing on its suspension when she severed the connection.

The aircraft pulled away, seemingly unaffected by the SUV ramming its left wing.

The jet engines blew a storm of stones and dust into the Navigator's windshield, blocking her vision, as Kim braked harder.

The big, heavy Lincoln slowed.

The distance between the Navigator and the Gulfstream widened.

Burke opened the passenger door and jumped out before the SUV stopped.

The Gulfstream was moving fast. Shooting its tires would not stop the jet now.

"What the hell are you doing? Reacher's in there. Our orders are to find him, not kill him," Kim yelled a second reminder into the jet engines' roar.

Burke rested on one knee, leveling the rifle at the aircraft just as the Gulfstream's nose gear lifted off the runway.

She realized he wasn't aiming at the tires.

He squeezed off six shots.

All six hit the aircraft but didn't slow it down.

The Gulfstream completed its takeoff, pulled up the undercarriage, and arced into the sky.

Kim stepped out of the Navigator and joined Burke, still kneeling on the runway. The wind and the jet's stench and roaring engines continued to fill the air for several seconds as they watched the Gulfstream become smaller in the distance.

"So close." Kim thumped the Lincoln's big door with the flat of her hand in frustration. Her palm had touched something wet on the SUV's paint. She rubbed her fingers together.

"Sticky," she said, her eyes following a line of drips up the SUV's door to the roof.

Burke stood up. "Fuel?"

"Smells like oil. Pink oil." She shook her head and looked into the sky, watching until the plane was out of sight. "Looks like one of us hit a vulnerable spot. He's leaking hydraulic fluid."

Burke nodded as if he'd known all along.

"Come on. That jet's in trouble. It might land somewhere soon." Kim jerked her thumb toward the driver's seat. She hurried to the passenger side of the Navigator. "We need to find a cell signal. I'll call Smithers and let him know the Gulfstream is in the air, probably flying on one engine now. He might still have a way to grab Keegan and Reacher before the jet crosses the border."

"We haven't had cell service for at least an hour. Where are we going to find it now? Rapid City?" Burke said, stashing the rifle in the backseat and himself behind the steering wheel.

"Head toward the monument. It's closer. Uncle Sam watches the place like a hawk. Tourists use their devices there every day. We'll find something we can use," Kim said, fastening her seatbelt as Burke punched the accelerator and headed toward the main road.

CHAPTER 51

Sunday, May 15
South Dakota
8:35 a.m.

A few minutes before takeoff, Keegan jogged up the jet stairs and entered the Gulfstream's interior, which was a luxurious sea of leather and giant armchairs. He plopped down into one of the seats by the wing. He reclined the chair, lifted the footrest, and closed his eyes.

He had barely slept last night. He'd found a tree to climb into and huddled among the branches for warmth, cursing Olson regularly. If not for her, he'd have had a warm and comfortable sedan to sleep in.

At first light, he'd waded through the waist-deep stream of icy snowmelt and then jogged along the rest of the trail to the hangar, fighting downed branches and ruts and holes all the way.

Keegan wasn't in the best physical condition of his life, and he hadn't jogged in years. It was slow going. By the time he'd made it to the runway, he was cold, hungry, thirsty, exhausted, and euphoric.

He'd made it to his destination a few minutes before the Gulfstream landed. Right on time. The pilot, Finn, was as reliable as ever, which was all Keegan cared about.

He'd had no time to talk to his new employee, but they'd have time for that later. They exchanged silent nods, and Garber used the flares to lead the jet onto the runway. Keegan watched him approvingly. Garber would be effective muscle, judging by the size of him. With luck, he'd also have half a brain.

The Gulfstream landed, the pilot opened the door and lowered the jet stairs. He waved them toward the plane.

Keegan entered first. Finn gave him a thumbs-up from the pilot seat.

"Just the two of you?" Finn asked.

Keegan nodded. "Yeah. Walsh and Denny didn't make it."

Finn shrugged. He'd worked in Keegan's organization for a long time. Finn knew the score. People got terminated. Death was a recognized hazard of the job.

Garber pounded up the jet stairs, ducked inside, snugged the door shut, and moved to the rear of the aircraft. Keegan glanced back to see him click his seatbelt.

The engines throbbed. A momentary vibration ran through the cabin, but the engine noise remained a distant rumble.

The aircraft accelerated at Finn's command. The wheels thumped over the rough runway. Canada was an hour away. Very soon, Keegan would be a free man once again.

His pulse quickened at the mere proximity to his final destination. He'd planned this for months. Thought about nothing else, night and day.

Hard to imagine he was only an hour away from the rest of his life. But his pounding heart and short, excited breaths assured him he was almost there.

Finn had never let him down before, and they'd done night runs under much worse flight conditions than this.

Keegan could almost taste the poutine and lager waiting for him at the end of the line.

The jet was still gaining speed on the runway, nearing takeoff. Keegan rolled his head to the left and glanced out of the Gulfstream's giant oval window. Something big and navy blue caught his eye.

He frowned. What was that?

A Lincoln Navigator came into full view, accelerating past the tails and straight up to the wing. A tiny Asian looking woman squinted toward the plane, lips pursed, frowning, hands gripping the steering wheel as if to hold herself up high enough to see.

She floored it. The Navigator was coming straight at them. Fast.

Keegan sat bolt upright.

He gripped the armrests. He couldn't believe it. What was that crazy bitch doing?

A moment later, the big SUV rammed the left wing.

The plane bounced and knocked Keegan sideways in the chair.

Finn shouted something Keegan couldn't quite hear, interspersed with a stream of incoherent cursing.

The jet kept rolling toward takeoff, picking up speed.

The Lincoln's roof rack meshed with the plane's wing and somehow got hooked on.

The SUV stayed connected for what seemed like ten minutes, although Keegan knew only a few brief moments had passed.

Surely Finn must have felt the weight pulling the wing down, even if he couldn't see the Navigator from the pilot's seat.

Keegan heard the Gulfstream's engines spooling down. Finn attempting to dislodge the Navigator, probably.

Somehow, the Navigator separated from the wing and decelerated, disappearing from Keegan's view.

Which was okay.

But the aircraft continued to decelerate, too.

Which wasn't okay. Not even remotely.

What the hell was Finn doing?

They couldn't stop now.

Keegan unlatched his seatbelt, drew his gun, and threw himself into the cockpit, ramming the muzzle into Finn's neck.

He shouted, "I don't care what's going on out there. We're leaving. Now. Got it?"

The pilot nodded and pushed the twin throttle levers forward.

The engines roared, louder this time. Keegan held the gun against Finn's neck. He'd already made up his mind.

He'd shoot Finn and take his chances if he had to. He had a plan B, like always.

Garber's résumé claimed he could pilot the plane. Which was one of the reasons Keegan had hired him. Redundancies had saved his life more than once.

A few moments later, Finn pulled back on the yoke, and they were airborne.

"We hit something," Finn said. "But there wasn't anything on the runway."

"Just fly this thing. We've got to get to Canada." Keegan gave him another jab with the pistol for emphasis.

Finn studied the numerous dials and lights arrayed in front of him and overhead. "Hydraulic pressure is low."

"We're flying. It doesn't matter," Keegan said. No need to get Garber up here just yet. Finn had come to his senses.

The pilot said nothing.

Keegan pulled down a jump seat. Unlike the comfortable armchairs in the passenger cabin, this seat was hard and flat. But keeping Finn suitably motivated was more important than comfort for the next hour or so.

Freedom was so close. All he had to do was press on. Finn was a solid pilot. Military training. He'd flown damaged aircraft before. They'd make it. They had to. He'd come too far to turn back now.

The altimeter showed they were climbing, but another dial showed what was obvious even to Keegan's eyes.

They were leaning to the left where the Navigator had hooked onto the wing.

Finn adjusted the controls. Keegan poked him with the gun.

"Trimming," Finn said. "We're losing lift on the left."

"We were hit on the left."

"By what?"

Before Keegan could reply a roar swept through the cabin followed by a heavy vibration.

The pilot's hands flew over the controls, flipping switches and pulling levers, nodding toward the controls. Much more calmly than the situation warranted, Finn said, "Fire."

"Fire?" Keegan said, alarmed. Fire on a plane was never a good thing. "Where?"

Finn nodded toward an outline drawing of the aircraft on the dashboard. A big red light glowed on the left engine.

Keegan leapt from the cockpit and returned to his seat, shoving his face against the big window.

He saw no flames, but black smoke trailed from the left engine.

Keegan returned to the jump seat. The vibration had stopped and the red light had turned orange.

"Fire's out," Finn said, too calmly by a factor of ten, at least. Pilots, like doctors and cops, were trained to be calm during emergencies.

"We can fly on one engine, right?" Keegan shook the gun for emphasis. "That's why the plane has two, isn't it?"

Finn gave a slow nod. "We...can."

"Then we will."

They flew in silence for a minute. They were no longer gaining altitude.

"What hit us?" Finn asked.

"An SUV. Rammed into the left wing."

Finn looked back, eyebrows raised and his mouth opening and closing like a fish. "The wing?"

"It's still in one piece. Keep flying."

CHAPTER 52

Sunday, May 15
South Dakota
8:45 a.m.

Keegan looked back into the cabin. Garber looked a little green around the gills and was still strapped into his seat. Great. An actual emergency, and the guy was completely useless.

A shrill buzzer sounded and several red lights illuminated in the cockpit.

"More fire," Finn said, urgently this time, flipping switches.

A small door to the luggage hold at the rear of the aircraft burst open with a whump. Keegan twisted around just as flames poured out into the cabin.

Keegan could no longer see or hear Garber sitting in the back. Was he belted into his seat, coughing in the cloud of flames and black smoke that quickly filled the rear of the aircraft?

Keegan's stomach lurched. He realized the Gulfstream was descending. He whipped his head around to the cockpit again.

Garber was on his own.

"We have to land," Finn said.

Keegan shoved his gun into the pilot's neck. "Not back to where we came from."

Finn shook his head. "Fat chance. Couldn't go back there if we tried. We're not going to make it more than a few miles."

The smoke curled into the cockpit, hovering along the ceiling, swirling around the air vents. It stung Keegan's throat and eyes.

He grabbed a small fire extinguisher.

Finn shook his head. "Waste of time. Won't help."

Keegan hurled the bottle into the flames in the cabin, which had engulfed the rear seats. Garber had disappeared in the smoke. Good riddance.

The pilot pulled down an oxygen mask. Keegan grabbed the copilot's mask as it hung from the ceiling. As he inhaled, the oxygen flowed with a plastic tang, but it relieved his throat. And he was still alive.

The horizon showed they were rolling left. Keegan pointed.

Finn nodded. "We've lost all lift on the left. And we've lost the hydraulics."

"Meaning?"

"We're going to crash," Finn paused. "At best."

"Parachute?"

Finn shook his head. "Get real."

Keegan watched the altimeter needle as it spun past four thousand feet.

The pilot wrestled with the yoke, pulling back, the muscles on his arms bulging.

Outside, a carpet of green trees stretched ahead crossed by the occasional road. None looked to be on their flight path. Was that a good thing? Or not?

Keegan shoved his gun in his belt, reached over, and pulled back on the copilot's yoke. The aircraft's nose inched up, climbing out of the dive with agonizing slowness.

"We're going to pull out," the pilot said. "Once we're level, we'll have to take our chances in the trees. If we're lucky, we can crash and survive."

Keegan kept pulling back on the yoke. Engines and air roared as aerodynamics fought weight.

He glanced left. His heart missed a beat.

A massive rocky outcrop towered above the sea of green. Roads and a cluster of buildings surrounded one side.

The rocks were rough, jagged, and directly in their slowly curving flight path. He turned the yoke right.

The controls responded, pushing the pilot's controls right as well.

Finn shook his head. More alarms were sounding. "We've lost roll control."

Keegan had no idea what that meant, but he pointed to the looming rocks ahead. The four famous faces carved there seemed to stare him down, like four disapproving fathers.

Finn nodded. "Mount Rushmore. God willing, we might clear it."

The Gulfstream's nose climbed above the horizon, but the altimeter still ticked downward. Like driving a car out of a skid, changing the jet's direction took longer. It seemed to hang too low for too long.

In a rush, the trees outside changed from a wide swath of evergreen to individual trunks. Keegan could see distinct branches, limbs. He saw them swaying in the wind.

They slapped against the belly of the aircraft, sending shock waves through the cabin.

Alarms continued to sound, more and louder, into a single cacophony of ear-splitting noise.

Treetops whipped by the windows in the cockpit.

From the corner of his eye, Keegan saw Garber's hulking form emerge from the black smoke and fire in the cabin.

"Garber!" Keegan shouted as he dropped the oxygen and moved to let Garber take the copilot's seat.

Garber stood aside to allow Keegan into the cabin.

The fire and smoke overwhelmed him. He coughed and scrunched his eyes shut against the stinging smoke.

The belly of the plane bounced along the treetops, making him queasy.

Before he had a chance to retch, out of nowhere, Garber's big fist landed a solid blow to Keegan's solar plexus.

Keegan yelled and stumbled backward toward the smoke, bent double with the pain.

Keeping his head down and his eyes screwed shut while tears ran down his face.

Over the unrelenting noise, he felt the passenger door open.

A rush of wind entered the cabin, clearing smoke but feeding the fire.

The plane bounced upward, like a great weight of ballast had been thrown overboard.

Had Garber bailed out?

Jumped out of a speeding jet?

Was he too stupid to live or what?

Half a moment later, Finn rammed the working right engine to full thrust.

Somewhere in the fire and smoke and the rush of cold air through the open maw feeding the flames, the plane responded, howling like a banshee.

For a moment Keegan opened his eyes. He saw through the doorway that they had been headed straight down, farther into the trees.

And then they weren't.

Miraculously, the nose picked up, emerging from the vegetation.

The jet was gaining altitude.

Pulling out toward the sky again.

Keegan released the painful breath he'd been holding in his screaming belly.

They'd lifted from the bottom of the dive.

Garber was nowhere to be seen. Whether he'd jumped or fallen out or whatever, Keegan no longer cared.

Finn had pulled it off. They didn't crash. They were airborne once more.

Keegan fist-punched the air. "Yes!"

Through his stinging eyes the parking lot flashed by the cockpit's windshield. Visitors. Rubberneckers.

And then he saw nothing but the monument.

Presidential faces. Regal. Blank stone stares.

Keegan still had his hand in the air, declaring victory over the forces of gravity, when the plane hit the mountain, head on.

CHAPTER 53

Sunday, May 15
South Dakota
8:45 a.m.

"I've got binoculars in the side pocket of my backpack," Burke had said, as he drove the Navigator as fast as he dared over the abandoned dirt road, heading back the way they'd come. He gestured toward the bag in the wheel well.

Kim had unzipped the small pocket, found the binoculars, and aimed her gaze to the sky. She watched the path of the jet as it traveled north and slightly west of the runway. The sun glinted off the Gulfstream's sleek body, twinkling in the early morning light.

"Looks like Keegan wants one last flyover of the monument before he leaves the country," Kim said, noting the jet's trajectory.

The jet's flight was often blocked by the trees and the bends in the old road, but she kept the binoculars trained on the north by northwestern sky.

Burke made it to the county road and turned toward Mount Rushmore. Once he'd reached the pavement, he accelerated to speeds well above the posted limit.

The park and the monument were ten miles away, but at cruising altitude, the Gulfstream could fly at five hundred miles an hour, and the Navigator's top-end speed was closer to one hundred.

Kim gasped and sucked in a great gulp of air as the plane came into view again.

"What?" Burke asked. "What do you see?"

"The jet's trailing black smoke. The hydraulic fluid leak must have caused the engine to overheat. It's on fire!"

Kim reported what she saw when she saw it, while Burke pressed the accelerator closer to the floor and took the curves in the road at an alarming rate of speed. The top-heavy Navigator tipped dangerously sideways and bounced down onto its tires and kept going.

"The jet's in trouble...It's losing altitude...The pilot's trying to lift it out of the dive...It's too close to the trees... It's coming up, but too slow..."

Kim's commentary continued as the Navigator finally turned the last big curve. Now, she saw the monument straight ahead, miles away.

Through the binoculars, she had an unobstructed view of the Gulfstream as it headed straight toward the monument.

And slammed, head on, into the side of the mountain.

"Dammit!" Burke slapped his palm against the steering wheel, and the horn blasted a quick, sharp, exclamation of its own.

Kim's gut clenched and roiled while she watched through the Navigator's big windshield, horrified. A sharp "No!" escaped her lips before she slapped her palm over her mouth.

Twenty tons of metal and fuel and passengers gone in a millisecond.

Kim had seen plane crashes before. She knew what to expect. She watched the crash unfold reduced to slow motion in a trick of time, understanding the developing events that investigators would confirm later.

The cockpit had crushed into the passenger cabin.

The wings were tossed to the wind.

The tail of the plane spiraled through the air and landed somewhere.

A fireball blossomed outward, sweeping over Jefferson and Roosevelt.

Yellow and orange flames. Black smoke followed.

The wreckage of the once sleek and beautiful Gulfstream fell against the giant sculptured backdrop as if in exaggerated frame-by-frame motion.

Tumbling and rolling.

Flame on flame.

Black scorch marks as wide as a highway scraped down the rock face.

The twisted wreckage of the now destroyed jet splayed over the scree to burn out, eventually.

There was no longer any reason to rush toward the monument to thwart Keegan's escape and capture Reacher.

Burke pulled the Navigator to the shoulder. They got out to stare, knowing there was nothing more they could do.

The park had opened at sunrise. Emergency vehicles were already on site. They deployed first.

More emergency vehicles were on the way. Sirens began to wail in the distance.

The monument was twenty-three miles from Rapid City. Helicopters were no doubt already in the air and firefighters en route on the ground.

But they had no need to hurry.

Handling the fire and locating potentially injured tourists were the only emergency efforts required. The park's first responders could get the situation under control quickly enough.

Kim's mind sorted through the facts that were important to her now.

Mount Rushmore was a terrorist target. It also attracted three million tourists every year.

Video cameras would have recorded the crash from a dozen angles.

Within the hour, the news stations would have the story on the air around the country and the world.

Reports would be written. FBI, FAA, DHS, and an alphabet soup of Federal departments. They'd all have their own take. Their own angle. Their own area of expertise.

But each report would contain one common statement about the Gulfstream crash.

No survivors.

If Reacher was on that plane when it exploded, he'd be as dead as the presidents on the monument.

She shook her head slowly.

Hard to believe. She'd been chasing him for six months now. Through one impossibly dangerous situation after another, Reacher had seemed invincible.

It simply couldn't be true. Could it?

How could Reacher possibly be dead?

CHAPTER 54

Sunday, May 15
South Dakota
9:30 a.m.

Burke kicked the dirt with the toe of his boot and stuffed his hands into his pockets. "Well, I guess that's that. Plane hits the side of a mountain. There's not much left. They'll be lucky to find DNA in the ashes for a positive ID on Keegan and Reacher and the pilot when all this is cleaned up."

Kim replied, "I'm gonna need to see the video."

Burke widened his eyes and stared at her. "Why? You saw Keegan and Reacher get into that plane. You watched it crash and burn. Why do you want to see all of that again?"

"Because I don't believe it. I need to confirm it for myself. And we can't examine the actual crash site until all the experts release it. Which will take weeks if not months," she explained, running a palm over her face. She inhaled deeply. "So video is the best we'll be able to do."

Burke shrugged. "Suit yourself. Where are you planning to get this video?"

Kim pulled the Boss's cell phone from her pocket and showed it to Burke. As she'd expected, she was able to get a cell signal here, closer to the park.

The phone rang several times, and Cooper didn't pick up. She left a message. "Looks like Reacher was on the plane. He may be dead. We didn't have a clear view. Please confirm. Check the video from eight-thirty forward."

Burke made his way to the Navigator and restarted the engine. Before she joined him, Kim called Gaspar.

He answered on the first ring. Kim smiled. She could always count on Gaspar.

"I'm watching the video again now," he said.

"And?"

"And it's…inconclusive."

She felt her spirits lift slightly, which was odd. "Inconclusive how?"

"The Gulfstream was damaged when you and Burke hit it at takeoff. A fire started in the hydraulics, at the back. It would have moved through the plane from the back to the front," Gaspar said, thinking aloud.

"Things happen fast. Pilot loses control, struggles to land. Passengers panic. Lots of smoke. Lots of fire. Lots of stuff happening to mess up the controls, the wiring, everything. Chaos inside. Alarms of all kinds going on," Kim said, repeating what she knew from airline disasters past.

"Which is why I can't say for sure," Gaspar agreed.

"Can't say what for sure?"

Gaspar took a deep breath. "It looks like maybe the passenger door opened when the plane took that last dive."

"What?"

"The belly of the jet was scraping the tops of the trees. The branches are in the way. I'll keep looking for a better angle, but as of now, I don't have a clear visual on the Gulfstream at that point."

Kim felt a prickle along her scalp. "But?"

He took another breath. "I'll send you the video now. You look. Tell me what you see."

Emergency responders were coming closer. Two noisy helos overhead coupled with multiple sirens from all sides made it impossible to hear anything else.

This was just the beginning. Soon, federal, state, and local personnel would overrun the monument and the crash site. To say nothing of the media and the gawkers.

She realized she'd heard nothing more from the phone for a full second.

Had Gaspar hung up? Or had the call been compromised somehow? Lockdown of communications was part of anti-terrorism protocols. Either way, the call was over.

She slipped the phone into her pocket, walked back to the Navigator, and climbed into the passenger seat.

Two fire trucks sped past, sirens wailing.

"What are you thinking about?" Burke asked as if watching the wheels turning in her head. Gaspar used to say that. He claimed he could tell when she was wrestling with a knotty problem.

"We brought that plane down," she said, troubled by the idea.

"That's a good day's work. I'd say," Burke replied. "Wouldn't you?"

She shook her head. "When I rammed into the wing, I thought the pilot would abort. We'd take them into custody."

"And then when he didn't stop, I guess my SEAL training kicked in, and I shot at the plane which didn't make the pilot stop either," Burke shrugged. "That's not on us. The guy must have had a death wish or something. He had to know he couldn't fly far with all that damage."

Kim said nothing.

After a few moments of silence, Burke cleared his throat. "I talked to Smithers. He's got teams in place. More help is on the way."

She raised the binoculars to look at the crash site. Controlled chaos had descended in the past few minutes. The scene would be overwhelmed for hours and closed for days.

"Smithers is more than competent for the situation," Kim replied as she pulled her laptop out and connected to it the secure satellite to download Gaspar's video. "Would have been nice to hear from the Boss. But I guess that's asking too much."

Burke said, "He called. I told him what happened. He's on it."

Kim cocked her head. "On it how?"

"He didn't say. Said to stand by. He'll call back," Burke replied, clearing his throat.

Kim nodded and opened Gaspar's file. The video filled the screen. Images only. No audio.

She watched as the Gulfstream approached the monument. The jet was clearly in trouble shortly after takeoff.

The point Gaspar flagged had happened shortly before the crash. The jet lost altitude and dipped way too low. At the bottom of the dive, it seemed to perch in the trees for a few moments, like a bird.

When the plane came back up, gaining altitude again, the passenger door was open. Absolutely.

"What have you got there?" Burke asked.

Kim turned the laptop screen toward Burke. She played the video again, enlarging the image.

They watched the Gulfstream dip and rise.

Burke jabbed the screen. "Right there. The door was closed as it went down and open when it came up."

"Are you sure?" She was certain. Gaspar was, too. She wanted unanimous agreement.

"No question," he said, sounding more irritated than the situation warranted. "Play it again. You'll see it."

She replayed the video.

"Pause it. Right there," Burke demanded angrily as if she were arguing with him. "Door was opened in that dip. No doubt about it."

Kim nodded. She agreed. So did Gaspar.

Did the door open because of a malfunction? Perhaps a failure of the locks caused by the fire inside the cabin?

Possibly.

But it was also possible that one of the passengers opened the door deliberately.

Which passenger?

Surely not the pilot. He had managed to bring the plane up out of the trees again, so he must have been at the controls in the pilot seat.

Would Keegan have known how to open the door? Maybe.

But Reacher was the one who had closed it before takeoff. He would definitely know how to open it again.

When the plane was low enough, Reacher could have jumped into that stand of trees. Definitely.

Was he still alive?

Smithers called Burke and asked them to assist with backup. He said they were stretched thin until additional personnel arrived.

He said a tourist had found Fern Olson, unconscious behind the steering wheel of a disabled Chevy on one of the backroads. She was alive and en route to a hospital in Rapid City. She'd be debriefed when the doctors allowed.

Burke mused, "So Olson met with three clients before the prison break. Two are dead, Denny and Walsh."

"What about Petey Burns?" Kim asked.

"Smithers says he's still at large. He probably stole another car and managed to avoid the roadblocks and get away from Bolton," Burke shook his head with a wry grin. "Turns out Burns actually is the kind of guy who learns from his mistakes, I guess. They might never find him."

"And Keegan wasn't a client, but he's dead now, too. What did Smithers say about that?"

"Still working on it. But preliminarily, they think Keegan was passing instructions to Olson through Walsh and Denny, and maybe Burns. Seems like they were all pals, one way or another." Burke had pulled onto the roadway again. "Smithers will debrief Olson and try to get the whole story."

"Olson's phone records may help with that, too," Kim replied.

"Hopefully." Burke nodded. "Smithers thinks Keegan has been using Denny like that for a long time. They were cellmates. Smithers says seven years back, when Reacher was here, Denny was the guy who passed along intel to Olson's now dead law partner."

"Seriously?"

"Yep. And since Denny wasn't all that smart, Smithers thinks Keegan was the mastermind who got a lot of people killed back then. People Reacher cared about, apparently."

"So Smithers thinks Reacher came back for revenge on Keegan and Denny?"

"That's the working theory," Burke said. "Not that anyone will ever be able to prove it."

Made sense. If there were people Reacher cared about, people he felt responsible for back then, coming back to set things right was exactly the sort of action he might have taken.

Which left a couple of open questions. Was Reacher planning to reach Keegan and Denny while they were locked up? Or did he have advance notice of the prison break?

Could have gone either way. But if someone told Reacher about the prison break before it happened, then...

Kim cocked her head and thought about it for a while, but every scenario she tried seemed implausible. So she tucked the question away in her mind, along with all the other unanswerable questions she'd stashed there before.

Then she turned her attention back to the things she knew for sure.

She watched the Gulfstream crash video a few more times while Burke drove the last miles to the park's entrance. She closed the laptop and locked it.

There was no time to do more.

She and Burke manned the phones and assisted with crowd control and various other tasks until official replacements took over.

But the questions weighed on her mind.

Was Reacher really on that Gulfstream? Burke had said so. Emphatically.

More to the point now, if he was on the plane, had he bailed when the Gulfstream dipped into the low trees?

Where was he now? Had he been burned beyond all recognition in the crash, like Keegan and the pilot surely had been?

When they returned to the Navigator hours later, Burke said, "Where to?"

"You've heard nothing from the Boss?" she asked.

Burke shook his head. Kim wasn't sure whether to believe him or not. Their relationship had been tense from the start. She wanted to trust him, and yet she felt uneasy.

Had he been sent here to spy on her? Report to Cooper when she preferred not to?

Maybe.

Or maybe she was just a little too paranoid.

She couldn't put her finger on any specific issues, so she tried to let her suspicions go.

Perhaps her relationship with Burke no longer mattered anyway.

If Reacher was dead, the assignment was over. She'd return to the Detroit Field Office and Burke would go wherever Cooper sent him next.

She wasn't sure exactly how she felt about all of that. Disappointed, certainly. Worried, like always. Defeated, too, in a way.

She'd been sent to find Reacher, not get him killed.

If Reacher had died in that crash, then she'd failed.

And for Kim Otto, failure was never an option.

A glimmer of hope still burned in her gut.

Reacher couldn't really be dead. She couldn't have failed so spectacularly.

She'd hunted men before. Captured plenty of them. She'd never lost any. Not one.

Reacher was the most challenging assignment she'd ever attempted, sure. But she was more than capable for the job.

Wasn't she?

She looked at her watch.

2:55 p.m. Eastern Daylight Time.

Exactly sixty-one hours since Cooper's first text.

Sixty-one hours later, in many ways she was right back where this assignment had started in Margrave, Georgia, seven months ago.

Jack Reacher, dead or alive?

ABOUT THE AUTHOR

Diane Capri is an award-winning *New York Times, USA Today*, and worldwide bestselling author. She's a recovering lawyer and snowbird who divides her time between Florida and Michigan. An active member of Mystery Writers of America, Author's Guild, International Thriller Writers, Alliance of Independent Authors, and Sisters in Crime, she loves to hear from readers and is hard at work on her next novel.

Please connect with her online:

DianeCapri.com
Twitter.com/DianeCapri
Facebook.com/Diane.Capri1
Facebook.com/DianeCapriBooks